JFry

The Space Between Words

Center Point
Large Print

Also by Michèle Phoenix and available from
Center Point Large Print:

Of Stillness and Storm

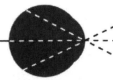

The Space
Between
Words

Michèle Phoenix

CENTER POINT LARGE PRINT
THORNDIKE, MAINE

This Center Point Large Print edition
is published in the year 2017 by arrangement with
Thomas Nelson.

The text of this Large Print edition is unabridged.
In other aspects, this book may vary
from the original edition.
Printed in the United States of America
on permanent paper.
Set in 16-point Times New Roman type.

ISBN: 978-1-68324-547-6

Library of Congress Cataloging-in-Publication Data

Names: Phoenix, Michèle, author.
Title: The space between words / Michèle Phoenix.
Description: Center Point Large Print edition. | Thorndike, Maine :
    Center Point Large Print, 2017.
Identifiers: LCCN 2017028426 | ISBN 9781683245476
    (hardcover : alk. paper)
Subjects: LCSH: Large type books.
Classification: LCC PS3616.H65 S63 2017b | DDC 813/.6—dc23
LC record available at https://lccn.loc.gov/2017028426

The Space Between Words

PROLOGUE

1695
Gatigny, France

My name is Adeline Baillard, and my life may end today. Or it may stretch its final throes into another dawn. Existence is a flimsy thing. I savor its fragility with every breath I take.

I made a promise weeks ago, the night my family tore apart, to trace the winding path that led us to the brink of our extinction. So I begin to write these pages from the shadows above the forge, because Story is sacred, insurgent in its power to unravel tangled roots.

Two generations warned us of the wrongs we face today. My grandfather passed on to us the tales his father told. The August night when the streets of Paris ran red with martyrs' blood. The savage slayings of Saint Bartholomew's three thousand. The wave that surged over city walls and seeped its crimson into provincial soil with tens of thousands more raped and branded, tortured and murdered for refusing to exchange their faith for the king's.

Their offense was being Protestant, believing in a God who needed neither pope nor priest to make himself known. Their sin was challenging the church and its fearmongering, its clergy and their profiteering. Their transgression was daring to dissent with a Crown whose authority depended on its people's docility.

The battles raged for decades, undeterred by truces and edicts. The wealthiest of the Protestants, named Huguenots, escaped to safer lands, often leaving everything behind, while the poor and courageous took to fields, caves, and dried-up riverbeds to worship and read from Bibles banned by the king and his court.

When the Edict of Nantes promised safe cities to the Huguenots, its "perpetual and irrevocable" protection ensured by the Crown's garrisons, my ancestors found asylum in places like Privas, a Rampart of Reform defended by its walls, its Protestant Seigneur, and his courageous men.

But the reprieve was short-lived, and the Huguenot church found itself, by time and power, stripped of the liberties the king had granted it. His forces rescinded our ancestors' freedoms with patient persecution and savage oppression, and we began to lose our way in mutinous revolts. We matched the soldiers' weaponry with zeal, their threats with desperation. We fought for our survival as they fought for our submission, some of us without conscience. Without mercy. Without God.

Privas fell in 1629. Those who had fled to higher ground before the siege began left only the old, the lame, and the brave behind. They listened, aghast, to the roar of fighting men, the cries of terrified children, and the wails of women forced to watch the torture of their kin. My grandfather was just a boy hiding in the hills that day. He saw his city burn and his brother marched off to the galleys, then he escaped with his mother into the mountains of Boutières.

His family settled on the outskirts of Gatigny, a village nestled in the heart of the Vivarais. We lived there for two more generations, beside the stream that ran among the mulberry trees of our modest silkworm farm. Harvesting the filaments and spinning them into thread was at the center of our lives, an intensive craft supported by the water-powered throwing machines my father invented and built.

We lived a good life on our farm, my brother, Charles, and I, then sister Julie when she came. My mother taught us every day a reverence for the written word, imprinting on our minds the call to tell God's story well.

And Father taught us honesty, nobility, and strength, repeating and embodying the principles we live by to this day: endure with courage, resist with wisdom, and persist in faith.

PART 1

ENDURE

ONE

The alarm went off at eight on the day my life imploded.

The springs in Patrick's couch clanged as I reached for my cell phone to turn it off. Vonda stretched and groaned on her thin mattress on the floor, then lifted the edge of her sleep mask to squint at me.

"Too early." Her voice was morning rough.

"Come on—get up. It's our last day here, and we're not sleeping it away."

I slipped off the couch and went to the windows, opening them wide to fold back their wooden shutters.

"Tell me it's sunny," Vonda mumbled from under her pillow.

"It's sunny."

"Are you lying?"

"It's Paris in November, Vonda."

She groaned again and forced herself to sit up, patting down the hair she'd dyed jet-black before our trip to Europe. "Those sirens are weird," she said as a police car navigated the narrow street two stories down. But it wasn't just French sirens she considered "weird." The traffic, the stares from strangers, the potency of the coffee, and the overcrowded Métro cars—all weird to the girl

13

from Santa Barbara whose most exotic world exposure had, until this trip, extended only as far as LA's Chinatown.

Back home in Denver, the three of us shared a townhouse—or we had until Patrick had headed to Europe for a semester of art classes at The American University of Paris. It came as no surprise to those who knew him that he'd decided to further his education at an age when most men were focusing on their children's academic ambitions. But we all knew that his studies, though earnest, were merely a pretext for living in a place where treasures hid in plain sight in attics, dumps, and flea markets.

Patrick's passion for picking was a galvanizing thing. It had led him to open Trésor three years ago, his eclectic store of vintage old world objects tucked away in a gentrifying neighborhood of Denver. The discovery of three rare, Napoleon-era coins in the lining of a corset he'd acquired from an online auction had financed the fulfillment of his lifelong dream to study abroad.

They called picking *chiner* in France. Patrick called it treasure hunting. And somehow—between his classes and homework—he'd found the time to travel the French countryside in his thirty-year-old Citroën 2CV, which the French lovingly called a *deudeuche*. The common knick-knacks he'd bought for a song in roadside shops and village fairs would be worth many times more back in his Denver store.

"Grab a shovel and believe in gold!" he always declared as he entered promising places. Given the impressive number of antiques he'd collected since his arrival in France, I could only conclude that his imaginary shovel had served him well.

Patrick and I had been a bit surprised by Vonda's decision to come along on our French adventure. She was nearly ten years younger than we were, and her interests diverged from ours in almost every way, particularly when it came to "digging for gold." But as opinionated, outspoken, and utterly without caution as she was, a quirky sort of friendship had evolved in the ten months we'd lived in the same home.

So she'd cashed in her vacation days to fly with me to the City of Lights. And since I'd left one job and had a few weeks to spare before starting another, I'd emptied the "Paris or bust" savings account I'd started on impulse seven years before, never really believing such a trip would actually happen.

But it had. Every morning for nearly a week, with Patrick wrapping up classes at the university and Vonda sleeping in, I'd strolled to my favorite café in Montmartre and sipped an espresso while watching the panache of city life pass by. The Seine and its quais were no longer foreign to me. I knew the churn of its *bâteaux mouches* and the hum of traffic on the clogged streets above its shores. There was a spot on the tip of the Île de la Cité that I particularly loved, and though the temperatures were in keeping with France's winter season, I'd bundled up on one occasion to sit there with a book and feel utterly, as Patrick put it, *"Ooh-là-là chérie"*—whatever that meant.

I felt drawn to France in a powerful way. Its vibrancy and history livened my senses and captured my imagination. I sensed the vastness and depth of its survival—the brutality of its mutinies and the surety of its rightful place as one of the world's most hard-won democracies. There was a homeness to Paris that felt both stimulating and soothing, unique and universal.

Patrick was in his element here, an art aficionado and self-proclaimed "clipster" who brought his own brand of class to the hipster movement. His confident exuberance was a natural fit in the fast-paced, artistically inclined city. I was a bit envious of the easy rapport he'd established with neighbors and *commerçants* during his four months in Paris. His interactions were effortless and genuine. They greeted him like a friend as he engaged with them in French. The pace and drama of his speech sounded fluent to my ears, though he assured me he still had a long way to go. Perfecting a language he loved had been just one of his motivations for moving to the City of Lights.

Patrick and I had met only four years ago, when I rang the doorbell of his Denver townhouse in answer to the "roommate wanted" ad I'd found on an online bulletin board. I was convinced that securing stable lodging would allow me to relocate to the city more permanently from the small town of Lamar, where my dad owned a body shop, my mom managed a grocery store, and everybody knew both who and whose I was. I'd moved in and out of their home so many times in the twelve years since college that I hoped a more distant location would prevent yet another embarrassing return.

It had taken me a few false starts to find the kind of employment that would finance such autonomy. After earning a pre-dental degree from a low-cost community college, I'd decided that cleaning teeth wasn't really my thing. I worked as a receptionist for a medical office for a while. Then I tried my hand at being a barista, followed by stints as a teacher's aide and finally an insurance agent. The job wasn't inspiring, but it felt stable and grown-up enough for me to move to Denver.

I was nervous but determined the day I answered Patrick's ad. "I'm here about the room for rent," I said when he opened the door, bow-tied and smiling. "I called you earlier . . . ?"

He gave me a once-over, and his blue-green eyes seemed to linger on my scuffed, utilitarian shoes a bit longer than warranted. He cocked his head when he looked up. "No drugs, no drunken orgies, and no messes in the common areas. You cool with that?" The words were blunt, but his expression was friendly.

"Uh . . . sure."

"I'll need one month's deposit, and payments are due on the first. We split utilities three ways, and each person has a shelf in the fridge. If that works for you, it works for me."

"I . . . Don't you want to interview me or . . . ask me questions or something?"

"I have radar for good people."

"Oh."

He raised an eyebrow and crossed his arms. "So—you want the room or not?"

I looked into his direct and honest gaze and couldn't think of a reason to hesitate. "Sure," I said.

He extended a hand. "Welcome home."

⸻⊰⊱⸻

And here I was in France, just over four years later, embarking on yet another adventure with a man whose kindness and impulsivity had drawn me into a friendship as solid as it was unpredictable. There was a nobility to his eccentricity, a keen curiosity, and a humane generosity.

Patrick and I were polar opposites in many ways. I proceeded with caution where he leapt with abandon. I chose the outskirts of crowds while he shone in their center. I was happy with plain while he thrived on fancy. In our grooming alone, the differences were evident: my shoulder-length brown hair in need of a trim and the impeccable blond pompadour he retouched twice a day.

Patrick burst through the door of his Parisian studio holding a paper bag aloft. "I've got croissants!" he declared, his voice more con-quering hero than early-morning shopper. By the looks of the butter stains seeping through the bag, I could tell he'd gone the extra mile and picked them up at Chez Paul, the bakery we'd elected Best in Paris within hours of our arrival.

Nothing motivated Vonda like the promise of decadent carbs. She was pulling a jar of Nutella from the kitchen cupboard before Patrick got there with his loot. "Kitchen" was a bit of an overstatement. There was a microwave, an electric burner, and practically no storage. The studio was small—too small for one person to inhabit comfortably, let alone three. And with Vonda's mattress bridging the space between Patrick's twin bed and my couch, the floor was all but invisible.

"Eat up," Patrick said after I'd pulled a plaid button-down on over my nightshirt and joined him.

"Way ahead of you," Vonda mumbled around the croissant already in her mouth.

I grabbed my own and reached for the Nutella jar while Patrick unloaded the plastic bags of groceries he'd carried up two flights of stairs. Sandwich fixings, fruit, pasta, canned goods. "You realize we're leaving tomorrow, right?" I asked.

"And all of this," he said, waving at the food like a game show hostess, "is going with us. The beauty of an Airbnb is that we can cook for ourselves."

Vonda rolled her eyes and gave me a long-suffering look. Then she turned back to Patrick. "But before we go off on your Dumpster-diving adventure," she said, a bit of derision in her voice, "you've promised me a day of touristy sight-seeing. Right?"

"If we must," Patrick said. "But we're not climbing the Eiffel Tower, and we're certainly not posing for tacky charcoal portraits on the Place du Tertre."

Vonda smiled. "Got one yesterday."

"So what's on the tour?" I asked.

"We can hit the Musée d'Orsay this morning, then the Latin Quarter for lunch. And . . ." He brightened a bit and made a production of pulling three tickets out of his breast pocket. "The opening of an art exhibit in the 14th arrondissement this evening!"

"I'm not spending my last night in Paris at a stuffy art exhibit," Vonda said.

"Come on," Patrick reasoned. "What better way to finish our time in 'Paree' than standing around with a bunch of rich people, commenting on obscure art and drinking free champagne? It doesn't get much more ooh-là-là chérie than that."

"It doesn't get much more *yawn* than that," Vonda corrected him.

"My prof gave me his passes."

"So you're not wasting any money by doing something else."

"Patrick's let us crowd his space for a week," I said to Vonda, fearing the skirmish might escalate into a debate. "Maybe going to this exhibit can be our way of saying thanks?"

Vonda looked at Patrick. "She's in crisis-prevention mode again."

"And we haven't even started cussing at each other," he said, grinning.

"We'll go to the art show," I told him.

But I hadn't taken into account Vonda's inability to abide by an established plan.

⸘⸘

"They're great—they're fun," she said later that afternoon, extolling the greatness of the "new friends" she'd made in a grunge-inspired clothing store while Patrick and I sat in Le Centre du Monde finishing up an order of crème brûlée. She looked from me to Patrick with expectation. "How often do you get offered free tickets to a concert?"

"A death metal concert, Vonda. Do I look like the type of person who'd enjoy that kind of thing?"

21

"All the more reason to try it," she insisted. "Come on—be daring! It's free. It's Paris! Ditch your paintings and live a little!"

Patrick gave her a look through the steam of his espresso. With a fancy art exhibit as an alternate option, his refusal was immediate and firm.

"Listen," she said, hands on hips and brown eyes firing. "I've let you drag me to every artsy-fartsy store and dusty flea market in Paris *for days*. I'm going to this concert, whether you two come with me or not."

"Vonda," I tried, "you've only known these people—what—ten minutes?"

She straightened to the full stature of her five feet eight inches, and I could tell by the way she tossed her hair over her shoulder and jutted out her chin that the outcome of the debate was a foregone conclusion.

So Patrick had gone off to his art gallery without us, and I'd reluctantly agreed to tag along with Vonda. Attending a concert populated by head-banging youth and jaded metalheads held absolutely no appeal to me, but her insistence that this would be "a side of Paris no one else sees" and a reticence to let my foolhardy friend venture out with virtual strangers had eroded my resistance.

Tomorrow we'd begin a road trip to Southern France in Patrick's dilapidated Citroën. We'd stop at every *brocante* we found along the way. We'd explore bustling cities and crisscross peaceful countrysides.

That's what I expected as we said good-bye to Patrick and made our way by Métro to the Bataclan concert hall on that mild November evening in the City of Lights. None of us could have imagined how the rest of the night would dismantle our lives.

TWO

Images flashed across my memory like a gruesome montage, slamming me with the horror again and again. The gunfire following me to the bloody exit door. The bodies I jumped over as I fled into the alley. The woman screaming, hanging by her fingertips from a second-floor window ledge. Cell phones shining through closed windows, capturing my flight.

I remembered being dragged into an alcove. There were voices—urgent, whispering voices—but my mind lacked the focus to translate what they said. Someone putting pressure on the left side of my waist. Pain screaming through my synapses. Then the welcome darkness of unconsciousness.

Later I heard more voices, their sureness and calm somehow hopeful to my ears. Hands lifted me and laid me on a stretcher. Flashing lights. Sirens. A rough, swerving drive. Nausea. Pain.

Hallway lights flashed by. Words I couldn't fully understand. Medical words. The sound of curtains being pulled. Hurried activity swirling around me. Scissors tearing at my sweater. A woman's gentle voice. A hand on my arm. Kindness. It made the horror I'd survived that much more terrorizing.

I remembered asking for Vonda—begging for someone to find and tell Patrick. And my parents. I needed them to know I was all right—but I wasn't sure I'd actually spoken the thoughts.

There was the dim pain of IVs being placed—one in each arm. Beeping instruments. A raised voice barking orders.

Then I remembered a groggy swim toward consciousness. The shivering. The reassuring pats and whispered conversations just out of reach. The slow ebb of anesthesia. Auditory chaos that separated into recognizable sounds. A beeping monitor. A gurney rolling by. A male voice. "Jessica. Jessica." I recognized his accent. France. I was in France. I was at the concert when . . .

As memories assaulted me, I willed my mind to sink back into insentience, to reverse its slow rise out of darkness. There was nothing in the brutal light of reality that wouldn't reverberate with the sound of gunfire bursts. Nothing that would shield me from a full remembering. From a full resuffering.

The world around me continued to come into focus, insisting on my consciousness. I commanded myself to resist, a plight as futile as fighting against gravity.

"*Jessica, vous m'entendez?*" The same male voice. My mind flashed to a sneering, menacing face, and my body convulsed—trying to escape. Trying to . . .

The pain was brutal. It seared its way across my abdomen and down my spine. "*Non. Non, non,*

non." His voice was gentle but urgent, his accent thick and comforting. "Don't move, okay? Don't move, Jessica. It will open your incision."

Incision. My eyelids felt leaden. I struggled against their weight. My mind was still locked on the massacre. Snapshots of the terror assailed me with every breath—with every heartbeat. I needed to open my eyes. I needed to . . .

A face swam into focus. That accented voice again. "Hello, Jessica." I squinted to see more clearly. A middle-aged black man in scrubs smiled down on me. His wasn't one of the faces imprinted on my mind.

"My parents," I tried to say. What came out was more croak than whisper. I cleared my throat. "Has someone called my parents?"

He leaned close. "Please repeat." His concern seemed genuine.

I took a deeper breath and tried again. "Do my parents know I'm here?"

The nurse leaned back and laid a hand on my shoulder. "Yes. I think so. The—how do you say—*emergency.* The emergency nurse found your phone and police took it. I think they called. I will ask, okay? I will ask."

"My friend. Vonda . . ." I took a couple breaths as a wave of nausea swept through me. He patted my shoulder until I could speak again. "Vonda— she was there with me. Do you know if she . . . ?"

He shook his head. "We have no list of names

yet. It's too soon. Too much—too many people."

"She was in the balcony . . . Were people killed in the balcony?" Just uttering the words stole the breath from my lungs. People killed. People killed.

I felt tears gathering in my eyes and running down my cheeks into the hair at my temples. "Please," I whispered. "I need to know if Vonda's okay."

⁓⁂⁓

It was night when I fully woke again. Pain medication weighed down my body and slowed my thinking. There were at least two other patients in my room. I'd heard them speaking to the nurses. Curtains drawn between the beds offered flimsy privacy.

I lay immobile, the pain somewhat bearable as long as I didn't try to move. Memories converged again. There was no use trying to evade them. Death had burned its savagery into the fabric of my consciousness. I felt stained. Branded.

When a nurse came to check on me, I didn't ask the questions grating through my mind. I craved and feared their answers.

"Are you comfortable?" the young woman asked in nearly perfect English. "How is your pain?"

"I'm okay." My voice still rasped over stunned vocal cords.

She put a call button in my hand and wrapped warm fingers around mine for a moment. "If you

27

need anything, you push the button, yes? I'm in the *couloir* outside the door."

More tears. The kindness wounded me. "I need my phone. Can I have my phone?"

"It isn't here. The police, they have to look at it. If you have pictures they can use to . . ."

"I didn't take any. Not after the . . . Not when the . . ."

"I'll bring it to you when they return it."

"Please." I tamped down the sob that threatened to escape. "Please," I said again, swallowing hard.

"I'll get you more medicine. Maybe you can sleep a little now."

I grabbed the nurse's wrist as she was turning to leave and bit my lip to stifle a yelp of pain. "Did a lot of people die?" I asked. I had to know.

The nurse nodded, and I saw tears in her eyes too. "Many," she said. Then she took a deep breath and added, "But many survived." She patted my hand where it still gripped her wrist. "I know you are *américaine*, but you are French now too."

Patrick had found me. I woke to see him sitting at my bedside, his eyes closed behind horn-rimmed glasses. He leaned forward in his chair, elbows on knees, hands clasped, his eyebrows drawn together in thought. Or fear. Or relief.

"Patrick."

His eyes snapped open and found mine. He

didn't move. He didn't touch me. But somehow—in a way that had bound us to each other since we'd met four years before—his strength bridged the space between us and eked into my bloodstream.

"You found me," I said, my voice sleep-rough and horror-hoarse.

"No easy task."

"You found me," I said again, dread softening into tears.

"And you're alive." I felt the miracle in his voice. He moved then. Just far enough to rest his forearm on the mattress beside me and lay his fingers against mine. "You're alive," he repeated, as if the warmth of my skin had sealed the unthinkable.

"It hurts."

"What?"

"Everything." Moving. Breathing. Thinking. Forgetting. It all hurt.

A muscle worked in Patrick's jaw.

"I had to have surgery and . . ."

"I know." He expelled a long breath. "The nurses caught me up. It could have been so much worse, Jess. With the amount of blood you lost between getting shot and being brought here . . ." He paused. "But the bullet missed your major organs and they got in there to fix what it damaged, so . . . It's a small, clean wound—that's what they said. A small, clean wound. That's good. That's amazing."

"I'll get out in a few days," I said, as much to prepare myself as to reassure my friend. "Once they're sure there's no infection."

Patrick's expression softened. "It could have been so much worse, Jess."

A wave of panic washed over me. "Vonda," I said. Fear drove the breath from my lungs.

His fingers tightened into a grip on my arm. He leaned forward. "She's fine," he said, urgency in his voice. "Jess, she's fine."

"Did she get out? When they started . . ." I closed my eyes against the memories. "Did she get out?"

His voice softened into a soothing tone. "She did. She's fine. She wasn't hurt."

I looked toward the door, half expecting to see her standing there. I needed to see her. I needed proof that she was alive. "Is she . . . is she coming?"

Patrick's head dropped forward before he answered. "I don't know," he said. When he looked up, I saw frustration in his eyes.

I fought a twinge of betrayal. She knew what I'd endured—what I was still enduring. "She's scared," I said, trying to excuse her absence. "Right? That's why she's not here."

"With what she saw . . ." He stopped himself short and sat up straighter in his chair. I felt a chill where his hand had been. "With what you both saw," he amended, "I guess she needs . . ." He hesitated, and I could see him trying to inject certainty into his expression. "She'll come," he finally said. "She'll come to see you when she can."

"I want to go home," I said, betrayal yielding to desperation.

"I know."

"I want to get as far away as . . ."

"I know, Jess."

I looked into my friend's face and felt overcome with powerlessness. "I thought . . ." I hiccupped on a sob. "I thought I was going to die."

The silence that followed felt overfull—heavy with the gunfire and screams in my mind. All the terror I'd controlled until then flowed out of me in tears and groans and spasms. Patrick pulled his chair up closer to the bed and wrapped an arm across me, shielding me from the horrors I couldn't stop reliving. There was a sacredness to that moment. Little was said, but everything was spoken as the injustice and bliss of survival washed over me in jagged waves.

When the worst of it passed, Patrick pulled away again.

"I don't want to sleep," I whispered. "Every time I close my eyes I see . . . I don't want to sleep."

There was nothing he could say—no gesture he could make—to diminish the weight of my trauma. So he sat next to me, hour after hour, our silence binding my wounds. He stayed through the night, upright in his chair, a sentinel poised to rescue and soothe. He squeezed my arm and wakened me when nightmares filled my sleep. He whispered comfort, his face near my pillow, when memories scraped my courage raw.

Patrick was still there when I woke the next morning. We waited for the doctor to come by, but he didn't. Nurses filled us in on what they knew as they changed my dressing. An incision five inches long extended around my waist. I'd had the best surgeon, the nurse said. He'd come in from the suburbs when news of the attacks first broke. "They all came. *Comment dire?*" She searched for the English words. "All the medical people could not stay home. We needed to help."

"*Merci,*" I said.

Patrick repeated his thanks. "Thank you. Thank you so much."

⸙

Vonda came the next day. I sensed a presence in the doorway and turned to see her standing there. Her face was blank—pale.

"Vonda." Tears flooded my eyes as I reached for her.

She entered slowly, tentatively, and stopped a few feet from my bed. "I'm sorry," she whispered.

"Sorry—?"

"I can't stay in Paris. I have to go. The nurses told me you're going to be fine and . . ." She held up a plastic bag. "I brought you a few toiletries. And some clothes—clean underwear, a couple shirts, and some yoga pants for when you're . . . when you're better. But, Jess . . ." She closed her eyes and shook her head, as if she were trying to clear it. "I just—I can't stay here."

I felt myself frown, confused by her calm. By her distance. "Vonda . . . You're—you're just . . . leaving?"

"I'm taking the train to Luxembourg in a little over an hour. And I have a ticket from there to Denver. The airports . . . It's the only way I could get out of France. After the attack, and . . ."

I saw her shudder. Her shoulders drooped. She reached for the railing at the bottom of my bed to steady herself. When she looked at me, it was with horror in her eyes. "I thought you were dead," she said. She bit her lip and inhaled a tortured breath. "I got out through a skylight. There was a storage room a bunch of us ran to and . . . somehow we all got out that way. We ran across the roof and climbed in someone's apartment window and waited for the police to release us. I could hear the gunshots," she said, a sob escaping her tight control. "The whole time we were waiting, I could hear the gunshots and I didn't know . . . I didn't know if you were alive until the hospital called the apartment."

I lay back and felt tears run into my hair.

"They held us for hours," Vonda continued, her voice lower and more resigned now. "The police. They had to question everyone. I kept trying to call you until they took my phone, but you didn't answer and . . . I didn't know what to do when they released me. I've been cowering at Patrick's, just . . ." Anger stiffened her shoulders, and a look of disgust crossed her face. "Just cowering. And I can't." She squared her shoulders. "I have to leave."

"Okay." There was nothing else to say. I felt abandoned. Stranded.

Vonda came closer, grasping my hand in both of hers, but avoided eye contact. "So this is good-bye," she said. I heard brokenness in the word.

"Stay until Patrick comes back," I begged.

"Jess . . ." She frowned as tears brimmed in her eyes, then ran down her cheeks.

"He just left to get some coffee."

"I can't."

"Vonda—please?"

"My taxi's waiting and . . . I have to leave." She released my hand and laid it back on the white blanket. She didn't look at me again but turned, picked up her purse, and walked out of the room.

THREE

"Honey . . ." My mom's voice on the other end of the phone was relieved and distraught. "Honey," she said again, a sob in her throat.

After nearly two days of being unable to reach me, and with the American Embassy offering little information in the chaos that followed the attack, my parents had grown frantic. A phone call from a police liaison officer had finally informed them that I was alive, but in La Pitié Salpêtrière—a hospital.

"I'm okay, Mom," I said into the phone.

"Your dad's right here next to me. We've got the phone on speaker." She hesitated. "Are you—?"

"We don't know anything," my dad interrupted. "The woman who answered the phone just put us through to your room, so . . . please tell us what's going on."

"I was . . ." There was something terrifying about putting words to what had happened. Articulating the horrors felt like grafting them to me. Me to them.

I took a deep breath and felt the stitches in my side pulling. I had to speak—they had to know—but the burden felt overwhelming. "I was at the Bataclan when it started," I began, hearing the tremor in my voice. "It happened so fast and I couldn't get out and . . ."

"Oh, Lord," my mother groaned. I could imagine my dad reaching for her hand to calm her.

"I'm okay," I hurried to say, though I doubted my own words. The reality stunned me. "I was . . . I was shot through the side. It was . . ." I stumbled. "They did surgery and . . ."

"What kind of surgery?" My dad's voice had hardened. "Honey, what did they do to you?"

I knew they wanted details. I knew they needed to understand what I'd endured two nights ago. And since then. But I couldn't bring myself to look the memories in the face. They'd already seeped too much of their paralysis into my mind.

"The nurses tell me I was lucky," I said, straining for a confident tone. "Really. They had to repair some damage to a portion of my intestines, but . . ."The image of a blond man lying in a pool of his own blood flashed into my mind. I shook my head to dislodge it. "But I was lucky," I said. *Lucky.* The word felt insufficient. Insulting.

There was silence on the other end of the line for a moment. Then my dad cleared his throat. "I've got our travel agent finalizing tickets, honey. We'll get there as fast as we can."

"No." The word was out before I had time to soften it.

"But . . ." My mom sounded surprised. When she spoke again, it was with more conviction. "Honey, we are not staying here while our daughter is in the hospital in France."

36

"It's already taken care of," my dad said. "We'll let you know when our reservations are confirmed."

"No," I said again. Even more firmly this time. I wasn't sure where my reticence came from, but I knew beyond a doubt that I didn't want them here. "It's just . . ." I tried to soften my tone. "I may not be in the hospital much longer. The nurses say I could be out in a couple days. And Patrick's arranging for a flight back for both of us." It was a lie. We hadn't so much as mentioned an exit plan. "I can stay in his apartment until I'm well enough to travel. Really. There's no reason for you to come here when I'll be back there in a few days."

"But . . . you're injured."

"I know, Mom." Impatience stirred. "But I'm not an invalid. They have me up and walking." I thought of the massacre, of the savagery I'd witnessed. "I'm alive," I said. My breath caught. Guilt and disbelief. "I can walk out of this hospital, when others . . ."

"We want to come," my dad said. I heard understanding and need dueling in his voice. "We just feel so useless sitting here. If we flew over, we could help you with—"

"Patrick will help."

"Honey, we've been so scared." My mom began to sob. I heard the muffled sound and felt remorse. They needed to come. They needed to see me breathing. But something in me rebelled at the thought of their presence. I didn't want their fear—their trauma—magnifying mine.

"I've been scared too," I admitted. Then I took a breath and strove for clarity. For resolve. "I'll be fine," I said. "Patrick's been here every day. He's promised to help me until I can fly out. He's . . ." I remembered how much my parents had balked when I'd moved in with him. They'd wondered about the optics of me living with a man. About his motivation too. "He's taking care of me. You know how he is. And . . . and I'm fine."

"Are you in pain?" The concern in my dad's voice nearly undid me.

"A little," I admitted. "But nothing awful. My doctor says I'm recovering quickly."

My mother's sobs reached me from across the ocean again. "What you've been through . . ." she said, shocked and broken.

"It's okay, Mom. I'm okay." I lay my head back on the stacked pillows behind me and stared at the ceiling. Every cell in my body wanted to flee— to get out of Paris as quickly as I could, the way Vonda had. To escape the pall that clung to every person, every place. But with impotence and immobility strangling the life from me, I needed this one decision to be mine.

They tried to persuade me for a few minutes more, as fatigue descended over me. "It's getting late," I finally said. "And I'm too tired to think straight."

"Of course." It was the same voice my mom had used when I was sick as a child. Calm and soothing. "You need to rest."

"Don't buy the tickets."

My dad didn't want to surrender. "Jessica . . ."

"Don't buy the tickets. Please."

There were a few moments of silence. I could picture them looking at each other, weighing the benefits of ignoring my wishes. "Let's talk again tomorrow," my father finally said. "Can we reconsider then?"

I sighed. "Sure."

⁂

They called again the next day, when Patrick was in the room. They repeated their reasons for wanting to fly to Paris, and I tried once more to dissuade them of their plans. Seeing my distress, Patrick whispered better arguments to me, facts and reasons that would convince them not to come.

Gratitude lifted my spirits as I heard them edging toward concession. He'd given me all the right words—the words a parent wants to hear—about my condition, my recovery, our strategy. "I'll fly back as soon as my doctors allow it," I finally said. "I'm in good hands. I promise you I am."

"Are you sure?" my mom asked one last time before hanging up. "If you're not . . ."

"I'm sure, Mom."

There was a pause. Then a sigh. Then my dad's voice. "Okay. We can't wait to hug you, honey. Can't wait to see your face."

"I'll be home soon."

I should have been elated, but there was a shroud over my mind—a muddied weight that seemed to prevent clear thought and, often, words.

I was moved to a private room the next day. My parents had made the arrangements, and friends and strangers in my hometown had pledged to cover whatever cost my insurance didn't. The quieter environment was comforting and terrifying.

I tried a couple times to speak of what had happened with Patrick, fearful that my silence would anchor the memories to my DNA.

I caught him looking at me across my dinner tray one evening.

"I was standing over by the left side of the stage."

He nodded courage.

"I wanted to get a close-up picture of the band. For you. To show you we were having fun without you." I drew in a ragged breath. It all seemed so trivial now. "I was just about to snap the shot when—"

My thoughts froze at that moment, as if the memories were sparing me from reexperienced terror. A sudden amnesia seemed to deaden my senses. I felt relief and fear. Relief that the details suddenly seemed scrubbed from my mind and fear that the loss was beyond my control.

Patrick must have seen the battle playing out on my face. He rose and came to sit beside me on the bed, his soft voice comforting. "Give it time," he said. "You'll know when you're ready."

I nodded.

"Just give it time," he repeated.

I tried again before he left that night. And still the memories that had been unbearably clear the day before escaped me. I could feel their impact—the full brunt of their damage—but had lost the sights, sounds, and words of the ordeal. Part of me was grateful for the selective amnesia. Another part wondered if I had lost much more.

⁂

The pall that hung over the hospital right after the attacks had begun to lighten. I could hear laughing nurses in those dark hours when residual pain kept me from sleeping. Not the leaden silence that had followed the influx of casualties overwhelming the hospital's services.

As my condition improved, traces of Patrick's exuberance reappeared again. He distracted me with tales of his quartier's happenings—the fishmonger caught selling three-day-old sole, squatters kicked out from the apartment across the street. There was something about the banality of the stories that allowed my mind to disengage—to focus for a moment on the ordinariness I feared I'd never know again.

When Patrick saw my disposition changing, he redoubled his efforts to bring brightness to my world. He wore his favorite striped blazer on my fourth day in the hospital, a red and beige monstrosity that somehow looked chic on him.

"Do not adjust your TV set," he said as I squinted at his getup when he entered my room. "This city needs some optimism, and I am *bringing it* in the form of vintage Pierre Cardin."

"You look like a candy striper."

"And you look like a patient. But you're out of bed—that's a step in the right direction."

He grinned and propped a hip on the medical cabinet just inside the door. "You okay sitting up?" he asked, eyeing the pillows a nurse had propped around me in the big armchair by the window.

"It's fine," I said. The pain was decreasing every day.

"Good—then let's talk travel."

He spent the next few minutes trying to talk me back into the expedition we'd planned before the attacks upended our worlds.

"We'll head south—take it as slow as we need to," he said.

"Patrick . . ."

"No," he said, pointing at me. "We do not let the bad guys derail our plans."

I thought of those who'd lost their lives, not just

42

their plans, and felt a too-familiar weight press into me.

Patrick sensed it and moved to sit on the end of my bed, facing my chair. There was hope on his face. "We'll find the most beautiful places. We'll soak in some sun. We'll hunt for the dirtiest attics and barns we can find and dig for treasure until the next bakery calls our name too loudly to ignore."

"I'm recovering, remember?"

"Fine. So I'll do the digging and you can do the eating."

"My parents want me home with them."

"Of course they do."

"And . . ." I took a deep breath and looked down at my hands, ashamed of my fear. "And I really just want to get out of France."

"Honey," Patrick said. He propped his chin on his clasped hands and gave me courage with his eyes. Not judgment. Not pity. "If you need to go home, do. Do what's right for you, and of course I'll fly back with you, but . . ." I saw a glint of rebellion cross his face. "But you're alive. And the deudeuche is gassed up and rarin' for an adventure, and if ever there was a time to thumb your nose at predictability by going on a treasure hunt with your slightly demented friend in a car that is really a go-cart with a rollback roof . . ."

"I don't want to stay in France." I took a breath. "I'm a rational thirty-four-year-old woman who knows in her head that this country may be safer today than it's ever been, but I'm terrified of staying here because I'm thinking like a four-year-old."

I could see optimism and understanding battling in Patrick's face. He'd brought to the past couple of visits a deliberate enthusiasm, likely hoping it would seep into me if he shone it long enough. But he'd also brought a caring heart—the same that had locked us into an enduring friendship—and I could see him evaluating the toll of his cheerleading on me.

"Aren't your parents concerned?" I asked him. "Don't they want you home too?"

He gave me a look. "Jessica." Of course. He was estranged from them—had been for years. They likely didn't even know he'd come to Paris for the semester.

"I think I'll go either way," he said. He held up his hands. "That's not a threat or an attempt at guilting you into coming along. I just want you to know that it's happening. If you decide not to come, I'll fly home with you—that's nonnegotiable—then come back over and do this trip."

"Patrick . . ."

"No pressure. Just an open invitation. Okay?"

I nodded, but knew I wouldn't join him. This city I'd loved—this country I'd come to with anticipation and excitement, wondering if I'd put down roots here someday and stay awhile—had become the scene of horrors too soul-shattering to measure. Distance felt like a reprieve. The slow resumption of life in a world untouched by tragedy.

I swallowed hard against the tears clogging my throat. "I could have died," I whispered. "More than a hundred people did." Those sounds—those awful, brutal, fatal sounds—reverberated in my mind again. "I want to leave."

Patrick pondered my words, a gentle, sad smile on his face. After a moment, he shook his head and expelled a long breath. "Of course you do." There was only concern in his gaze.

FOUR

"Are you sure it's safe for me to go home?"

My favorite nurse, Lilly, had just handed me a prescription bottle with a two-week supply of painkillers and informed me that she had my discharge papers ready. Though the doctor had been by to check on me the day before, there was nothing in his demeanor that had hinted at my release.

"The doctor thinks yes," she said, her voice more lilting now than in those early, somber days. "You can wait a little more time before you go back to *l'Amérique*, if you prefer," she added. "And you need someone for your suitcases, yes? To lift them for you. I have instructions . . ." She leafed through the papers she held in her hand but couldn't find what she was looking for. "I will print them and bring them before you leave. It says no lifting heavy things for a few weeks, but as long as you listen to your—how you say? To your *instinct,*" she said, pronouncing the word the French way, "then it is okay for you to go home today."

I was stunned. And excited. And terrified. "So I can . . . leave?"

"Yes, yes," Lilly said, smiling broadly. "Do you want me to call your friend—the one you say you stay with?"

"I'll try to reach him," I said, pulling out my phone. "He doesn't live far."

⸙

I hadn't anticipated the frenzy Lilly's news set off in my spirit. Having waited so long for permission to go home, knowing I'd have been released much sooner from a hospital in the States, I wasted no time after the nurse left my room.

I went to the closet and pulled out the few items Vonda had brought for me the day she'd said good-bye. I changed into them slowly, careful not to pull too much on the incision in my side.

When I reached for my wallet, the thin leather billfold I'd tucked into my pocket on the night of the concert, I saw dark stains on one corner. Blood. I felt my pulse speed up as the static in my mind crescendoed. Memories lurched and I fought them back. There was an urgency in me—a desperation to get out, to see the sky and breathe the air outside hospital walls. I took the credit cards, euro bills, and Patrick's apartment key from the wallet and tossed the rest into the trash can by my bed.

Then I sat down, unsettled and agitated. But I couldn't wait for Lilly to return.

Looking back later, I'd have little recollection of my departure from the hospital. I left my room and rode the elevator down to the main floor. I didn't think of unpaid bills or discharge procedures, but focused instead on the sliding doors and the daylight beyond them. Somehow I found a taxi and gave the driver Patrick's address. I must have paid the fare, but even that was just a blur.

I climbed the stairs to my friend's studio apartment slowly and let myself in when he didn't answer my knock. I locked the door behind me, went to the couch, and lowered myself into its familiar softness.

-ॐ-

Patrick was home when I woke up—sitting by the window in his vintage chair, looking melancholy. Maybe wistful.

"Hi," I said.

He looked at me and cocked an eyebrow, melancholy replaced by relief. "Did they let you go or did you break out?"

I adjusted my position to prop my feet on the couch's armrest. "I'm cleared to fly when I feel up to it."

"And do you feel up to it?"

I closed my eyes to take inventory of the aches and pains that had steadily decreased since the night of the . . . "Better every day."

"So . . . are we booking tickets?" There was a plea in his voice. A reluctance.

I knew he wanted me to stay. I knew he thought it would be better for me not to run from a place that was now defined by terror. Yet the thought of staying intensified the panic that hummed constantly, like static, in the recesses of my mind. "I think I'll feel up to it in a couple of days," I said, attempting a smile. "My parents are getting antsy, and it hurts a lot less to move, so—yes. I think we're booking tickets."

The thought of leaving caused a brightening in my spirit. Putting distance between us felt like a welcome reprieve.

Patrick sat in silence for a moment, his eyes on me. Again, there was no judgment there. Just that trace of the sadness I'd seen when I woke up. "We can wait until morning," I said, hoping the delay would allow him to warm to the idea of leaving.

He nodded. "So I've got—what?" He checked his watch. "Half a day to convince you to stay?"

"You have half a day to get used to my leaving."

He didn't like my answer. I could tell by the frown he tried valiantly to suppress. "But first we eat," he said in typical Patrick style, diverting my mind from flight to food.

"Got anything tastier than what I had in the hospital?"

He hitched his chin toward the kitchen counter, where stacks of the groceries he'd bought a few days earlier, in anticipation of our trip, still lay. "I'm thinking I can rustle something up."

"Thank you, Patrick." Tears blurred my vision.

Perhaps it was the comfort—the homeness of his place. Or maybe the relief of being out of the hospital. Or maybe the reassurance and understanding of his friendship.

He feigned confusion. "For making dinner or . . . ?"

I smiled. He understood.

It was the easy nature of our relationship that had confounded my parents when they first met Patrick. They'd come up to Denver for a weekend and demanded to meet my "roommate." They said the word with underlying disapproval. They'd taught me better than that. A woman was not to live with a man. It didn't matter to them that three of us shared the apartment. They were sure there was something sordid I was keeping from them.

So Patrick had met us for dinner in a kitschy chain restaurant, the type of place he'd never have set foot in were it not for the attempt to ease my parents' qualms. Though they'd come to our meeting expecting to dislike him, they'd been charmed nearly instantly by his authenticity and wit.

As I drove them back to their hotel that night, my father said, "So, are you going to marry him?"

"Henry!" Her husband's penchant for bluntness had always made my mother squirm.

"We're not getting married, Dad." I was grateful for the traffic that kept my attention focused forward.

"You seem to get along well," he said.

"We do."

My mom's intentions were subtler, but just as obvious when she said from the back seat, "It's nice to see you so comfortable around a man."

"Mom . . ."

I'd never really had a serious romantic relationship, so there was no comparison on which to base her assessment. The men of Lamar were not what I was looking for, and I'd been so busy since my arrival in Denver that I'd scarcely had the time to consider a romantic life.

Granted, Patrick had done his best to improve my track record. He'd signed me up for an online dating site just weeks after I moved into his townhouse—completely without my knowledge—then spent a couple more weeks perfecting my bio and weeding through potential suitors, discarding the ones he didn't like and communicating with others on my behalf.

After my initial consternation, I'd agreed to a couple of handpicked dates, and Patrick had declared himself my stylist and my coach. But despite his best efforts, the encounters had been awkward and my matches either arrogant, disinterested, or dull.

My father turned toward me. "You should bring

him home for Thanksgiving. He looks like he could use some of your mother's cooking, and we'd get to spend more time with him."

"He's not coming for Thanksgiving."

My mom said, "We just had the guest bedroom recarpeted. He'd be the first to use it."

The conversation had gone on from there—my dad with his prying questions, my mom with her passive-aggressive enthusiasm, and me trying to explain, with words and exclamations, that Patrick and I were not "that kind" of friends.

My parents hadn't been the only ones to broach the topic. After yet another barely veiled comment by a mutual friend a few weeks later, Patrick finally brought the subject into the open.

"You've seen *Sleepless in Seattle*, right?"

I was a bit taken aback. We were sitting in our usual chairs in his apartment, catching up on the shows he'd saved to his DVR. "Uh, yes. A few years ago."

"So you know the meaning of MFEO."

I pushed pause. "What's this about?"

"Made for each other. MFEO."

"I know the meaning of MFEO."

He pursed his lips and looked at me, but I could tell his mind was on choosing the right words. "I'm just going to come out and say it."

I rolled my eyes. "The suspense is killing me."

"People think we're MFEO."

So this was the topic that had made him so

fidgety all evening. "They do. And none more than my parents, despite my constant denials."

He stared for a moment again. "I just want to . . . I just want to make sure we're on the same page. Because people keep trying to be cute about hinting at—things—and I . . . I just want to be clear."

I turned so I was facing him and tried for the most earnest expression I could muster. "Patrick."

He suddenly seemed uncomfortable. "Wait—are you going to say something awkward?"

"We're PMFEO."

He squinted at me. "Probably made for each other?"

I laughed and rolled my eyes again. "Platonically made for each other!"

"Oh." He looked away, giving the term some consideration. "I like it," he finally said. "Succinct and unequivocal."

I shrugged. "I'm a big fan of both." We smiled at each other until it got weird. "Can I go back to my show now?"

"We're okay?"

"Patrick."

"Just want to be sure!"

"We're okay."

"Good. Then you can press play."

The conversation had defused a tension I hadn't acknowledged until that evening. There was a muddiness to mature adult friendships—

the expectation that they would lead to some-thing more. That they *should.* And after that night, with our relationship more clearly defined, we'd moved forward more freely, autonomous and intertwined, an unusual duo bound by similar passions and complementary interests. Patrick and I knew that what connected us was rare. It didn't matter anymore how others wanted to define it.

-⧜-

When I woke up on my first morning after my release from the hospital, in Patrick's tiny studio near the Rue de Rivoli, he was ready to launch a campaign of persuasion. He spent the better part of the morning calmly and fervently reiterating the reasons I should stay in France and go adventuring with him.

"We can buy you a ticket home," he kept interjecting, holding up his hands as if I were accusing him of derailing my plans. "But consider this . . ." And he'd go off on another impassioned plea for me to reconsider my decision.

At the end of that first day, after I'd made tentative reservations for us with Air France for three days later, Patrick sat on the edge of my bed—his bed, which he'd graciously ceded to "the patient"—and tried one final approach.

"This is the last I'll say about this . . ."

"I don't believe you."

He frowned. "This isn't about me."

I opened my mouth to speak, but he cut in. "Yes, I've been planning this trip for months, but it doesn't matter. Jess, believe me, it doesn't matter anymore to me. You do. What's best for you is what matters now."

He was as sincere as I'd ever seen him. "But?"

He sighed. "If I were you—and I know I'm not—but if I were you, I think I'd want to stay. Not because I feel safe. I know you can't feel safe anywhere right now. None of us can, but you—you've seen . . ." He looked up at the ceiling for a moment, then back to me. "You're a survivor. You've survived a nightmare, Jess. And the reason I keep hoping you'll change your mind and stay here and drive that silly deudeuche around France with me is that I want to see you taking something back—making your next step a decision, not a—"

"I was shot, Patrick."

He hung his head. "You were. And I can't imagine how that feels."

"I just want to go home."

"I get that. I'm a jerk for suggesting anything else."

"You're not a jerk . . ."

"I guess I just want to give the bad guys the finger—to prove that they didn't destroy you, no matter how hard they tried."

"They might have." The words should have appalled me, but I felt numb to them.

"They didn't. You're here. You're breathing." He paused and looked at me for a moment. "But I can't use you to send them my message. It's unfair and selfish."

"They're dead," I said. The nurses had joyfully told me they were all gone. "No messages to send."

"But their intentions aren't. They wanted you to feel so scared that you'd never step foot outside again without looking over your shoulder and expecting more of the awful you've already been through."

"I *am* scared," I whispered. "Every time I close my eyes or hear a loud noise or—"

"I know." He took my hand and gave it a firm squeeze. "I know. I know, Jess." Then he sat back and blew out a loud breath. "I won't mention it again."

This time I believed him. "You can."

"I won't. This is your life. It's your *spared* life. And you know what you need, so . . ." He smiled a little sadly. "You take your pain pill?"

"I'm trying a night without any."

"Okay." He nodded. "Then I'll see you in the morning?"

"Patrick, you're sleeping right over there." I pointed at the couch just feet from the bed I lay on.

"Right, but . . . you need to sleep and I said I'd be quiet, so . . ."

"I'm turning out the light now."

"Okay."

"And I'll see you in the morning."

"Right."

"Good night, Patrick."

"Good night, Jess."

FIVE

Three days later, I wasn't on a plane bound for Denver. I was in a small, loud, bare-bones car headed south. I wasn't sure how I'd reached the decision to postpone my flight home, though everything in me craved an escape. Patrick had eased up on his persuasive pitches after that first day out of the hospital, discussing potential plans only after I brought up the subject.

So I wondered, as we rumbled off the *périphérique* in our faded orange deudeuche and followed signs to Orléans, how my determination to leave France had morphed into agreement to give it one more chance.

"You're not just doing this to make me happy, right?" Patrick had asked after I told him I'd changed my mind. We hadn't left the apartment since I'd returned, the thought of venturing out still causing tingles of panic in my mind. He hadn't pushed me to step outside or take a shower or distract myself with TV or books. He'd cared for me by occupying my mind with his inimitable conversation, by feeding me from the stash of food we'd purchased for the trip—before the nightmare, before the carnage—by letting me go silent when memories tried to force their way past my mental barricades.

"I'm not going for you, Patrick," I assured him. "I'm going because . . ." My thoughts trailed off. As sure as I was that this trip was what I wanted, I couldn't identify a cogent reason for my change of heart. Except an impulse—a quiet instinct that had whispered above the deafening fear fueling my flight from France. It had coaxed a reluctant relinquishing from me. I sensed, in some unexplainable way, that this was the right choice to make.

The feeling had persisted as I gathered enough belongings for our southern adventure. It persisted as Patrick pulled out a map of France and showed me again the itinerary he'd planned, assuring me that it could be modified if I needed to take it slower. It persisted despite the anxiety that grew from a dull hum to a roar as we left his apartment, stowed our baggage in the backseat, and made our way slowly down familiar streets.

I tried not to see the French flags hanging from windows, the flowers and candles and notes piled high on the Place de la Réunion. But there was no ignoring the alterations in this post-attack France. The buildings and shops and cafés hadn't changed, but the air around them felt fragile—almost brittle—with the wounded disbelief of the Parisian spirit.

"We'll be out of the city soon," Patrick said, sensing my anxiety, as we followed the Seine on the Quai du Point du Jour. "Once we hit the périphérique, we'll be free and clear."

I closed my eyes and tried to remember the beauty that had lulled me into daydreams of moving more permanently to the city. The markets and their voluptuous aromas—flowers and baked goods and fresh fish and crêpes all intertwined and warm in the cold morning air. The grandeur of Notre Dame. The decadence of Quai des Orfèvres. The simple enchantment of the skyline at dusk.

But they were all bloodstained now. Tainted with terror. Steeped in the stench of unexplainable hatred. So when we left the road that looped around the capital and set out toward Orléans, it was relief, not regret, that permeated my thoughts.

We stopped for the night in Moulins at a little Airbnb I'd reserved for us online. It was an extra stop from our original itinerary, one that would shorten the hours we spent in the car on our first day.

"You're picking our lodging," Patrick had said the morning before as he dropped a pair of white linen pants into his vintage leather suitcase.

"Are we going treasure hunting or yachting?"

He gave me his don't-mess-with-me look and began folding the striped jacket he'd worn to the hospital. "I've packed plenty of common clothes," he said, infusing the last two words with his usual disdain. "These are just in case our modest adventure intersects with someone else's extravagant expedition."

"Your optimism is astounding."

He didn't respond. I watched him folding more clothes and fitting them neatly into his organizational masterpiece and knew he was thinking of me. Of optimism. Of the fact that I'd been hopeful once too. I knew he worried, as I did, that that part of my life had been amputated by fear.

"So why am I the one planning our overnight stays?"

"Because you're the one with a bullet hole in your body." His countenance softened. "I want you to be comfortable. You pick the beds, I pick the attics."

I hadn't reserved traditional B&Bs, daunted by the prospect of conversations with strangers. So we were staying in a coach house that night, on the outskirts of Moulins. We'd found a note on the door with instructions to work the keypad. The space was small and comfortable, recently renovated, and far from the frantic pace of a city. There was some comfort in that. We ate what we'd bought at the local Auchan store, and I went to bed early.

I wanted to be excited. I wanted to give Patrick the companion he'd invited on this trip. The energetic, intrepid friend he'd chosen to take along. *Maybe tomorrow,* I thought as I turned off the bedside lamp. Light from the living room shone under the door. I pictured Patrick on his foldout couch, reading a historical novel or scouring the map for the villages we'd visit when we got to the first stop of our picking pilgrimage. Not for the first time, I thanked God for this friend.

Then I remembered the attack. And God seemed suddenly less worthy of my gratitude.

⋰⋱

It took us two more days to get to Balazuc, a small town perched on a rocky outcropping in the Ardèche region of southern France. I'd chosen the location because the online pictures were beautiful—a rugged village that still looked as it would have hundreds of years ago. And Patrick had approved of it because there were enough flea markets in the area to have him happily sifting through junk for the four days we'd be there.

The tall stone bridge leading to Balazuc was just one lane wide, and the roads got narrower from there. They flowed like water through the little town, around centuries-old constructions unbound by draftsmen's plans. We pulled up to the B&B in the late afternoon, weary from the drive but fascinated by the place we'd found. Like the rest of the village, the cottage was built of chiseled limestone. Single-storied and stoic, it stood in the shadow of an austere manor house.

We circled around the cobblestoned courtyard

in our loud deudeuche and parked in the spot labeled *Visiteurs* near the cottage's front door. Patrick took off toward the gate as soon as he was out of the car. "Hey," I called after him. "Where are you going?"

"Checking out the antique store we passed back there. These places close at five, and it's nearly quarter 'til!" He jogged around the gate and out of sight.

I shook my head and stretched in the afternoon sun, careful not to pull the still-healing incision in my side. I hadn't even noticed the store he was referring to, but Patrick had a radar for the junk he called treasure.

A door opened in the manor house across the courtyard from our cottage and a woman stepped out, waving at me before she'd crossed the threshold. Though I'd expected a greeting in French, she spoke to me in English.

"Hello, hello! You must be the Jessica who reserved online."

"I am," I said, surprised by her American accent.

She closed the gap between us. "I saw from your credit card info that you're from Denver." Holding her arms out wide, she declared, "From one American to another—welcome to Balazuc!"

"I . . . Thank you. It's a beautiful little town."

"It is indeed. Charmed us the first time we set eyes on it."

"You're from the States?"

"California. Redding." She hitched her chin toward a freckled face peering around the open door of her house. "Although that little guy remembers more of France than he does of the States by now." She called to the child. "Come say hello, Connor!"

The boy ducked out of sight, then peeked around as he reached out with one hand to push the door closed.

"He's only shy when he first meets someone," she said, shaking her head. "And since you're here for four days, you'll be wishing he were shyer by the time you leave again."

I looked around the courtyard, where every window was adorned with flower boxes and green shutters. They softened the harshness of straight angles and gray stone. "How long ago did you renovate?"

She threw back her head and laughed. "Oh, honey, the renovation's ongoing. The old barn over there is the current concern. We're turning it into a youth hostel of sorts—cheaper rooms, tighter quarters. We put a new roof on in the fall so Grant can work inside over the winter, but I've made him promise he won't start until after breakfast in the mornings so you won't be disturbed by the noise. Here's your key, by the way. And my name is Mona—did I say that before?"

"You did not. And it's nice to meet you."

I took the key from her and glanced back at the gate. No sign of Patrick.

Mona opened the door to the cottage and preceded me inside. I took in the Provençal décor—shades of blue, whites, and accents of yellow. The space was clean and welcoming. A kitchenette in the far corner was bigger than the one in Patrick's Parisian studio, and the view from the window right next to it was stunning—the deep, rocky riverbed of the Ardèche and rugged cliffs rising up toward an intense blue sky.

"The bedroom's through here," Mona said, opening the door to a bright space in which twin beds stood on either side of a courtyard-facing window. "Feel free to pull the shutters closed for privacy," she said. As she led me back out toward the door, she pointed at the phone on the kitchen counter. "Need anything, give us a call. Number's next to the phone, along with a bunch of information about the area. Breakfast's at eight, if that works for you. I'll bring it over here so you can eat in peace. And if you'd like to go out for dinner in town, there's a *crêperie* just past the church that makes the best buckwheat crêpes around."

She paused and took a breath, as if trying to reel herself back in. "Oh, and coffee . . ." She went to the kitchenette and opened cupboard doors. "Everything you need is right here. Coffee. Sugar. Creamer's in the fridge. A couple boxes of cookies if you get a midnight hankering. Just scrounge around and if there's something you can't find"—she pointed at the phone again—"call me."

"It's beautiful," I said. "And just what we were hoping for."

She gave me a pleased but quizzical look.

A shadow crossed the doorway and I turned, expecting to see Patrick, but a larger man stood there, backlit by the afternoon sun.

"Grant!" Mona exclaimed. "Come on in and meet our guest."

"I'm dragging around a day's worth of construction dirt on my boots, so . . ."

Mona held out both arms, as if warding off an evil force. "You stay put—we'll come to you!"

As we crossed the living room and stepped out of the sunlight pouring through the doorway, more of Grant came into view. He smiled a bit nonchalantly, hands propped on dusty hips, a ball cap coated with dirt on his head. "Grant," he said, pulling a work glove off his hand to shake mine. "But I guess you've already figured that out."

"Nice to meet you." I had to look up to return his smile.

"Got any luggage I can carry in for you?"

I looked past him. Still no sign of Patrick. "I'd appreciate that. It's all in the back seat."

He smiled. "The trunks on those deudeuches are a joke, right?"

There was something calming about him—I wasn't sure if it was the deep voice, his imposing frame, or the aura of sturdy composure that emanated from him. "So is the suspension," I said.

He was standing by the car already, pulling the bags out of the back seat. "Just inside the door okay?" he asked as he carried them back toward the cottage.

"Not okay—mandatory," Mona said, watching him closely as he set down the luggage. "Those boots come nowhere near these floors." She turned to me. "Holler if you need anything." And with a friendly wave, she backed out of the house and closed the door.

I dragged my suitcase into the bedroom and left it on the floor by one of the beds. Then I went to the window to look out.

Grant and Mona were still standing in the courtyard, their attention trained on the barn. They looked right together, somehow. Though Mona's frame was much smaller than Grant's, there was a sturdiness to it that spoke of strength and reliability. A strand of sandy blonde hair escaped from the clip that held it in a loose roll at the back of her head. It blew across her face, and she tucked it behind her ear as Grant pointed at the roofline and said something that made her shake her head in what looked like dismay. They walked slowly toward the open front door, where Connor—who looked to be maybe five years old—leaned against the doorframe, arms crossed, just the way Grant had stood in mine.

The boy straightened as they approached, and Grant ruffled the boy's bright-red hair before bending over to take off his boots. I heard Mona's voice again, unintelligible from this distance, then they all disappeared inside as the door closed behind them.

⤛⤜

"You missed all the fun," I said when Patrick returned a few minutes later.

"Sorry. Not worth it."

"The fun?"

"The store. Overpriced antiques and under-friendly staff."

"Find anything?"

He shook his head. "I like my treasures rough and moldy, not sweating under layers of slapped-on varnish."

I told him about Mona and Grant. "We should do that," he said.

"Do what?"

"Start a B&B!"

"Patrick."

I could see his wild imagination already conjuring up the future. That he was able to do so astounded me. I felt incapable of projecting beyond today.

"Think about it—a B&B-slash-brocante. A comfy house and a picker's paradise. People would come from all over the world for the Ealy-Jackson experience."

"So your name comes before mine in this little fantasy of yours?"

"Jackson-Ealy? That make you feel better? And if we could get a place with this kind of view . . ." His voice trailed off.

I'd started to pick up on a pattern since my release from the hospital. What little energy I could muster to do "real life" seemed to seep out of my system during the day and usually hit its lowest point just before dinnertime. The now-familiar slump came on suddenly as I watched Patrick standing by the window, visions of the Jackson-Ealy B&B brocante brightening his features. My muscles seemed to grow heavy. My mind less clear. My ability to process and communicate all but gone.

Patrick sensed my depletion. "Sinker?" he asked, using the term he'd coined for my end-of-day fatigue.

"It's the injury, right?" I asked, fear stirring. "Not something permanent."

He gave me the look that made me feel known. "You lie down and rest. We'll deal with dinner later."

As it turned out, dinner was boxed cookies and a few slices of the dried sausage we'd picked up at the butcher stand of an open-air market the day before. I told Patrick he was losing credibility in the "ooh-là-là chérie" department, and he informed me that I was in no position to insult the chef.

I went to bed early again that night, knowing how difficult sleep would be. Even in my childhood, when the worst of my fears were of monsters in closets and snakes under my bed, nighttime had fueled anxieties.

And now, in the vacuum of insentience, undefined memories surged back, laced with acid and barbed with terror. They'd lain dormant for a while—muted, perhaps, by subconscious self-preservation, but they'd resurged since the beginning of our trip to southern France.

I willed myself to stay awake until my medication kicked in, fearful of the twilight sleep between wakefulness and slumber when snapshots of the horror hurled themselves—blood-streaked and shrill—against the backdrop of my mind. But there was little I could do when my will surrendered to memory's onslaught.

Daylight didn't erase the macabre, but it diluted it somehow. There were moments when the beauty we encountered brightened the edges of the darkness that consumed me. But I couldn't seize the light that glimmered out of reach while my strength was still held hostage by the burden of surviving.

With Patrick's bed just feet away from mine, I woke on our first night in Balazuc to find him leaning over me, saying my name and rubbing my arm. "It's just a dream," he whispered when my eyes found his in the dark room. I shook my head against the pillow and fought the urge to back into the wall, draw up my knees, and sob some of the terror from my mind. "I hate this, Patrick . . ."

"I know."

He sat on the floor next to my bed with his hand resting on my arm as the acid of terror seeped out of my veins and the ticking of the alarm clock lulled me back to sleep. When residual fear snapped my eyes open again, I found him there, his head propped on his hand—a look of sadness and compassion on his face. "Still here," he whispered.

I let my eyes drift closed again.

SIX

By the time eight o'clock came the next morning, I was hungrier than I'd been in a long while. When I saw Mona coming across the courtyard with a tray, I yelled at Patrick, who'd just finished his shower, that food was on the way and opened the door before Mona had reached it.

"Good morning!" She carried the tray to the small table next to the kitchenette and unloaded a basket of croissants, a steaming baguette, and a small platter of jams, honey, and Nutella.

"Just press the plunger to the bottom and pour," she said, motioning to the French press she'd wrapped in a kitchen towel. She surveyed the table. "Did I forget anything?"

"It all looks wonderful."

"Excellent." She went to the door through which crisp morning air was pouring. It felt reviving. "Big plans for the day?"

"We'll lay low this morning, then head out into the countryside this afternoon looking for brocantes."

She gave me a look again.

"This trip is more treasure hunting than sight-seeing," I clarified.

"Well, don't miss the one about fifty kilometers down the N102 from here. Go west toward

Langogne and keep an eye out after you leave the town. Can't remember the name of the place—there's a big white sign on the stone wall out front. Looks like a dump, but it's a gold mine. We found that fixture there." She pointed at the rustic chandelier above the table. "Well worth the visit."

I thanked her and saw her to the door. "Does he have his water bottle?" she yelled across the courtyard.

Grant was walking toward the front gate with Connor. He waved off her concerns and disappeared around the corner.

"How old is your son?" I asked.

"Five and a half. And more than ready for first grade."

"He's a doll."

"He's Grant's mini-me too. The only kid in *maternelle*—that's kindergarten in France—who wears a Sacramento Kings ball cap to school, but whatever Grant does . . ."

"Imitation's the sincerest form of flattery, right?"

"Something like that." She shoved her hands into the pockets of her wraparound apron. "Need me to draw you a map?"

I shook my head. "Fifty kilometers west on the N102, just outside Langogne."

"That's quite the memory you've got. Let me know if you find any treasures!"

The truth was that my mind craved details to

remember—innocuous, practical details to take the place of those I just could not forget. I closed the door and leaned back against it, repeating Mona's instructions to myself, hoping the place they took would push the memories further from my consciousness.

But I knew they couldn't.

-ᘓ⊷ᘍ-

Patrick and I headed north as we left Balazuc, circled through scenic villages and towns, then found the N102 and came home through Langogne, just as Mona had suggested. We found Passé Composé on the outskirts of the village, a ramshackle barn with a fancy calligraphed sign. Patrick whooped as we turned off the road onto the potholed driveway that led to huge barn doors. Just to the right of the brocante, several old cars languished, dented and rusty, under the collapsed roof of a decomposing carport. A dog chained to the house on the other side of the structure barked a warning to its owner.

"You think they'd let me dig through to those cars?" Patrick asked as I pulled the lever that released the deudeuche's door.

A bony man in farmer's overalls, a fisherman's hat, and rubber boots came out of the house, a cigarette dangling from his mouth. He nodded approvingly at our car, then turned his watery eyes on me.

"I think that's what you call a once-over," Patrick mumbled.

The man ambled toward us, tilting left. "*Bonjour!*" he yelled, raising an arthritis-clawed hand in greeting. "*Vous voulez voir à l'intérieur?*"

I waited for Patrick to use his French and confirm that we did indeed want to see inside—and glared at him when he didn't.

"He's got eyes only for you, Jezebel. I'm guessing ears too."

"Oh, please." I smiled at the man. "*S'il vous plaît,*" I said, trying for my very best accent.

The old man slapped his thigh, and a cloud of dust billowed up from his gray overalls. "*Anglaise?*" he said, his interest clearly piqued.

With Patrick still standing there, silently enjoying himself, I said, "No. Not English. American."

"Yes!" the man exclaimed, clearly thrilled by foreign visitors. "*Venez,*" he said. "You come! You come!"

"That's French for 'swipe right, swipe right,' " Patrick said under his breath, this time eliciting a smile from me.

"You're a freak."

"Yes, but I'm your PMFEO freak."

The barn was epic. I'd expected a few tables laden with dusty relics and maybe some larger furniture pieces standing alone—like what we'd found in the other brocantes we'd visited. But this was a chaotic, overstuffed, and overwhelming

75

space where every square inch was occupied and stacked high. An open second floor, accessible only by ladders, was equally cluttered.

"Holy—"

"Don't say it."

"It's the freakin' Taj Mahal of exquisite excrement."

"Only you could make that sound poetic."

"You look," our host instructed us with a heavy accent, sweeping an arm across the expanse of the barn. He seemed to search for words. "Many things!"

"Yes. Many, many things," I agreed.

He smiled and nodded, then pointed from his chest to the table near the barn's broad entrance, where stacks of old buttons had been partially sorted into Mason jars according to color. "Me here, yes? I wait here."

He turned and walked back to the desk.

"Pick up a shovel and believe in gold," Patrick said as he walked past me to the darkest corner of the barn.

We spent over an hour digging through the piles of books and linens, opening every drawer in every piece of furniture we passed, sorting through tarnished brass window handles and doorknobs, porcelain dolls with moth-eaten clothes, military paraphernalia, kitchenware, and building tools.

When we'd filled our arms with items we wanted to buy, the old man appeared with a large wicker basket for us, then disappeared again. We dropped our loot into it and continued the exploration. For the first time since Paris, I felt excitement stirring. Our hands were black with dust and our eyes were tired from squinting in the barn's dark interior, but we were finding treasures. An 1880 prayer book inlaid with mother-of-pearl, sterling silver dessert ware engraved with a nobleman's crest and stamped with the maker's mark, and—when we dared to climb one of the ladders to the open space above—an antique map of Paris.

"That'll look fantastic framed and hung on a wall," Patrick said, excitement in his voice and gestures.

"Or under the glass top of a coffee table."

He nodded approvingly. "Good call, grasshopper. I've taught you well."

He had. The four years we'd known each other had been an apprenticeship of sorts. I didn't know as much as he did, but I'd come a long way. It felt good to have adrenaline pulsing through my veins again. I felt . . . alive. And that, somehow, felt utterly wrong.

Claustrophobia clutched me suddenly—the walls seemed closer, the air staler, the light dimmer. I stepped away from Patrick to catch my breath.

"You okay?" He'd asked the question a hundred times—more—since he'd found me in the hospital.

I gave him the usual response. "I'm fine." He

watched me make my way back to the ladder and descend it on shaky legs. I glanced down to see how much farther I had to go, and a small wooden box perched on top of an oak wardrobe caught my eye. It would have been invisible from below, but it was clearly defined from this angle in the glow of a bare lightbulb. There was something about it that arrested my attention and distracted me from the discomfort that had caused my descent. I went down two more rungs and reached out, pulling it nearer by the small brass handle attached to its side.

There was no way to lift it with just one hand, but I knew, from what I could see of it, that I wanted to take a closer look. I clambered to the floor and located a wooden chair sturdy enough to stand on. Then I lifted the box from the top of the wardrobe and blew the dust off its lid. It was made of dark walnut—a rectangular base topped by a sloping lid in which a frayed pincushion was embedded.

I turned it from side to side, holding it directly under the dirty bulb. There was a hint of design in the wood, nearly imperceptible for the gray of age and mildew. I reached for a piece of newspaper in a box of wrapped china and used it to clear some of the dust from the front of the piece, where the porcelain knob of a small drawer extended.

"Patrick," I said loudly enough for him to hear me from above.

The barn's owner looked up. "*Ça va?*"

I waved him off. "I'm fine! Thank you."

Patrick's head poked over the edge of the second floor. "Found something?"

"Come see this."

He made quick work of descending the ladder while I turned to lay the box on a vintage dresser. Patrick leaned in to get a better look at it. "You see the detail in the wood?"

I tilted the box back and looked more closely at the portion I'd cleaned with the newspaper. "Is it parquetry?"

"And top-notch too."

"It's a sewing box, right?"

"What gave you the first clue?"

I ignored his sarcasm and used the pincushion embedded in the top to lift the lid, exposing the partitioned shelf beneath. "Probably held all kinds of sewing paraphernalia in its day," Patrick said, leaning in close. "Thread, needles, scissors, embroidery yarn."

I pulled out the small, shallow drawer and found it empty too. There was something about the box that spoke to me. "I like it."

Patrick nodded. "You've got a better eye than you realize. What era do you think it is?"

"I don't know. Maybe seventeenth or eighteenth century?"

"More likely seventeenth. And a couple steps above provincial, which is good. Check the bottom . . ."

I turned the box over, careful not to let the drawer

slide out, and found the artisan's stamp burned into the wood. "Looks like a *C,* an *S,* and an *F.*"

"The mark increases the value."

I realized I was smiling and felt an impulse to smother the sign of happiness.

"Don't," Patrick said.

There was something so loving in his gaze that I felt tears come to my eyes. I looked back at the sewing box. "I want it."

"Then buy it." He nodded toward the barn's owner, still hunched over a pile of buttons by the door. "Guido over there might even give you a deal."

"His name isn't Guido."

"*Fini?*" the man asked, sensing our attention. "Finished?" It took him three syllables to say the word.

I glanced at Patrick. "Can we call it a day?"

"Yep. Let's get some dinner and come back tomorrow."

I tucked the box under one arm as our host lifted our basket and carried it toward his old-fashioned cash register. "We'll come back," I said to the back of his head. "*Demain,*" I said in French, proud of myself for remembering the word for *tomorrow.*

"*Avec plaisir!*" he said loudly, waving a hand in the air.

SEVEN

We brought crêpes from Balazuc's crêperie home to the B&B and settled in for the evening. There was a honk outside the door just as we were finishing dinner. At first I thought it was Connor playing in the courtyard, but when it came again, then again, I opened the door to find him sitting by the door in his Cozy Coupe.

"Hello," I said, a bit tentatively. I looked across the courtyard and saw Grant standing at the doorway to the manor house. He nodded and smiled, and I turned my attention back to his son. "Did you drive your car all the way over here?"

"I'm a devivery man." The word seemed too big for his mouth.

"A delivery man?"

He reached down for a plastic container and handed it to me out the Cozy Coupe's window. "It's leftover stew," he said with a bit of a lisp. "Mom says you can have it for lunch tomorrow."

"Well . . . thank you, Connor."

He pushed his car forward a bit and leaned sideways to glance into the cottage. "Does your friend like stew?" he asked.

It took some self-control to refrain from saying

81

"thtew" the way he did. "I think he does like stew."

Connor smiled, exposing a gap where one of his front teeth should have been.

"Did you lose a tooth?" I asked.

He gave me a look, as if I were asking an obvious question. "The *p'tite souris* has it," he said.

"The *p'tite* . . . ?"

"The little mouse, silly." He honked his horn again and pushed the Cozy Coupe around so he was facing home.

"Thanks for the delivery," I said, probably too quietly, as he rolled away over uneven cobblestone. Unsure of what to do, I gave a little wave to Grant, who nodded before descending the three steps to the courtyard. He grabbed the edge of Connor's plastic car and dragged it the rest of the way to its usual parking spot next to a watering can and a pair of rubber boots.

"What was that about?" Patrick asked, coming out of the bedroom. He plopped down on the couch and reached for the sweating glass of artisanal beer he'd left on the coffee table.

"Delivery from Connor. Stew for tomorrow."

"Catering isn't mentioned on the website, but I'll take it." A squeal reached us from the courtyard as I stowed the stew in the fridge.

"Cute kid," Patrick said.

"He is." I'd always found children a bit intimidating, and Connor, endearing as he was, was no exception.

"Please," Patrick said, sarcasm dripping. "Contain your enthusiasm."

I went to the bench just inside the front door where we'd left the sewing box and brought it into the living room, placing it between us on the coffee table and tilting it back to see the carpenter's mark again.

"So," I said, "do we try to find out who CSF is?"

"We can try, but if he was a local artisan he wouldn't be listed with the greats." He frowned. "Three initials is unusual—it's normally just two. That might actually be helpful."

I opened the lid and peered inside again.

"Remember what I told you about the mystery of picking?" he asked.

I looked at him.

"We don't find our treasures—they find us," he said.

It certainly felt true. This box with the parquetry and slanted lid had called to me the moment I saw it. "I think I believe you," I murmured.

Patrick leaned forward. "It may not be worth a whole lot," he warned. "More in the States than here, for sure, but . . ."

"It is," I said with unusual certainty. "It's worth something to me."

I pulled the small drawer open and it slid easily. There were small bits of debris loose in the bottom. I turned it upside down over the coffee table and most of it fell out. "There's something in the corner," I said, wondering if it was a remnant of its contents centuries ago.

Patrick leaned closer as I picked at it. It was some kind of reddish yarn that seemed anchored to the wood. When I grasped it with the tips of my fingers and pulled lightly, it broke off, frayed and frail from age. Just a hint of it remained in the crack between the edge and the bottom of the drawer. I tried to get ahold of it with my fingernails, but it was too short to grasp.

I went into the bathroom under Patrick's watchful eye and retrieved the tweezers from my toiletry bag. Back at the coffee table, I used them to grab the tiny piece of yarn and pulled. The bottom of the box bent a little as the yarn came loose. I squinted at the knot that had been hidden under the wood until I pulled it free. Then I looked at Patrick, something I couldn't quite identify scratching at my mind. "There's a knot. It was under the edge of the . . ."

He leaned back. The look on his face—the calm, knowing, melancholy expression—somehow felt frightening to me. "Patrick."

He smiled. "It found you."

I frowned. "What are you—?"

"So," he interrupted, "your job now is to figure out why it did."

I looked more closely at the knotted yarn still pinched between my tweezers, and that vague intrigue I'd felt a moment before crystallized into suspicion. "You think it's a . . . ?"

"Remember the rolltop we found at the flea market in West Virginia?"

I held his gaze, perplexed and still a bit disquieted by his serene and expectant countenance. I remembered the desk. We'd had to cancel airline tickets and rent a U-Haul to get it home. It was one of his most prized possessions. He'd spent months restoring it to its former noblesse, meticulously refinishing it, repairing its locks and the mechanisms that operated its hidden compartments.

Hidden compartments. "Do you think . . . ?"

He just raised an eyebrow and smiled a bit more deeply. I hurried to the kitchen for a knife with a thin blade and returned to the sewing box. It took a bit of pressure to insert the tip into the corner where the red thread had extended and pry it up. It gave just a bit before the knife slipped out—just enough to make me wonder if there really was a secret space below.

I tried again, moving the blade a bit farther from the corner this time. The wood arched up, but it snapped back into place when I pulled out the knife to move it down the seam. I continued to loosen the thin layer that seemed to be more of a veneer than a structural piece, returning to the corner and working the knife along the other edge. Inscrting and prying up. Inserting and prying up.

I could feel anticipation coming off Patrick like electrical energy. He watched my every move in silence, the master observing the apprentice.

I wedged a pen under the veneer when the gap was large enough to allow it, preventing the false bottom from snapping down again, and continued to loosen the edges. I glanced up at Patrick when there was enough give for me to grasp the wood with my fingers. He smiled. I smiled back. "Pull it up?" I asked.

He hunched a shoulder. "Only if you want to." The excitement in his eyes belied the nonchalance in his tone.

I pulled on the thin layer of wood and heard it groan against the edges restraining it. Then it was in my hand.

I looked into the inch-deep space, not really expecting to find anything there—maybe more dust or remnants of sewing items.

"Oh—my—gosh." The words were barely a whisper. I looked up at Patrick and said them again. "Patrick. Oh—my—gosh!"

His expression gave me pause, but only for a moment.

With shaking hands, I lifted a small notebook from the drawer—yellowed, handwritten pages bound together by a string inserted through two holes at the top of the sheaf. There were a couple loose sheets still in the bottom of the drawer.

"This is . . ." My words trailed off. I looked at Patrick again, and he laughed at the amazement on my face.

"Excitement looks good on you."

"We found a treasure . . ."

"Well, it could be some middle-school girl's idea of a practical joke, but . . ." He laughed. "Yep, there's a chance a treasure found *you*."

I ignored his subtle correction and stared at the pages in my hand. The writing was in ink. Though it looked brownish, I guessed it had been black at the time the words were written. Some of them looked like French, but others seemed foreign. I moved closer to Patrick so he could take a look and was surprised when he seemed to shift away. I looked at him, frowning. That melancholy was there in his face again. The melancholy and the peace. And maybe a hint of pain.

I felt fear coiling in my stomach but couldn't identify its source. "Patrick . . ." I reached out to touch his arm, then pulled back, dread and panic surging.

He shook his head.

"Patrick," I said again, questioning and begging. "What's—?"

It was as if he was fading—like old-fashioned slides, whitening and dissolving from the heat of a bulb. My voice was low and shaky. "Patrick—what's happening?" I leaned in to touch his shoulder, his face, to convince myself that he was here. That I was not alone. And I cried out when my hands felt only air.

Though he hadn't moved, an agonizing space broadened between us. "It found you," he said, his eyes settling on the box for a moment before making contact with mine again. His voice sounded muffled. Distant. But there was certainty on his face. Courage too. "Now you need to figure out what it's trying to say."

"Patrick!" I heard the scream through the cacophony of incomprehension and agony in my mind. It took me a moment to realize it was mine. "Patrick," I screamed again as he seemed to recede farther, to grow dimmer, to disintegrate. His smile was soft. Sad. Hopeful. The smile I'd seen that first night in the hospital, when I'd woken to find him there. Watching me. Shielding me.

A reality too unbearable to process descended over me like an inexorable weight. I felt it push me further into myself, deeper into a void that gaped, threatening and inscrutable, beyond my consciousness.

"No!" I screamed as Patrick's form faded even more. I clawed my way to the other side of the couch, where he'd been sitting—where he'd been talking—where he'd been smiling just moments ago, but he drifted farther yet. "Patrick!" I could see only his eyes now. Everything else had faded from sight. Then they disappeared too.

I felt a hollowing. A searing, insufferable hollowing. My body collapsed. My spirit reeled and spun apart. The air around me quaked and pummeled, seethed and roared.

Then darkness.

EIGHT

Reality surfaced slowly when consciousness returned. I lay on the couch, my legs drawn up, my arms crossed over my stomach. There was static in my mind. Loud and numbing and pervasive.

The room's swirling slowed. I took one deep breath after another and tried not to remember—not to think. But truth pierced through my defenses. "No!" I said, loudly enough to startle myself, willing the thoughts away.

But they returned larger and stronger, hurling themselves at my resistance until I could forestall them no longer. Grief breached its barriers and overflowed the levees of denial in my mind. I groaned and sobbed and screamed and pled.

When I could breathe again—when the onslaught of emotion and disbelief had passed—I rolled off the couch onto the floor, knocking the coffee table so hard that the sewing box fell off and the string holding the sheaf of papers snapped. Incomprehension and panic fueled irrational anger. I kicked at the pages and watched them scatter across the floor.

Then I lay there, paralyzed, mindless, emptied out, as the sunlight angling through the kitchen window crawled across the floor, then up the wall, then faded into dark. I pulled myself upright in the wee hours of the night. My eyes skimmed the surface of the room, barely lit by a single lamp. The coffee table. Patrick's beer glass wasn't there. The sink. Only one plate rested in the drying rack. The bedroom. Only one bed was unmade. Only my suitcase lay open on the floor.

I pulled myself up to a standing position and fought the nausea clawing at my gut. I stumbled toward the bathroom and dry-heaved over the commode. There was no razor on the vanity. None of Patrick's fancy soap on the shower's ledge. Tears fell silently from shell-shocked eyes and burned the chapped skin of my face.

I moved into the bedroom and felt loss liquefy my limbs, then I fell onto the bed—onto Patrick's bed, where neither sheets nor pillow had been disturbed. Despite my supplications, my mind rolled back over the days since the attacks, replacing what I'd known with a reality I couldn't bear. It was all there. All the absences imprinted on the fabric of my grief. Survival's masquerade.

I saw Vonda again. When she'd come to say good-bye. I heard the bustle of the hospital ward. "Stay until Patrick comes back," I'd begged.

"Until . . . ? Jess. Honey. What are you talking about?"

"He was just here and went out to get some coffee. He'll be back in . . ."

"Jessica." Her voice was broken and resolute. "Jessica, he wasn't here."

"He was. He's been here off and on since the—"

"Jess . . ." She was battling for composure. For words. "Jess . . . he's gone."

I laughed—shrill and desperate. "Vonda, I assure you that—"

Tears gathered in her eyes. "He left the exhibit early . . . came to find us at the Bataclan. Because it was our last night. That's what I think. Because we were supposed to spend it together. The police . . ." She halted. Swallowed hard. Took a deep breath. "The police called the apartment after I got back. He was—he was at the doors when the shooting started and—"

"No."

"He was one of the first to be killed, Jess."

"No!"

"I had to identify his body. I had . . ." She gripped the rail at the bottom of my bed. "I had to find his parents and tell them over the phone . . . They're trying to . . . The embassy is helping them get his body home. They'll come later. I don't know when. They transferred money so I could pay ahead on Patrick's rent until they can get here to take care of his studio and his things and . . ."

I shook my head—violently—against the hospital pillows, as the walls and ceiling began to buckle around me. She came closer, and I felt her hand grasping my shoulder.

"You have to believe me, Jess. This—this

pretending. It's not good. It's not real. You have to believe me, Jess."

"He's alive!" Anger acidified my voice.

"Jess—"

"Get out, Vonda. Get out!"

I saw it all, in retrospect. Horrific and obscene. I heard her words. I saw her leave—and I waited for Patrick to return.

⊰❦⊱

Time lurched. Night deepened over Balazuc, its void a magnifying force.

Then day—again. Unbearable and cruel.

I found the stew in the fridge and ate only a bite before nausea sent me staggering back to bed, begging for oblivion.

I didn't answer the knocking at the door. I didn't have the strength to see another person. It went on for what felt like forever. Loud and insistent. Then it stopped.

It resumed sometime later. More determined this time. "Jessica, it's Mona." Her voice cut through my despondence. "Jessica? Could you please open the door if you're home? Your car hasn't moved in a couple of days and . . . I just want to be sure you're okay."

I pulled a pillow over my head and closed my eyes.

"Jessica."

Time had passed, but I wasn't sure how much.

92

"Jessica?"

Her voice felt nearer this time—its closeness threatening. "Jessica." Feet hurrying to my bed. To Patrick's bed. Hands on my shoulders. Tentative. "Jessica, it's Mona."

I resisted her touch, curling tighter into myself. "No."

"Jessica . . ."

"No!"

I heard her feet retreating, the front door opening. "Grant! Connor, go get him—he's in the barn."

Footsteps returned. The mattress sagged as she sat next to me and lifted the pillow off my head. She pulled the hair back from my face, and I covered it with my hands.

"We're going to get you help. Jessica—we're going to get you a doctor, okay?"

More footsteps. Heavier and quick. "What's going on?" Deep voice. Concern.

"Get Docteur Fabian. He said to call him if we ever needed anything, and . . ."

Retreating feet.

Minutes later, muffled voices. French words. Being turned onto my back. A stethoscope. A pressure cuff. A flashlight in my eyes. Intrusion.

More words I couldn't really hear. One sounded like "shock," another like "hospital." Someone held a wet towel to my forehead.

I tried to force my mind to connect again. "No . . ." A whisper.

"Jessica?" Mona's voice.

"No hospital. Please."

"We need to know what's wrong—"

"Please . . ." I poured the shreds of energy I could muster into forcing my eyes open, squinting against the brutal light of day. Mona crouched by the edge of the bed, her face close to mine. Grant and an elderly man stood in the doorway.

Mona leaned in close. "Tell me what you're feeling. Have you been sick? Or taken a fall or . . . ?"

"I'm not sick." I cleared my throat and tried again, more loudly. "I'm not sick."

"But you've been holed up here for . . . You haven't been out, not even to eat. And . . ."

I could only imagine what it looked like to her. What I looked like.

"There's a retired doctor here. Docteur Fabian— he used to run the village clinic and lives two doors down. He's taken a look at you and . . . Let's just take you to the hospital and have you checked out, okay? He really thinks it's best. Just to be sure . . ."

I shook my head. "I'm not sick."

"Then . . . Jessica, what is it?"

I bit my lip as reality and pain surged back. "It's . . ."

Mona took the glass of water Grant handed her. "Here. Can you sit up a little?"

She snaked an arm under my shoulders to pull me up, and the world tilted a bit, then righted itself.

She held the glass against my lip and I sipped. The water felt reviving. I tried not to look at the two men standing near the bedroom door, a redheaded boy just a bit behind them.

Mona released me and I lay back against the pillow, looked into her kind, concerned face, and knew I had to speak the aching words.

"My friend died," I whispered.

Agony.

Mona's face softened instantly, and some of the tension seemed to fall from her shoulders. "Oh, Jessica. Oh, I'm so sorry."

Grant said something to the doctor, who was still standing near the door, while Mona used the wet towel to soothe my face. *"Elle est en état de choc,"* I heard the elderly man say. *"Il voudrai mieux qu'elle consulte un médecin à l'hôpital."* *She's in shock. It would be best for her to see a doctor at the hospital.*

"Please," I begged. "I don't need a hospital."

Mona hesitated, then said, "Let's give it a little time, okay? You rest for a bit and we'll reevaluate later."

Grant translated for the doctor, and I saw the elderly gentleman nod. Then he made a *tsk-tsk*ing sound with his mouth and turned to leave the cottage, a pitying look on his face. I tried to quell the sob rising in my throat. This was too much. This—was—too—much. The men stepped out as I began to wail.

• • •

After the torturous moment when reality resurged, my mind retreated into blankness and surfaced only gradually again. I felt its fits and starts like an actor and a spectator—overwhelmed and disengaged, consumed and removed. It was a schizophrenic, lurching re-emergence in which pain and apathy wrestled for control. Apathy soothed pain, and pain jarred apathy.

There were seconds—just seconds—as my eyes opened after sleep when the world felt unshrouded again. Then memory maimed.

Mona's kindness over the next few days layered guilt over grief. She stepped into my suffering with quiet words and gentle touch. She cared for me as if I were family, attentive to my every need and generous to a fault with her time and resources. It was she who coaxed me out of the bedroom and onto the living room couch on the day after she'd found me curled up on Patrick's bed, horror-stunned and paralyzed. It was she who stood outside the bathroom door after convincing me to shower, who brought me soup and ate with me.

We hadn't spoken about Patrick since she'd found me. She'd washed my sheets and replaced my towels and checked in frequently during the day. "I don't want to intrude, but I need to make sure you're well," she said on the third day since I'd lost Patrick. The illusion of Patrick. "I need to ask . . . ," Mona said after I'd stared at the surface of my soup for a while.

I nodded. She did. And she'd been patient. I looked up and attempted a smile.

"Is there anyone back home who knows you're here? Family members who should be told . . . ?"

Her question took me by surprise. I'd expected her to ask about Patrick—about how my friend had died. But it made sense, from the little I knew of Mona, that she'd also be concerned about those who loved me.

"I talked to my parents before we left Paris," I said, my voice rough from lack of use. "They know I'm on a trip and won't be in much contact, so . . ."

"Do they know about your friend?"

I blinked back tears. I didn't have the energy to cry. They thought I was traveling with Patrick and had sounded glad for the diversion, despite their misgivings, the last time I'd spoken with them. "They knew we'd planned this trip, and—"

"Jessica," Mona said, putting down her spoon to look at me with the same expression I'd seen a couple times before. She seemed to hesitate. "You keep saying 'we'—about leaving Paris and now about this trip . . ."

I hung my head. How many times had I spoken in the plural when those I spoke with had seen only me? "It's . . ." I didn't know where to begin. I didn't know how to fit words into a sentence so they'd mean what I needed them to say. I tried to look directly at Mona, but it made me feel too broken. "I thought I was traveling with Patrick," I finally said, my eyes trained on the poppies in the watercolor above the table. Saying his name out loud felt liberating. And shattering. "Patrick's my friend," I added, blinking again at the treacherous tears. "My roommate back home. I came to France to travel with him and—he died. He . . ."

I breathed. Once. Twice. Deeply. I didn't have the courage to describe the way he'd been killed, those final moments my mind played back incessantly in the darkness of the night. Mona gave me the time and space to still my roiling thoughts. "He died—" The words stunned me into silence again. "He died a few days ago. Nearly two weeks. And somehow . . ." I looked at her then. Desperate for someone to reassure me. To tell me I wasn't as crazy as I felt. "I somehow thought he was still alive. With me. In my mind, he was in that car." I felt myself frown. "He was *driving* the car. He was talking—joking. It was so real. He was so . . .there."

I shook my head and tried to make sense of the illusion that had been so viciously compelling. How had I believed—for such a long time—in the presence of a person who was not only absent, but dead? Yet part of me had known, since Vonda's visit to the hospital, that my friend was gone. I could see it so clearly now. Sitting alone in Patrick's apartment for days after my release. Letting my subconscious talk me into a trip that would allow the illusion to endure. Driving myself out of the city, into the comforting beauty of southern France. All the while believing the fantasy that I was not alone. That Patrick was speaking to me. Caring for me. Protecting me.

"He was right there," I said, a bit breathless, pointing at the couch where he'd last sat. "And . . ." I glanced into the bedroom where Mona had found me. "And in there too."

Mona reached across the table and squeezed my arm. I looked down and felt the humanness of touch. She was real. And Patrick hadn't been since . . . "The mind is a miraculous thing," Mona said softly. "And it can be a powerful buffer. It shields us as best it can from what we can't escape and . . . and I guess it thought it was doing you a favor by erasing your friend's—"

I had to shape the word in my mind before speaking it. "Death," I finally said. Then I added, "Murder."

Mona's head snapped up, and I could see her quelling the questions my admission had triggered. "Is it something you'd like to talk about?" she finally asked.

I wanted to. And I knew I should. But I wasn't sure my mind could bear putting words to what had happened.

"I don't think I can right now," I answered.

"Then you shouldn't," she said with a kind smile.

"I'm sorry," I whispered, finally looking directly into her face.

"No need for that."

"You've been so kind and so . . . Anyone else would have sent me to the hospital. Or put me out on the street. Or . . . or tried to call someone."

"Grant said to give it a couple days—to keep an eye on you and let you sort it out—and I've learned to trust his instincts." She stood and took our bowls to the kitchen sink to rinse them.

"How many guests have you turned away because I've overstayed my welcome?"

"None," she said. "This isn't exactly tourist season in these parts."

Fear fluttered in my stomach. "I know I need to—to make some decisions. And move on. Maybe leave in a day or two, if it's okay for me to stay a bit longer."

"Nonsense." Mona wiped her hands on a yellow dish towel and shook her head at me. "You stay until you're ready to go—in every sense. You won't find a quieter place than this to rest, and . . . I'd feel better if I knew you were a little less shaky before taking off again."

"I'm not sure—"

"Besides, I miss having guests here during our low season. If you'll agree to give someone back home a call and let them know that you're all right, I'll block out some more days for you." She looked at me—kind and compassionate—then leaned against the kitchen sink as her expression grew pensive. "Take it slow. Rest. Let your mind untangle itself. You'll know when it's time to move on."

She left our bowls in the dish drainer and went to the front door. "You need anything, you call. Same as the first day you got here," she said. Then she nodded at the sewing box on the coffee table. "I found it on the floor when I came in looking for you the other day. It's a beautiful piece."

The door clicked closed behind Mona. I sat at the table and stared across the room at the box I'd found with Patrick on our last treasure hunt together—on *my* treasure hunt, I corrected myself. On my treasure hunt alone.

NINE

My mother's voice was shrill with worry. She called for my dad to pick up the phone in their living room, and he got on the line too.

"We've been beside ourselves," she said. "You said you'd text us every day and—"

"Why didn't you?" My father wasn't one to show emotion. The fact that he'd asked the question was evidence of his concern.

"Are you still in southern France, sweetie? We've been so worried . . ."

I tried to picture my mom sitting at her kitchen table with the spiral phone cord stretching down to her from the receiver high up on the wall. My dad sitting in his light-blue armchair in a living room encased in floral wallpaper. The images were so serene—so unmarred by tragedy—that I hesitated to shatter them by explaining my reality.

"Are you there, Jess?"

It was the concern in my dad's voice that made me tell them, as briefly as possible, that Patrick had died in the attacks in Paris and that I was taking some time to gather myself again.

"But . . ." My mom sounded shocked and perplexed. I didn't blame her. "Didn't you say you were on this trip with him?"

"I've been . . . confused." The word felt anemic,

a pale expression of the grief that had sent me headlong into a merciful oblivion. I didn't tell them much more. There'd be time for that later. My father wanted to know details, of course— to understand what had happened. And my mom wanted to be sure that "my heart" was okay. Something in me resented the words she used, the sympathetic tone of her voice as she begged me to fly home so they could take care of me.

"You've been injured," she said, pleading. "And you're dealing with so much, honey. Between what you saw and . . . and . . ."

"Would you like me to look into a ticket for you?" my father asked. "Tell me what the nearest airport is and I'll get my guy at the travel agency on it."

It took several minutes to convince them that I'd be staying awhile longer, that I was in a beautiful, safe place, and that I'd contact them again soon. Though I could still hear the concern in their voices, they finally agreed to let me stay as long as I needed.

"Just communicate with us, okay?" my mother said. "We just need to be sure you're safe."

I hung up the phone, depleted from the exertion of trying to sound well.

⊰•⊱

I was woken from a nap by a knock on the door late the following morning. My muscles felt stiff as I got up from the couch. I wondered if sadness could cause physical pain.

Grant stood outside the door when I opened it, a large basket of kindling in his arms.

"Figured you might be running low," he said.

When I failed to answer, he asked, "Have you used the fireplace since you got here? I thought maybe with the cool evenings . . ." His voice trailed off.

"I—no, I haven't." Patrick and I had considered it on our first night in Balazuc, to take the chill out of the air, but . . . The force of the delusion slammed me again. Patrick had never been here. I glanced at the fireplace and its cast-iron grate, then looked at Grant. "I don't really know how to start one."

He raised the basket he was still holding. "Care for a quick lesson?"

I really didn't. There was nothing I wanted. Not a fire to sit by or a lesson on how to light it. But, reminding myself of my hosts' kindness, I moved out of Grant's way and pushed the door farther open.

Just a few minutes later, a fire burned in the hearth. The warmth felt life-giving, and I moved the sewing box onto the floor so I could sit on the edge of the coffee table, closer to the flames.

"Nice piece," Grant said, eyeing the antique.

"We found it at—" I stopped myself and took a breath. "*I* found it. At the flea market in Langogne."

I felt another wave of grief gathering and braced for its onslaught.

Grant acknowledged my correction with an inscrutable look, then turned to move the basket of kindling to the side of the fireplace. "So . . . paper, kindling, small pieces of wood, then large," he said again as he rose to leave. "In that order. You may need to blow on it a bit until the kindling catches."

"Thank you." I attempted a smile. "I'm used to fireplaces that turn on with a switch."

He smirked. "That's why I thought you might need a lesson."

I'd expected some discomfort from him as he came face-to-face for the first time with a woman he'd last seen wailing in the cottage bedroom, but there was only calm consideration in his expression. "Mona says you've been doing better."

I felt a flush of embarrassment and looked away. "I think I am."

Silence stretched.

"And she tells me you may be staying a few more days."

"She tells me the same thing." I tried for another smile.

"You'll learn that arguing with her is pointless."

"I've gotten that impression." I took a breath and gathered my courage. "I want to apologize for . . . for what you saw in here on Monday."

"Please . . ."

I held up a hand to stop him. "I'm—I'm a bit ashamed of . . ."

"Don't be."

I wanted to explain what he'd seen, to assure him that I wasn't crazy. But if I didn't believe it myself, convincing him would be a futile endeavor.

Grant watched the fire for a moment more, then turned his attention to me. "Do you need anything?" he asked.

Fatigue washed over me again as I thought through an inventory of my needs. What I wanted more than anything was to turn back the clock to those days before Paris when my perspective on the world had been infused with anticipation. Founded on sureness. My reality unsullied. My confidence in humanity—in goodness—unshaken.

"I think I'm okay," I said to Grant. I heard the uncertainty in my own voice and looked away.

He nodded and stepped toward the door, then looked back as he opened it. I could see him searching for words. "Have a good day," he finally said.

After the door closed behind him, I pushed back the coffee table to make room for me to sit on the floor by the fireplace, nudging the sewing box out of the way with something that felt like resentment. Though I'd found it enchanting in the shadows of the brocante, it now felt like a hostile thing, a reminder of the power of grief to distort truth. I scooped it up and took it to the kitchen, shoving it into a cupboard under the sink.

Then I went back to the fireplace and found a position on the floor that wouldn't hurt my still-healing wound. I let the warmth seep into my spirit and wondered what words Grant had just left unspoken.

Then I drifted into sleep

※

Connor was playing in the courtyard when I stepped outside a couple days later, a stack of Mona's food containers in my hand. A fireman's hat sat askew on his head. He brandished what looked like a vacuum cleaner attachment and made a *whoosh*ing sound as he waved it around. He saw me come out of the cottage and lowered his weapon.

"Hi, Connor," I attempted.

He waved the plastic tube at me in greeting.

"Are you putting out fires over there?"

"I'm fighting the Thiths. Wanna help?"

"I . . ." It took me a moment to figure out he'd meant to say "Siths."

"Isn't it *goûter* time?" Grant asked, approaching from the barn, his dark-blond hair gray with dust.

Connor turned toward Grant and hopped a couple times. "Hey, hey, hey!"

"Hey there, tiger," he said, ruffling the boy's hair.

Connor pulled Grant down to his level and looked wide-eyed into his father's face. "We went to Fabrice's house to see the baby pigs, and he let me ride in his eclectical car all the way to the end of the driveway! It was awesome." The curly-haired boy leaned in until their eyes were mere inches apart—Grant's hazel and Connor's darker brown—then he repeated, in his hoarse little voice, "It was *awesome.*" He drew out the last word for emphasis, and I caught myself smiling.

"Sounds like fun," Grant said, returning the boy's wide-eyed stare. "And I think you mean 'electric'—and no, we're not adopting one of Fabrice's pigs."

"Aw, come on!"

Grant straightened and turned toward me. "If Connor had his way, we'd turn the B&B into a working farm."

I looked down and found Connor's eyes on me. He leaned sideways into Grant. "You wanna see my lightsaber?" he asked me.

"I promise you that's not a euphemism," Grant said.

The boy pantomimed a vigorous saber battle for a couple seconds, complete with sound effects, then took off running toward the house, vacuum attachment raised, yelling, "To infinity and beyond!"

"He gets his favorite movies mixed up," Grant said, smiling.

"Hey, I get my favorite rap stars mixed up, so . . ."

"Those dawgs and diggities can be a real brain twister." He shoved his hands into the pockets of his dirty, slouchy jeans.

Another silence stretched. "I was just going to return these containers to Mona."

He nodded toward the front door, which Connor had left open. "How about some *goûter*?"

"*Goûter*?"

"Afternoon snack. It's a big deal for French kids."

"Oh, I don't want to intrude. If you'll just take these in to . . ." But his back was already turned, and he was walking toward the front door.

"I've got something to give you anyway," he said over his shoulder, not slowing his step.

Simply venturing out of the cottage had felt like a monumental milestone, but spending social time with people . . . That felt like an insurmountable challenge. Wondering how long my courage would hold up, I followed Grant up the stairs and preceded him into the house as he held the door open for me.

It was clear that this building, too, had been through extensive remodeling. Arched openings and tall ceilings gave the home an airy feel. A stand-alone fireplace divided the broad space into a living area and a kitchen, its rustic, naked brick an intriguing contrast to white walls and tiled floors.

Grant led me into a kitchen where splashes of red accented black-and-white décor. Mona stood by the sink and talked softly to Connor. The boy knelt on a tall stool, watching his mother take a dish towel off two loaves of unbaked bread.

"Can I now, Mom?"

"Go ahead. Poke your finger in the middle and see if it bounces back," she instructed.

Connor did as she said, and the hole he made filled in almost instantly. "Yep!" he said. "Can we put it in the oven now?"

Mona turned to open the oven door and saw Grant and me standing there. "Well, hello!" she said, her gaze landing on me as Grant exited the room. "How nice to see you out and about."

"I thought I'd return some of your dishes."

"We're making bread," Connor declared.

"My first attempt at brioche," Mona said, gently inserting the loaf pans into the oven. "I'm not convinced it will be successful, but you never know until you try, right?"

"Right, right, right!" Connor punctuated his agreement with a swoosh of his vacuum saber.

"Now how about a cup of tea?" Mona was already reaching for a cup on the open shelving above the counter.

"I'm not sure I . . ."

"Listen, the bread's got to cook and Connor needs his snack, so—cup of tea?"

I smiled. "Sure."

"How about you, Grant?" she asked as he reentered the kitchen.

He gave Mona a look that made her laugh. "Right. Coffee. Tea's for sissies," she explained, winking at me as she put a kettle on to boil, then handed Connor a flaky, chocolate-filled pastry.

Grant placed some printed pages on the table in front of me. "I did some research on the antique box you found," he said.

I looked down at the picture on the front page. It was of a sewing box similar to mine. A French article from an antique dealer's website was printed on the next few pages, followed by a rough English translation.

"It's seventeenth-century," Grant said. "French, obviously. I'm guessing yours is walnut with a cherry inlay. Worth about two hundred here, but probably four times that much in the States."

"I got it for twenty-five."

"Nice investment."

I looked through the pages he'd printed out for me. "You didn't have to do this," I said.

He shrugged. "I like mysteries."

I held up the French article. "You speak French?"

"Grant's the linguist in the family," Mona said before he could answer, dropping two tea bags into a white teapot. "Four years of high school French and ten months of construction over here, and he's practically fluent."

"I'm not fluent," Grant said quietly, pulling a

111

stool up to the kitchen island where I sat. "I know enough to get by," he said to me.

Mona laughed. "In my world, anything beyond 'Frère Jacques' is fluent! Don't know what I would have done if Grant hadn't stepped in when . . ." She covered Connor's ears and whispered, "When my husband walked out on us." She removed her hands and kissed the top of her son's head.

It took me a moment to realize what she'd said. I looked from her to Grant. "Wait. You're not— you two aren't . . . ?"

"It's a common misconception," Grant said with a faint smile.

"This little venture," Mona said, waving a finger at her surroundings, "started out as a team project. It turned solo when one member of the 'team' decided France wasn't his thing." She covered Connor's ears again and whispered, "His family either." He pried her hands away as she went on. "And then it turned back into a collaboration when a certain brother of mine decided to take a sabbatical from flipping houses in Redding and come flip houses—and cottages and barns—in Balazuc instead."

" 'Sabbatical' might be a bit of a misnomer," Grant mumbled. He raised an eyebrow in my direction as I tried to absorb this new information.

Connor clambered off his stool and onto the one next to me, leaning in to take a closer look at the articles Grant had printed out.

"Is it a treasure?" he asked.

"It's a sewing box."

My social energy was fast declining, and Mona seemed to sense it. "Probably not the kind of treasure you're thinking of."

"I think it was Captain Sparrow's," Connor said to Grant, eyes wide and hopeful.

His uncle pursed his lips, a smile behind his serious expression. "I don't recall him doing a lot of sewing, kiddo."

TEN

There was some comfort in the routines that emerged in the following days. Though my thoughts and emotions were still erratic—rare moments of stability derailed by bouts of anxiety—I found relief in the predictability. Mona no longer brought food to the cottage, having convinced me after my first foray into the manor house that venturing out might be good for my spirits.

I fended for myself at breakfast, often entertained by Connor's voice echoing in the courtyard as he went off to school. Midmorning, I headed out for the trails around Balazuc, always in sight of the village, forcing my mind to acknowledge the natural beauty Patrick would have loved as I sought to regain some of my strength and stamina.

We'd have lunch at the manor house when Connor came home at noon, then Mona and I would chat over cups of tea while Grant went back to work. When I was tired, I returned to the cottage to rest. When I felt up to it, I helped Mona with her projects around the house and the culinary experiments that kept her busy during the winter months. She called the latter "research for the café coming soon to a Balazuc near you." Mona was a visionary, relentlessly optimistic, and I wondered if proximity would rub some of it off on me.

Evening meals were typical French fare—soup, bread, cheese, and a salad. We ate them together. We were clearing dishes after dinner one evening when I asked Mona what the next project would be, once the barn remodel was finished.

"The conservatory," she said, anticipation lighting her features.

That took me aback. I pictured the music department of a stuffy college back home and couldn't imagine such a thing in a small town like Balazuc. "There's a conservatory in town?"

Mona laughed and led me through the entrance hall to a tall door tucked away on the other side.

"Meet the conservatory," she said, turning the brass knob and pushing the door open. It was a striking space with a high ceiling and elegant windows, furnished with a couple of old bookshelves, a faded couch, and a chair. A dusty chandelier illuminated the peeling gold-and-blue wallpaper, and an old piano stood in the middle of the room.

"Looks like a big project," I said.

"It will be, once we get around to it. But until then, this here is a reminder to myself that chaos can be comfy. Keeps my raging perfectionism in check."

"The piano is . . ." I didn't know how to describe it. Then I remembered Patrick. "My friend would have called it Decay-Deco."

Mona nodded. "Decay-Deco. I like it!" She ran a hand over its open lid. "I found it in here when I bought the manor house. Termites did a number on the wood, some of the keys are missing, and the finish is all but gone, but look at the character it brings to the space."

She was right. There was something regal about her Decay-Deco piano despite its state of disrepair. It anchored the room with history and whimsy.

"I was considering refinishing the dining room chairs," Mona said. "You know—to pass the time when the weather gets bad. And I'm thinking this room might be a great place to do it."

There was something in her tone that sounded like a hint. "Would you like me to help?"

She smiled. "I thought you'd never ask."

As I took on the project, part of me knew that she'd initiated it for me—to give me a goal, as minor as it was. On days when my listlessness turned the work into a chore, I reminded myself of Mona's kindness since I'd arrived in Balazuc. And on days when my mind seemed more able to concentrate, I derived a certain pleasure from my hours in the conservatory, revealing the rich wood beneath several layers of gray paint.

⸻ ❧ ⸻

The evenings were the hardest for me. Too quiet. Too reflective. On one such night, after I'd leafed again through all three magazines in the basket

116

next to the coffee table, I went to the cupboard where I'd stored the sewing box.

I wasn't sure why I'd left it hidden until then, but as I took it out and carried it to the couch, my mind stumbled back to our trip south, to conversations with Patrick that hadn't happened and to the plans that never would. To the flea market and our dusty dig and the excruciating walnut-and-cherry memento that had stolen my breath and swayed my sanity.

I set it on the cushion next to me, recalling the look in Patrick's eyes when I'd pried up the suspended piece of wood and found the notebook underneath.

I pulled open the drawer with its false bottom now removed. I wasn't sure who had gathered the pages—perhaps I'd picked them up myself or maybe Mona had when she'd found me—but there they were, back in the drawer from which they'd come.

I lifted them out and turned the first couple of sheets over, recognizing some of the words so gracefully handwritten but unable to decipher many of the others. The script was small and impeccably even.

"They found you for a reason," I heard Patrick say as clearly as if he'd been sitting right next to me. I'd shared that notion from the start, when the sewing box had first caught my attention—a siren call too subtle to describe and too visceral to ignore. And I wondered now, with Patrick gone, if this treasure was a fragile thread he'd left to link himself to me.

I felt the stirring again, the anticipation and connection, as I leafed through the jumbled pages, some upside down and mostly out of order. Three of them were slightly larger than the rest, their text clearly printed—not handwritten—on thin, numbered pages.

A rustling sound reached me from the courtyard. I leaned sideways to look out the window and saw Grant covering a trailer full of Sheetrock with a plastic tarp. A look at the sky explained the precautionary measure. On a whim, and with some hesitation, I went outside with the handwritten pages in my hands.

He saw me coming and jutted his chin toward the 2CV that still sat in front of the cottage.

"They're reporting hail a few kilometers up the road. Might want to move the car under the overhang. That canvas roof looks like it could use some protecting." He motioned to the sheltered space where the roofline extended from the barn, propped up by rough-hewn beams. "There's room next to the table saw," he added.

I hadn't driven the car since our trip to the brocante nearly two weeks ago. Though I now realized I was the one who drove it from Paris to Balazuc, I had no memory of sitting behind the wheel, and the thought of moving it felt unsettling.

"I can do it if you'd like," Grant said.

"Oh—thank you." I hurried back to the cottage to get the keys, relieved and grateful.

"Been doing some writing?" he asked, noticing the pages I was still holding.

I took a deep breath. "I have a question . . . a favor to ask—"

Grant looked up as the first raindrops fell. "Hold that thought."

I watched him push the driver's seat back as far as it would go before folding his tall form into the low-riding car. It rattled to life when he turned the key, but he seemed to struggle with the gearshift. He finally found reverse and backed up enough to turn toward the barn's overhang.

"So—what's the favor?" he asked after jogging back to the cottage through the intensifying rain.

I was standing in the doorway, still holding the loose pages of the notebook. "These were in the drawer of the sewing box."

He raised an eyebrow. "Really." He took the pages from my hands and hitched his chin toward the living room. "Mind if I come in to take a closer look?"

I shook my head. He toed off one shoe, then the other, and walked over to the couch, already flipping through the loose-leaf pages. "They were just sitting in the box?"

"No, they were . . ." I went around him and crouched in front of the antique, retrieving the false bottom from the upper tray, then pulling out the drawer to show Grant where it used to rest. "They were under here. That string there held them all together, but they got—the string broke and they scattered. The first handwritten page said 1695 when I first pulled them out . . . It's in there somewhere." I pointed at the three printed pages still sitting on the coffee table. "And these were in there too."

He reached for them. "Ezekiel," he murmured, reading the single word at the top of the page. He looked up at me. "These are from a Bible—but you probably figured that out already. By the looks of the French"—he squinted at the paper—"not a recent edition."

"That's what I assumed—that they were from the same era as this journal. And if the box is from the seventeenth century . . . is it possible that all of this dates back to then too?"

Grant arched an eyebrow. "Possible."

Something that felt like excitement fluttered in my stomach. "Okay," I said. "That's what I thought."

"So—about this favor . . . ?"

I hesitated. "I want to know what the handwritten pages say, but . . . I don't know enough French to even put them back in order."

"Where did you find the box again?" Grant asked, lifting it onto his lap to take a closer look at the secret compartment.

I sat in the chair across from him and said, "Passé

Composé," stumbling over the pronunciation. "Mona suggested we go there, and . . ." I stopped short as memories of being there with Patrick made my sense of reality waver. I could picture the barn, the old man with the limp, Patrick climbing the ladder to the second floor and calling out to me when he found the map of Paris. I could hear his voice and sense his nearness even in hindsight. But with newfound lucidity, I could also remember that the old man had eyes for only me. How could I have been so sure—so grounded—in the illusion that Patrick was alive?

I shook my head to clear it of the static that seemed to swell when memories of Patrick came to mind. "Mona suggested that *I* go there," I corrected myself. "Me. Just . . . me."

Seconds of silence ticked by. I picked at a chip in my chair's wooden armrest.

"I'm sorry. For what you've been through." Grant's voice was soft. Sincere.

His words made me feel fragile, so I pointed at the sheaf of paper he'd set on the couch beside him and turned the conversation back to more neutral things. "Do you think you'd be able to help? I tried to translate some of the pages on my own, but a lot of it just didn't make sense. Not even with a search engine doing the work for me."

He picked up the pages and glanced through them again.

"Looks like archaic French," he said. "*Vieux*

français. It's not surprising the search engine failed."

"Is it much different from modern French?"

"Not impossibly so. Alterations in spelling and sentence structure, vocabulary, too, and they've swapped some letters out for others in the . . ." He paused to think. "In the more than three centuries since this was written, but I'm sure it can be done. Just might take some time."

The challenge was daunting. I felt my shoulders sag. "I know you're busy with the barn and keeping things running around here and taking care of Connor, and I feel bad asking you to—"

"I'd be happy to help you with it."

"But . . ." I saw no hesitation on his face. He merely hunched his shoulders and smiled. "Are you sure?"

"I've spent every evening since I got to France either reading books or watching dubbed episodes of old American shows on French TV. This kind of a project might actually be a nice change."

"I can help you," I offered, surprised by a flutter of anticipation. "Type it up as you figure it out— or Google words you don't understand."

"We'll need a place to work," he said. "And maybe some resources other than the Internet."

"I don't want you to spend anything."

"Docteur Fabian's the town historian. He'll at least point us in the right direction if we can't figure it out on our own."

"You're sure you're okay with this?" I said, afraid I'd pressured him into something he didn't want.

He shrugged. "I like mysteries, remember?" There was something that looked like anticipation in his gaze. "We can work in the evenings. After Connor goes to bed. Maybe in the conservatory?"

"Only if you feel like it."

He smiled. "I will. And if something comes up, we'll play it by ear."

It felt a bit frightening to have committed to the project, but as I looked at the pages Grant still held in his hands, I sensed again that the sewing box had found me for a reason. There was something of Patrick in the mystery it harbored, and I wasn't ready to completely let him go.

"So," Grant said as he stood, dwarfing the small space with his height, "do we start tomorrow?"

I shrugged and hoped it looked casual. There were butterflies in my stomach. "If you're okay with that."

ELEVEN

The Revocation of the Edict of Nantes came as no surprise, nearly ten years ago. It legitimized the hardships we'd already been enduring. Hardship is a toothless word. What we'd survived were atrocities too inhumane to comprehend. In reality, the Edict had been annulled for years in incremental ways, well before the Revocation was decreed: our "places of safety" left defenseless, land confiscated, crops destroyed. Friends labeled us heretics, and neighbors sold us out for the king's promised reward.

It was my brother, Charles, who first warned us that something ominous was afoot. Thirteen at the time, he'd been out in the thick brush around Gatigny collecting rabbits from the traps he'd set the night before. He saw three horsemen approach the village from the north and crest the hill across the valley from our farm.

Despite his age, Charles knew enough to be concerned. Though our parents had tried to spare us from the horrors emanating from the capital, we'd overheard whispered exchanges about threats, reprisals, and fast-spreading unrest.

Charles ran back to the farm and found our father and me loading bales of raw silk onto our cart.

"Father!" he yelled. "The king's men! I just saw three of them ride into town."

Our father's gaze narrowed, his eyes nearly black in his somber, weathered face. To Charles and me, he was the epitome of Man: strong, unflappable, driven, and astute. In every way, he lived up to his name. Pierre. The rock. "They're there now?" he asked in his deep, soft voice.

"I think so," Charles answered, a bit breathless from his run.

Father was already striding toward the barn. He lifted a saddle from its shelf.

"Can I come with you, Father?" Charles asked. "I can ride Caprice!"

Our father installed the saddle on his Percheron's back and tested the straps. "You two stay here," he said, his tone calm and commanding. Then he looked at me. "Tell your mother where I've gone."

❧

It was dark by the time Father returned. Charles and I had climbed up to the loft above the sitting room, where we slept, and had tried to stay awake as we waited for his arrival.

Our mother sat beneath us, next to the crib

where baby Julie cooed, repairing a tear in one of Father's shirts. When he unlatched the door, we inched closer to the loft's edge to peer down. Mother looked up as he entered, but she said nothing while he ladled some soup into a bowl, then joined her.

Charles and I looked at each other, impatient, but didn't make a sound as our father ate in silence. Though he was a year younger than me, there was something about my brother that evoked courage and calm. I sensed, as we waited for Father to speak, that those traits would be tested by what we were about to learn.

Father soaked up the last of his soup with a piece of black bread, put down the bowl, and leaned back in his chair. "It's as we feared," he said. As I write, I can still hear the disquiet in his voice.

"The king?" Mother asked.

He nodded. "Three messengers brought the decree and nailed it to the church's door." He leaned forward and propped his elbows on his knees. "The Edict has been revoked."

"Pierre . . ." She put down her mending and stared, a hand fluttering to her chest.

"What we've endured until today, I'm afraid, has been only a prelude to the hardships we will know."

"How can he do this?" Mother asked. "How

can he reverse the laws that have ensured our safety and freedom?"

I looked at Charles and he looked at me. I could see the fear he tried to conceal. For this news to shake my intrepid brother's bravery was more frightening to me than the words our father had uttered.

"We were inconvenient to the Crown before," Father said, a sort of hollowness in his face. "But we're intolerable now. There are no more limits to what our enemies can do." Rising from the chair seemed to require great effort. He looked down at Julie in her crib, then went to the stove, opened its door, and shoved a few pieces of wood inside. "Our faith has become criminal. Either we convert to King Louis's religion or we risk losing everything. And if we're found meeting together, reading together, singing . . . It's all punishable by death now."

"Pierre." Mother sounded breathless. "Death?"

"Or the galleys. Death delayed."

"What can we do? There must be something we can do."

"There is nothing."

They stared at each other for long moments as tears trickled down my mother's face. Beside me, Charles breathed fast and hard, distraught by what he'd heard. He inched closer to me in the shadows of our loft. We didn't know what words to use for the emotions tightening our chests. So we lay there, side by side, long after our parents had finished speaking, and listened to the silence reaching us from below.

-ॐ॰ॐ-

By declaring that we must be converted or destroyed, the king unleashed a virulent strain of persecution among the loyal who followed his decree. In the decade after the Revocation, they closed our schools and colleges, forbade employers from giving us work, and offered even more enticing rewards to those who would convert us. Even Charles, who for years worked as a carpenter, was forced to shutter his shop in Gatigny, resorting instead to clandestine labor for allies who kept his activity from the authorities.

When the mere threat of reprisals failed to extract enough Huguenot abjurations, the king ordained that we be made more miserable yet and enlisted his dragoons as hammers sent to shatter us.

The soldiers stopped at nothing to break the bowed and straining resistance of the Huguenots still clinging to their faith. Dozens of our churches were destroyed, their walls torn down, their Bibles burned, their pastors tortured or killed for preaching to the few who remained faithful. The dragoons poured boiling water down the throats of women, bounced the elderly in blankets until their old bones broke, and ended the lives of the most headstrong of men with dismembering racks they constructed in public squares.

The Protestant community was brought to its knees by the persistent brutality of the king's decree and its subjects' inhumanity toward the Huguenots they martyred. We heard rumors of conversions by the thousands in towns and villages surrounding us, but saw only a few among the Huguenots we knew.

Until the dragoons arrived in Gatigny.

They rode into town nearly two years ago, invested with the authority to live in our homes, to confiscate our belongings, and to convince us to recant by any means they believed justified. Half a dozen soldiers were assigned to our small town. We were a people besieged. A community of faith oppressed and ostracized.

The dragoons pitted horror against horror in their macabre attempts to steal our souls from our God's clutches, and their efforts were rewarded. After they forced his feet into boots filled with hot grease, Brother Sebastian was the first to recant his beliefs. His wife, Marie, converted, too, after they brutalized their daughters, only to savage her as well despite her desperate abjuration. For months after the attack, Sebastian sat hunched outside his home, his feet and livelihood destroyed, his spirits broken by his forced conversion.

"Depart from me, for I never knew you," he mumbled incessantly. No salve could soothe the anguish in his soul.

When the house where I held classes with a handful of our children came under the dragoon's surveillance, Serge, our blacksmith and our friend, offered the loft above his forge as a much safer place to study. Our numbers had dwindled from fifteen to only three, but I found joy and divine purpose in deepening their knowledge and heightening their skills.

So we read the Bible and learned to write God's truth by lamplight there, removed from the prying eyes of disloyal neighbors and surrounded by the smell of coal fires and burning hooves. The students staggered their arrival, and Serge helped them in through the alley-facing window at the back of the shop. We sat close enough to hear each other over the hammering and hissing down below. Sometimes we forgot about the danger that lurked outside our walls and Serge had to remind us to keep our laughter down. So we muffled the freedom-giving sound with hands over our mouths and let our joy of living and believing become silent.

Many of Gatigny's believers vowed to continue worshipping together despite the threat to our shrinking congregation. We met by torchlight in the hills of the Boutières, timing our movements to limit suspicion. Our intimate knowledge of every wildlife path and clearing in the deep, dense woods around our village was an advantage we used to outsmart the king's henchmen. We moved in silence on familiar soil, agile and quick, to the meeting places arranged by word of mouth a day or two before our gatherings. Then, like our ancestors before us, we sat on the bare ground, on fallen trees and rocks, buffering our resilience and drinking from the Holy Book we kept hidden on our farm.

"The faith that unites us cannot be extinguished," my father, our pastor, declared at the end of every service, unbowed in carriage and in voice. Yet we'd already seen our numbers dwindle, our losses the result of fear, of prudence, or of capitulation.

Though we acted as if our gatherings could go on unimpeded by the threats against our lives, we knew in our hearts that a marginal community could only subsist for so long. After one of our own was captured and tortured by dragoons for information about our meetings, we knew our safety could no longer be ensured.

• • •

We gathered in secrecy for the last time, two months ago, to honor our union and finalize our parting.

My father stood deep in the gully carved by winter's thaw, and we sat on the embankments, Charles and his wife, Isabelle, Julie, and me. The weight of grief pressed into us as I held my sister close. She was just twelve and overwhelmed, her tears a testament to the loss of our dissolving. We knew we'd never meet this way again. Of the forty-some families that had formed our congregation, only nine remained. Those who could afford it had moved to safer countries. Others had restricted their faith to the privacy of their own homes. And others yet had bowed under the threats and harassment of the king's vicious envoys.

Father reached into his bag and took out the Bible we kept hidden behind loose bricks in the well next to our home. It was missing half its pages now, as we'd given portions of it away to nearby gatherings whose Scriptures had been confiscated and burned by the king's men. Father held what remained of our Bible in both hands and declared, "This is the Truth that binds us to each other and to God. These are his words exhorting us to faithfulness and strength. These are the pages that emancipate our faith from the dictates of a king. We will carry them with us as a testament to our resistance, as a reminder of all the Huguenot community has endured."

He was silent for a moment, peering into each of our faces with a sincerity and conviction that lent valor to discouragement. Then he stepped up to a boulder and held the Bible aloft. "We are neither bowed nor broken, neither fearful nor bitter. We stand today a strong, victorious people, sharpened by affliction and united by our God."

He rested the Bible on top of the boulder and took a knife from his belt to slit its binding. "Let the head of each family come forward," he said. Using his knife, he divided the Book into several sections and handed one to the elder of each family, instructing some of them to take an extra sheaf for those who hadn't made it to our final gathering.

"The Word of God," he said once all the pages had been passed out, holding our family's with one hand and covering them with the other. "Thus far the Lord has helped us. As his Word has endured, so will the God who spoke it and those who find in him salvation for their souls."

He prayed a blessing over our disbanding church in a voice rich with authority, soft with emotion, and strong with purpose. He described the peace we could know in spite of all our losses. Then we sang a final hymn in the quiet tones we'd learned to use since the Edict's Revocation and separated into the night, each family timing its departure and charting its return to avoid the dragoon's detection.

⸙

"I think this is God's will," Charles said as we sat around our parents' cast-iron stove several weeks later. He'd come to tell us of a plan that seemed to me both dangerous and wise. His voice was solemn, his expression grim. "With a baby on the way, I think we need to flee." He looked around at each of us: his wife, Isabelle, our sister, Julie, our parents, and me.

His plan was simple: to travel by night to the coast and, from there, on to the safety of England. It wasn't without risk. We knew it was a crime to flee, punishable by death, not only for those running, but for the families they left behind as well. Charles knew the dangers. My father knew them, too, when he gave the plan his blessing.

"Please. Come with us," Isabelle begged after Father and I said that we would stay in Gatigny. Her hand grasped my mother's while her eyes implored me. "If you stay here . . . If you stay here and they find we've left . . ."

Mother patted her hand and tried to smile. "Whatever may come, the Lord is with us."

"He'll be with us as we travel to England too," Charles interjected, urgent and earnest. "Please," he said. "Please come with us."

"You should go, Constance," Father said to Mother. "There's no need for you to stay here. You'll be safer with Charles and Isabelle."

She shook her head. "My place is with you. And at my age . . ." Tears filled her eyes. "My place is with you."

"You'll take Julie," Father said to Charles. Mother's hand fluttered. She looked away. I felt my breathing stop as dread and certainty settled in my chest. In every way that mattered, Julie was my child. The countless nights I'd rocked her to sleep, the long days we'd spent spinning raw silk onto skeins, the twelve years of laughter and love we'd lavished on each other had woven a bond that could scarcely be described. Yet as Father spoke, I realized I could not let my selfishness deprive her of life.

Julie's eyes were wide with disbelief. "But I don't want to run," she said.

"You must," I whispered through a tight throat. Letting her go felt utterly wrenching, yet it was completely right.

Julie murmured, "Adeline . . ."

"You're not safe here."

"Then you aren't safe either." Her lip began to tremble, and I reached out to draw her close. "I don't want to run," she said again, her face pressed into me, her arms tight around my waist.

"I know," I said against her hair. This bright, enchanting child who would soon be a woman, this skilled student and avid reader, this lover of nature and of God was a part of me I desperately longed to keep close and just as desperately needed to send far from the dangers that threatened her life.

In a moment of clarity, I saw her future unfurl in front of me, as if God himself were showing me that she would be safe if we'd just find the courage to send her away.

Heartbroken but certain, I untangled Julie's arms and pushed her back so I could look into her face. She was shaking her head, eyebrows drawn, before I began to speak. "Adeline, no," she said, her voice tremulous.

"Do you remember when we learned that God has a plan for each of us?" I asked. We'd talked about the story of Moses just a few days before.

Julie bit her lip but didn't respond.

"And do you remember the many ways God speaks to us to reveal his will?"

She pinched her lips together and frowned, determined not to be convicted by my words.

"I believe God is speaking," I said. "Father, Mother, and I love you." I paused to blink back tears. "We love you too much to keep you here when Charles and Isabelle can lead you to a safer place." I tilted up her chin so she couldn't avoid my eyes. "No one wants to say goodbye. But I believe—" I looked at my parents and my brother. "We all believe this is what God wants."

"But . . ." She turned her eyes on my father, begging for a concession. "Father . . . God will protect us. You said it yourself: he is our refuge."

We'd seen too many die to believe that our faith would grant us immunity from danger. But Julie was just twelve, and in her mind our God would shield the family from destruction when hundreds, maybe thousands, in our community had already died, tormented and tortured for a faith they'd refused to reject.

I saw my parents exchange a knowing look, then turn their eyes on Julie. "He has made no promises that we would be unharmed," Father said, his voice resonant with sadness and conviction. "He has promised to be with us, but never that our lives would be untouched by man's worst deeds. If you stay here—" He paused and swallowed hard. "What Adeline has said is true."

I ran a hand over Julie's cheek when she turned back to me. "I believe this is God's will, sweet Julie. This is what he wants. For you to reach England and begin a new life there. For you to extend in that distant place what he started here in Gatigny."

⚜

"Are you sure?" Charles asked as he and Isabelle prepared to leave for their home later that night. There was pleading in his eyes when he repeated his question. "Are you sure you won't come with us?"

We knew with a clarity that rendered us speechless that staying in Gatigny would put us at risk. We did so willingly, aware of the peril. My parents would stay for what remained of our congregation, providing comfort to the grieving and guidance to the lost. I would stay for my students, the few who still came to study, most mornings, in the loft above the forge. I drew courage from the certainty that as long as our children were able to read and convey God's Word, our faith—our very existence—would never be extinguished.

Charles stood in front of me as strong and determined as I'd always known him to be. From our childhood to this season of our tearing apart, we'd been more than brother and sister to each other. We'd been companions, accomplices, and friends. As I looked into his face, I saw the man he had become, his protective instincts now aligned with the duties of impending fatherhood. He had to move his family out of harm's way, but he still feared for those he'd have to leave behind.

"You go," I said. "You, Isabelle, Julie, and the baby. It is good and right for you to go. But I must stay here, Charles. This is the place where God has planted me."

He held my gaze for a moment longer, then he nodded his understanding and turned slowly to leave.

—❦—

We stood outside my parents' home a few weeks later, and, in a ceremony similar to what we'd experienced as a church, Father divided our pages of the Bible into smaller sections, handing a sheaf to each of us and keeping another for himself.

"Are you still sure?" Charles asked, trying again to talk me into leaving.

"I'm sure."

"If you get caught teaching the children . . ."

"I'll be careful."

"We'll look out for her," my father said.

We said good-bye past midnight, in the courtyard of my parents' farm. Charles and Isabelle seemed serene, but there was fear in Julie's eyes. They had packed only what they could carry on their backs and wore dark clothes to blend into the late June night.

Charles pulled an object from one of the bags he'd brought with him to the farm. "This is for you," he said, handing me a sewing box I knew he'd made himself. The inlaid wood and smooth finish were signature features of his work. I took it from him, captivated by its beauty and exquisite detail. There were tears in his eyes when he said, "It's the last thing I made in my shop. I finished it just this morning."

"Charles . . ."

He pulled out the drawer and tugged on the red thread extending from its corner. The bottom of the box came up easily, revealing a space beneath it. The look he gave me was intense with conviction and loss. "Hide your pages here. Your pages of the Bible. If they find you with them . . ." He grasped my shoulders. "Hide them here."

"I will," I promised him. "I'll keep them safe."

I turned toward Julie, her face a mask of reluctance and sadness. "And you, sweet sister," I said, putting down the sewing box and reaching into my apron's pocket. "I made this for you to take on your journey." I pressed into her hands the parting gift I'd confected through blinding tears.

"You made it?" Julie asked.

"It's small enough to carry, and what you're about to live . . ." Losing her was a physical ache. "You'll write your story here: the places you go and the lessons you learn," I said as her arms wrapped around my waist. I remembered all the times I'd held her since the morning she was born. "And God's Word too," I added. "You'll carry it with you and share it with those who follow after us."

From the corner of my eye, I saw Isabelle fold her hands over her still-small belly. She understood. Though distance would soon diverge our journeys, their common roots would bind us to each other.

"I'll write it all," Julie said, understanding as only a sister could how important story and family were to me. "I'll write it the way you taught me." She stepped into my arms again and I held her close, reluctant to release her, but eager to let her go. This voyage away from me would allow her to flourish in a safer and more peaceful land than France.

"Will you tell your story too?" she asked, still pressed into my chest. "So we can share them with each other when we meet again?"

"I'll write it all," I whispered near her ear, but as confident as I was that God would ensure her survival, I had no such certainties that my life would be spared. I stroked her cheek and tried to smile. "Story is sacred, and I will tell mine."

When I released her, she melted into Mother's

embrace. They didn't try to muffle the keening of their grief. Their sadness was the measure of their love.

⸺⸙⸺

Ten days have passed since Charles, Isabelle, and Julie left. As I write these words, I realize how precarious all our lives have become. My parents and I have no illusion of safety. Our end feels inescapable. Our courage stretched taut. Our faith firm, but weary.

For all its scars and strife, this world still speaks the beauty of its Maker. I rise each morning seeking glimpses of his heart. In simple ways, I see him moving in Creation with serenity and grace. He looks kindly on the good that still reflects his loving purposes and binds the wounds inflicted by the wicked and depraved. He is our hope and refuge still. Though our lives have been dismantled by the cruelty of man, God in his faithfulness has scattered flecks of gold amid the debris of our loss.

TWELVE

Most evenings Grant and I sat in the conservatory at the gouged antique table we'd moved in for our project. We'd stolen a couple reading lights from around the manor house, as the bulbs in the chandelier barely illuminated the space. It had taken us a while to put the pages back in order. Sometimes the color of the ink, which varied in opacity and shade, was the only sign we had that one sheet led to another.

We sat side by side with a dictionary and a laptop, slowly and deliberately translating Adeline's words. When I pushed for us to skip ahead, past sentences that didn't seem to make sense, Grant dug in his heels. "Let's figure this out first." He'd gone to Docteur Fabian only once, when the meaning of an archaic idiom eluded us for hours. The rest of the work we'd done alone as night descended over Balazuc, our minds and efforts trained on Adeline's account.

"You realize there are people around here who could give you a hand with the French," Mona said, probably for the third time that week, as she brought coffee for Grant and tea for me.

"And give someone else the satisfaction of deciphering this?" There was low-key excitement in Grant's eyes. He seemed as fascinated by the task as I was.

His expression grew grim as Adeline wrote of the atrocities she'd witnessed. When she made reference to a *boîte à couture*, I entered the words into the online translation engine and froze. Grant had been working on the previous sentence and felt more than saw my surprise. He swiveled the laptop so he could see the screen. "A sewing box." It was a statement—as if he'd been waiting for the confirmation.

I got up so fast that my chair toppled backward, and I heard Grant chuckle as I hurried from the room. I found the box where I'd left it by the fireplace in the cottage and returned to the conservatory with it. We pored over Adeline's description of the gift again, just to confirm what we already knew.

"Looks like a match," Grant finally said.

"It is. It's . . ." I felt tears come to my eyes. "It's Adeline's sewing box." I missed Patrick so fiercely in that instant that it took my breath away.

My mind flashed back to the moment when we'd found the compartment hidden inside the shallow drawer. To Patrick's statement about our treasures finding us.

"He knew," I said to Grant before I'd had time to consider the words. I ran my hand over the sewing box. "Patrick knew what this was. The story it held. He knew."

I felt Grant lean back in his chair. His eyes were on me when I looked up. "Before he died?"

There was something about our shared discovery that made me trust the moment. I shook my head. "No. When I . . . when I found the box at Passé Composé."

"I see."

I looked down again. Away. Anywhere but at Grant. "I would have missed the box if not for him. That's the part I don't—I don't understand." I struggled with the conflicting reality and squeezed my eyes shut to remember more clearly. "I'd gone up the ladder to the second floor where he was looking through old maps." The memories were treasonous. "I saw him." I said it again because it had been so real. Because it still felt so real. "I saw him . . . but he wasn't really there," I added, as much for myself as for Grant.

"But you thought he was."

"Did Mona tell you?"

He nodded.

I blinked back tears. "I was sure he was. I can picture him standing by that collection of maps as clear as . . . as clear as *you're* sitting right here." I wondered if the pain and shame of the illusion would lessen with time. I doubted that they would. "He told me it was a good find."

"It was."

"But he wasn't really *there,*" I said again.

Grant sighed. "In ways that matter, he was."

I found it reassuring that he was neither laughing at me nor questioning my sanity.

"He told me the box had found me—that there was a reason for it. That afternoon when . . . before he . . . before Mona found me."

"Do you believe him?"

"I don't know. I want to."

He stretched his neck from side to side, and I heard something pop. Then he leaned forward in his chair and gave me a considering look.

"I'm not crazy," I whispered, as much to convince myself as to persuade him.

He gave me his usual half smile. "Your mind gave you the illusion it needed to survive."

I pulled the sewing box closer and opened its lid, imagining the items Adeline would have kept in it. "Why did you need me to know your story?" I whispered to the box.

Grant chuckled. "Okay, *now* I might have some questions about your sanity."

I felt myself blush. Adeline's face, the way I imagined her—long dark hair, pale skin, deep and earnest eyes—floated into my consciousness. Hundreds of years later, her courage still moved me. "Do you think she lived for long? After her family left?"

"Adeline? I'm guessing the rest of her journal might tell us."

"She could have survived," I said, wanting to believe that she had.

"She could have."

We sat in silence for a while. "I want to know," I whispered.

He grinned. "I want to sleep."

I glanced at the time on my laptop's screen and saw that it was nearly two in the morning. So I placed the pages of Adeline's notebook back in the box's bottom drawer and pushed it closed. "Back at it tomorrow?"

"Sure."

Grant walked me to the door.

-⸰⸱⸰-

In an attempt to learn more about the Bible pages we'd found in Adeline's sewing box, we drove to a Huguenot museum seventy kilometers away in Mialet. From the outside, it looked like just another historic farm nestled into a wooded hill, but on the inside it offered a modern, thorough exploration of the region's religious past.

The curator, a distinguished gentleman by the name of Yves Vivier, seemed pleased that we'd come to him in search of answers. "They were in a drawer?" he asked in barely accented English as we stood near the welcome desk. Though he appeared to be nearing seventy, the sparkle in his eyes was youthful.

"Under the false bottom of a sewing box's drawer," Grant confirmed.

"Astounding." He led us into his office and

offered us coffee, which Grant accepted and I declined. He motioned for us to sit, then opened a document on his computer, clicked a few keys, and finally turned the monitor around so we could see what he'd found. It was a printed page in Old French—and it looked just like the one we had.

"Lucky for us, someone thought it would be a good idea to scan all the pages of rare editions of the Bible," he said. "Ezekiel, right?"

Grant and I looked at each other while Monsieur Vivier clicked around on his computer some more. When he turned the monitor toward us again, a page identical to the first one of Adeline's was on the screen.

"Notice the lettering, the layout on the page . . . What you've got here," Monsieur Vivier said, turning the monitor back to himself, "is a rare edition of the Bible, published probably around 1688 in Geneva." I could tell by the glint in his eyes that he was intrigued by our find. And I could tell by the matching glint in Grant's that he was just as relieved as I was to have the pages authenticated. "Tell me again what the woman said—the one who wrote the text you found with these pages."

Grant and I told him about Adeline's family, their church in Gatigny, Charles and Julie's flight to England.

"This was around 1695?"

"Yes."

He went to the shelves that lined one wall of his office and climbed onto a footstool to reach for two books. "You'll find information about the refugees who fled to England in this tome," he said, handing a thick book to Grant. "And this one here will give you some insight into the life that awaited the Huguenots who made it acrossthe Channel." He handed the second book down to us. "Somewhere around chapter fifteen, I believe . . ."

"How soon do you need these back?" I asked.

He waved off my concern. "Whenever you return them is fine. And if I find anything else, I'll send you an email."

Grant took one of the B&B's business cards from his wallet and handed it to Monsieur Vivier. "Email's at the bottom."

"Balazuc?" he asked after glancing at the card. When we nodded, he said, "You'll likely pass right by the place where Gatigny used to be on your drive home from here."

"Used to be," Grant repeated.

"Not much to show for it now, of course. It was the only town in the Vivarais to have been struck by the Great Plague of Marseille—in the 1720s, I believe—and they wasted no time burning it to the ground. What little was left of the structures they buried for good measure."

I caught Grant's eye as Monsieur Vivier went

on. "They found the town's foundations when a— what do you call it?" He thought for a moment, smoothing his mustache with his index finger. "A commercial complex, that's what it is. They found it when a commercial complex was being built on the site several years ago and did some excavating. But there was little there worth unearthing, so they went back to bulldozing the area where Gatigny once stood."

"So there's nothing left of it," Grant said.

Monsieur Vivier shook his head. "It wasn't much of a village to begin with. But there was a strong Protestant presence there—that's what drew the king's attention. I suspect nefarious souls alerted him to it."

"Are there any records that would indicate if Adeline ever married, if she had children, where she was living at the time of her death?" I asked, intent on learning all I could about her fate.

"I'm afraid you'll find no such records," Monsieur Vivier said, frowning. "One of the king's more insidious decrees was that no Huguenot milestone—whether it be baptism, marriage, or death—could be legally recorded unless it was recognized by the Catholic Church. The Protestants of that era, as unwilling to recant and submit as they were, would have wed in secrecy and buried their dead in private services, often in unmarked graves."

"So . . ." I could feel my hope of tracing Adeline's lineage decreasing. "There would be no paper trail to validate that they existed?"

"I'm afraid not. The law essentially erased their lives from the region's records. But . . ." He went around his desk and pulled a torn and dog-eared map from one of its drawers, then waved it in the air as he continued his thought. "It isn't much, but you can at least see the place where the village used to stand. Here—let me show you." He unfolded the map on top of the stacks on his desk and took a moment to orient himself. Then pointed at a spot not far from the town of Vallon-Pont-d'Arc. "Right here—just off the D290. That's where it was. Look for the Carrefour grocery store on the left as you come into town and mark a moment of silence for the history under its floors."

⁂

"So they built a mall over Gatigny," Grant said as we drove back to Balazuc. We were in Mona's Peugeot 308, a significant upgrade from the 2CV.

"Life goes on, right?" I was surprised at the cynicism I heard in my voice.

Grant glanced at me but didn't say anything for a moment. When he did speak, it was with surprising perceptivity. "Life goes on and people forget."

It was a grim assessment, but I knew it was

151

accurate. The Paris attacks had happened less than a month before, and many in the country had already turned their attention back to trivial concerns.

I sat back and watched the countryside flash by, immune to the sights that would have charmed other tourists. Though talking about Patrick with Grant and Mona had allowed some light into the sepulchral darkness that had haunted my spirits since Paris, it had also heightened my sense of his absence. The intensity of missing him was a physical ache. I just wanted to have my friend back. To have him real and breathing next to me.

I allowed my mind to conjure up his voice, the way he always sat, how he leaned forward when he spoke with friends—even with strangers. I tried to recall every detail of who he was, unsettled by the notion that time moves on and life builds malls on the graves of those who are no longer here. I crossed my arms to ward off a sudden chill, and my hand settled over the incision in my waist. I realized how grateful I was for a reminder that wouldn't fade.

It was a strange imbalance—the newfound ability to function almost normally, even light-heartedly, for minutes and hours at a time, and the underlying strain of all I had endured, quick to blindside me when I expected it the least. The unpredictability was confusing and destabilizing. So was the subtle tension that sometimes wedged itself between Grant and me. I hadn't identified it yet, but I heard its hum in the lulls of our conversations.

Thirteen

I was teaching my three pupils in the shadowy space above Serge's forge when Brother Ludovic arrived. I shushed the children when we heard the clatter of his horse's hooves, and we edged toward a spot where I could see him and Serge down below.

"Something wrong with the shoes?" Serge asked.

Ludovic had come just the day before to have his horse reshoed.

"They're heading toward the Baillards' farm," he said without preamble, his voice low and urgent.

Serge said, "The dragoons?"

"Five of them."

Both men looked up as I clambered over the edge of the loft and descended the ladder.

"How long ago did they leave?" I asked Ludovic, dread chilling me.

"Just now. I came as soon as they were out of sight."

I reached for his horse's reins. "Can I borrow him?"

The men exchanged glances and Serge said, "It may not be safe."

"Please."

Ludovic hesitated. "I'd go myself . . ."

"You have children," I said. "And the dragoons won't be surprised to see me at my family's farm."

Serge moved around the horse to help me into its saddle. "Go with God," he said.

I rode through the broad doors of the forge, unconcerned by who might see me, and set off toward home by the less traveled path that ran along the stream, arriving at the farm ahead of the dragoons.

I had just begun telling my father what I knew when they crested the hill and came into view. Father motioned for me to step back, and he stood in the barn's doorway, waiting as they approached.

"Pierre Baillard?" their leader called as they rode into our courtyard.

Father nodded, but said nothing.

"Where is your son?"

"He isn't here."

The white of Mother's apron drew my attention to the house. She stood on the doorstep mouthing words I imagined were a prayer.

The soldiers dismounted, and the leader approached my father as the others hung back, surveying the farm, the land, my mother, and me. "Where is your son?" he said again, more ominously this time.

"I answered your question. He isn't here."

The dragoon's next step brought him so close to my father that they stood chest to chest, Father's lean lines a contrast to the other's bulky form. "You know it is a crime against the Crown to flee the country."

My father didn't flinch. "I know."

"Where is your son?" The dragoon's voice was getting sharper. Shriller.

"He isn't here."

"Where has he gone?"

"He isn't here."

I knew my father wouldn't lie. No matter how much the soldier yelled and threatened, Father would not lie.

"And your daughter?" the dragoon asked, instantly drawing his men's attention. He glanced at me. "The younger one, thirteen or so, I think?"

"She's not here either."

"Search the house and the barn," the dragoon ordered quietly.

Two men set off toward our home, and two more walked into the barn. My father turned to follow them, but the soldier drew his sword and barred his way. I saw my mother flinch as the men shoved past her into the house.

I could feel the head dragoon's bloodshot eyes following me as I crossed the yard to her side. "Mother . . ."

"You shouldn't have come," she said, her voice shaking, her face pale.

A horse whinnied in the barn. I saw my father start when it cried out in pain. One of the men inside let out a long, shrill cheer. Then our second horse whinnied, the sound cut short with a bloodcurdling cry. They came out of the barn, and one of them casually drove a sword through the neck of Ludovic's stallion too. Mother reached out for me when my legs grew unsteady, but her eyes didn't leave my father.

Inside the house, furniture crashed and pottery shattered. The men called out and egged each other on. I heard their footsteps on the ladder to the loft, to the safe space that had witnessed the best of my childhood.

The dragoon's leader prodded Father away from the barn with his sword, into the center of our courtyard, then turned on him again. "Where is your son?"

Father stood facing the man whose soldiers had slaughtered his horses and still threatened his family, ashen-faced and unyielding.

"He isn't here."

The dragoons' leader stood back to get a better look at my father. "You'll do well in the galleys. All that farmer's muscle . . ." He turned his salacious gaze on Mother and me. "And they'd do well . . ." He leered. "They'd do well in my captain's bed."

I felt my blood run cold. Mother reached for my arm and pulled me nearer. Then she stepped in front of me, shielding me with her body, a desperate, futile gesture.

The men who had been ransacking the house stepped out and grabbed us from behind, their breath sour against our necks, their hands groping.

I felt my father's eyes more than I saw them. His agony reached me across the space between us. "My son and my daughter have gone to Bourges," he said, perhaps trying to deflect the attention from us. Though his expression was impassable, there was fear in his voice. It was a sound I'd never heard before. "There's—there's a weaver there who buys our silk."

The dragoon struck him in the temple with the grip of his sword.

Father hadn't lied. They'd gone toward Bourges, and there was indeed a weaver there with whom we'd done business. But on this trip they'd gone to stay with a pastor who would provide food and lodging until they moved on toward England.

"You lie," the soldier sneered.

"I wouldn't lie," my father said, raising his voice to a persuasive pitch.

"For this lie, you should die." He pressed the tip of his sword into Father's upper arm and drew blood.

"I did not lie," my father repeated through clenched teeth.

The solder struck him again with his sword's grip, swift and hard to his left cheek.

"No." Mother tightened her hold on my arm as I tried to step forward. The drunken soldiers still standing behind us released us and stumbled toward my father, bloodlust on their faces. We watched as Father straightened. He touched his cheek, and his hand came away bloodied.

There was nothing we could do as they encircled him, propelling him back and forth between them like a rag doll. "Liar," they bellowed.

"What's your God doing for you now?"

"To the galleys with you, you Protestant filth!"

When Father lost his balance and fell, they began kicking him. He curled into a ball and tried to shield himself, but his strength and reflexes were too wounded for self-protection. My mother's knees buckled, but her eyes never strayed from her husband. I smothered my cries behind shaking hands and knelt beside her, certain that my father would soon be dead.

But they didn't kill him that night. They left him lying on his side, bloodied and motionless, his legs drawn up and his arms around his abdomen. The leader planted a boot on his bruised and swelling face and leaned low to growl,

"How about we make a deal, you peasant heretic? If they're not back here by tomorrow, we'll cut off your hand. The day after that, we'll cut off the other. And if they're still not back from Bourges on the third day, we'll return to this farm, send you off to the galleys, and move into your house to make your women ours."

He leered in our direction, then pressed harder on my father's face. "You hear what I'm saying, you Huguenot scum? Get your son and daughter back here or . . ." He ran his sword lightly across my father's neck, and I saw blood seeping from the cut as the dragoon looked up at us and winked. Then he ordered his men to set fire to the barn, and they rode away from our farm.

⊰⊱

We moved into town that night under cover of darkness. Though our home had been spared as the barn burned to the ground, we knew that our farm was no longer a safe place. One of our friends risked his own life by riding out to warn us that the king's men had stationed lookouts on the roads that led into the hills, barring our escape. With those routes blocked, we'd have to shelter in Gatigny for a while and put greater distance between us and our oppressors when they let down their guard.

Mother and I packed what we could carry

while my father lay on their bed suffering agony, then she went back into the house and returned with my sewing box in her arms. "I've put all our pages inside," she said. "In case they catch us before we reach the forge."

⸙

Serge wasn't surprised to see us standing at the back window to his shop, as the whole town had heard of the fire at our farm. He took one look at my father's battered face and crawled out the window himself to help us get him inside, his features hardening as my father groaned and grimaced with the pain of being moved.

"You weren't seen?" Serge asked.

Father shook his head. "We circled around to the west and took the alleys to the forge. I'm certain no one saw us."

"It was Jacques," Serge said.

My mother gasped. "Josephine's son? We've known him since . . . He was one of Adeline's children!"

"Collaborating with power is a heady thing," Serge said, leading us to the ladder at the far end of his shop. He motioned to the space above us. "If you clear away the materials Adeline uses for her classes, there will be space enough for all of you."

"We'll leave as quickly as we can," Father

said. "As soon as the dragoons think we're long gone."

"The caves?" Serge asked. How often had he and my father discussed such a plan, never thinking that our family would be the one in need of refuge?

"For now," Father answered this man who was putting his own life at risk to defend ours. "We know the risk you're taking, Serge. First allowing Adeline's students to study here and now this . . ."

A faint smile creased Serge's forge-weathered face. "We are a brotherhood. Brothers help brothers."

We settled into the low, narrow space at the back of the loft, clearing it of books and writing materials so we could all three lie down to sleep. Mother and I helped Father to the wooden floor. He grunted with the pain of broken ribs and bruised flesh, his face so discolored and swollen that I could scarce tell who he was.

We had a chamber pot, a couple blankets, and little else. No candle. No lantern to draw attention to our location. It was hot and reeked of coal fires and heated metal. But it was a safe place for now.

After we'd lain side by side, awake and speechless for some time, my mother whispered, "We should have died today." Her hand fumbled for mine and found it. I knew she held my father's too. "I thank God for his protection."

I thanked God, too, but I knew the soldiers' visit had set our lives onto a path that we could no longer control. What danger had already existed had been multiplied tenfold, and I envisioned with foreboding what might lie ahead.

❦

We spent seven days at the forge.

"You can't leave yet," Serge said on the third day, concern somehow audible in his usual monotone. "They're still watching all escape routes and promising rewards to anyone who turns you in."

That we'd eluded their game of cat and mouse before they'd had a chance to quench their thirst for Huguenot blood was an affront to their honor. To save face and reestablish power, they'd enlisted the dragoons stationed in neighboring villages to scour the countryside for signs of our passage.

"Yet every hour we spend under your roof puts you in greater jeopardy," Father said to Serge. He reclined against a pile of linens in the far end of the attic, the bruising in his face now faded and yellowish. The past days had been agonizing for him, the discomfort from his broken bones a constant misery. When I'd handed our chamber pot down to Serge on our first night in his attic, I'd seen blood there and

163

wondered how long my father could survive the injuries we couldn't see.

Serge's report was the same on the fourth night. The dragoons were still out en masse, making a flight to the caves too risky to consider. The fifth and sixth days marked a slight lessening in the number of them patrolling the environs, but their sights were still too keenly set on finding "those Baillard heretics." We could hear them going door to door through town, when the forge didn't resonate with the hammering and hissing down below, cajoling and commanding our friends and neighbors to report any sightings.

By the seventh day, Father was able to move a bit more freely. It took him some effort and pain to get up from the ground, but after nearly a week of being pulled up and lowered by Mother and me, it was significant progress.

"We need to get to the caves," he said when Serge came to update us that night.

"It still may not be safe."

"Serge . . ." The conviction and courage had returned to Father's voice. It was a relieving and disquieting sound. "It's time for us to go."

"You'll have to walk."

Father nodded. "By God's strength."

There was a moment of silence as Serge seemed to consider how much influence he could wield over a man as determined as my father. "I'll let you out through the back window when I'm certain it's safe," he finally said. "Be ready to go the moment I give you the signal."

"Thank you, my friend."

Serge looked at Mother and me. "With these two helping you, I believe you'll make it to the caves."

"I'm not going," I said. The sureness in my voice surprised me.

My mother turned anxious eyes on me. "Adeline . . ."

"I can't leave the children, Mother. They count on me."

"To write and read, yes. But, Adeline, is it worth your life to teach them these skills?"

"I'm teaching them the Bible," I said, conviction strengthening my resolve. "It isn't just school. You've told me so yourself."

"They can learn from someone else."

I squared my shoulders and tried to sound more courageous than I felt. "This is the task entrusted to me," I told her. "An appointment from God to endow them with the words and skills they'll need to tell the story he is writing. To keep our faith from dying, I'm willing to take the risk."

"I'll stay," Mother said, desperate. "I'll teach them. You can go." She turned to my father for reinforcement, but there was only pride in his eyes as he looked at me.

"I believe I'm the one God has chosen for this work," I whispered to them both. "This burden, this privilege, it comes from him."

"Are you sure?" my father asked. I could see that he already knew the answer.

"I'm sure, Father. You go with Mother and care for those who need you in the caves. I'll remain here and care for those who count on me in Gatigny."

My mother flinched and looked down. She knew arguments were futile.

"You'll allow her to stay on?" my father asked Serge. "To live and teach in this room?"

Our friend didn't hesitate for a moment. "She is bestowing eternity on our children."

"I am grateful, my brother," Father said, extending his hand to his friend.

Mother sank to the rough-hewn floor and covered her face with her hands. I knelt beside her and begged her to look up. "I'll come to you when the time is right," I whispered when she finally met my gaze. "I'll come when God tells me it's time to leave Gatigny."

Later that night, my father tucked his Bible pages into the burlap sack of clothing and food he carried on his shoulder, then he leaned down to kiss my cheek, wincing a bit at the pain the movement caused. "We'll wait for you," he said. "May God protect and strengthen you."

Serge and I helped him through the window

first, then we assisted my mother out. She seemed to have aged ten years in the hours that preceded their departure.

"Are you sure you're strong enough to make it to the caves?" Serge asked again.

"I am not," Father replied, honesty and bravery in his face. "But I'll be with Constance. If anyone can see us safely into the hills, it is she, the strongest, most resilient woman I've known." He smiled into her concerned eyes. "God knows what lies ahead. Of this I'm sure. He has gone before us, and if we're caught . . . he'll be there." He glanced at me and gave me courage with his gaze. "He will be there."

My parents draped dark blankets over their heads, and I had to keep from calling out when they turned to walk away, my father's hand resting heavy on my mother's shoulder.

The tears that had been threatening since I'd made the decision to stay finally fell. Serge let me return to the attic without a word, honoring the grief I'd chosen. We'd each followed a calling we sensed had come from God, my parents to their flock and me to my students.

⟞⟨⟩⟵

I've spent the last few days fulfilling my promise to my sister—chronicling the events that brought our family to this point. I write for Julie and for Charles, for a community oppressed, for loved ones hung, for slaughtered innocents. I write for our descendants, for those who will not understand the cost of our survival.

Though we've been bowed, the Huguenot people have not been broken. Our faith breathes on in the bravery of belief and in the insurgency of prayer. Sobered by the danger threatening our future, trusting in the sureness of God's unfailing promises, we will live out the vows embodied by my father: enduring with courage, resisting with wisdom, persisting in faith.

Fourteen

I'd moved out to the courtyard with a dining room chair and some sandpaper on a particularly sunny afternoon. The wind was cold, but it barely reached me in the corner between the cottage and the barn. The sun on my face felt reviving, but a bank of dark clouds rolling in made me wonder how long it would last.

A farmer had delivered a tractor-load of firewood earlier that day. Grant was set up not far from me, splitting huge logs into smaller pieces with an ax, then piling them neatly against the barn's wall. We hadn't spoken much, and I was grateful for that.

"Hey, hey, hey!" Connor stood on the edge of the porch and cupped his hands around his mouth as if he were calling across a canyon. "You gotta come see my fort!"

"Be there in a minute!" Grant answered, the ax around behind his back, then bringing it down hard on the round of wood in front of him.

"Not you—Jessica!"

Something warm curled in my stomach as I sat on the ground, sandpapering the rungs of Mona's chair.

Grant leaned on the ax and glanced at me. "She's kind of busy, tiger."

"But she's right there!"

"He's got a point," I said, dragging my cramped body into a standing position and imitating Connor's accent. "I'm wight here."

Grant rested the ax against the pile of split wood and propped his fists on his hips. "Why does she get to see it and I don't?"

"Because she's Jessica, silly." It was a perfectly logical reason to him.

Grant pulled off his work gloves and walked in my direction. "It's okay to say no, you know."

"I know."

He smiled. "Let's go check out his fort."

We set off toward the manor house, and Connor yelled, "Yes, yes, yes!" pumping his fist in the air.

"Have you noticed how he says things in threes?" Grant asked from right behind me.

"I have, I have, I have."

Connor's fort was little more than an afghan draped over the couch and two chairs, anchored in place by stacks of old books. "It's a fort *and* a pirate ship," he declared, crawling inside. He sat cross-legged and looked at me with expectation. "You coming in?"

Grant stood in the kitchen doorway drying his hands on a towel. "It might be a little tight in there for two."

Connor ignored his uncle and kept his frowning gaze on me. "You coming in?"

That's when a clap of thunder shook the air so violently that the windows rattled. Connor yelped and scooted far back into his fort as my body lurched with an instinctive fear, then froze. I tried to tell myself that it was only thunder, but I stood anchored to the spot, immobilized by a sound that had felt too much like terror.

I heard Mona say, "Better clear the courtyard," as she exited the kitchen and headed for the front door.

"Stay with him?" Grant said to me as he fell into step behind his sister.

I shook my head to clear the static the sudden thunder had set off in my mind, then looked around to anchor my reality to the living room of Mona's home. I could hear her and Grant dragging things to safety in the courtyard, pouring rain muting their voices.

"Help me with the tarp?" Grant's steady voice.

"Be right there."

I took a deep breath as lightning flashed and thunder rolled again, tamping down the fear that threatened.

"You wanna come inside?" Connor asked me, peering around the edge of the afghan. His tone was more urgent this time. "I'll scooch way back so you have more room."

The look in his eyes and the tremor in his chin brought the moment back into focus. I crawled into his makeshift fort, where the blanket hung so low that I couldn't sit up straight. Connor scooted back, his frightened gaze on me, his arms wrapped tight around his legs. He inched over when I adjusted my position to rest my back against the couch. When the thunder rolled again, he scrambled so close that his freckled face pressed against my arm. "I don't really like storms," he said in his broken little voice.

"I don't either," I whispered as some of the tension eased out of my limbs. There was something about his need that made me feel stronger.

"My teacher said it's because someone stepped on a ladybug."

"The storm?"

"No, the rain. Someone stepped on the *bête à bon Dieu* and now he's crying."

Another clap of thunder shook the ground. Connor started, then hunkered down against me. I tried to occupy my mind by translating the phrase the shaking boy had said. "God's bug" was as close as I came.

"So ladybugs are God's favorites?" I said, hoping to distract him.

"And it rains when somebody hurts them."

"That's what your teacher said?"

Connor nodded against my arm. "And then the ladybug turns shiny and . . . and whooshes up." He made the sound of wind blowing and raised his arms. "Like this. And then she disappears."

"Your teacher said that too?"

"No. Me. She doesn't know about the shiny thing."

"What kind of shiny are you talking about, Connor?"

He held out his hands, palms up, as if he were explaining something obvious. "You know—shiny. Like your friend."

"Like my friend?"

"Your yellow-hair friend. Shiny like that."

I felt my breath catch. "What yellow-haired friend?"

His cheek brushed against my arm as he raised his face to look at me. "Your friend that came in the car. He's a ladybug, right?" he said. "A shiny ladybug ninja with bright-yellow hair."

"Connor . . . there was nobody in the car with me."

He looked at me again. "When you got here?"

"Right. I drove here all by myself."

He frowned, then a look of suspicion crossed his face. "Are you being silly?" he asked.

"No, I'm . . . I'm telling you the truth."

"You're being silly," Connor said with a gap-toothed giggle, for a moment forgetting the threat of the storm.

My mind flashed back to the night he'd turned up on the cottage doorstep in his Cozy Coupe and asked if my friend liked stew too. It hadn't surprised me then—I was still living with the illusion of Patrick's survival. But this little boy with the earnest eyes had leaned around the doorframe to see if Patrick was there. Elation and grief stunned me in that moment. I didn't know what to say.

Another clap of thunder shook the house, and Connor pressed closer. "I really don't like storms," he said, lisping the last word.

"Connor, are you sure you saw my friend?"

He nodded. "He was a shiny ladybug ninja."

I blinked back tears and wrapped an arm around his tense little shoulders. "He wasn't a ladybug."

"Then what was he?" He seemed disappointed and confused.

"He was just my friend."

-&+&-

Connor didn't speak of the "ninja" again. Every time I tried to broach the topic, he looked at me like I was crazy. "Ladybugs aren't people," he said one day when I asked if he'd seen my ladybug friend again. It was as if our conversation in his fort, as the storm raged outside, had never taken place.

But I carried the image with me—the ladybug ninja with the shiny golden hair and the tears heaven shed for the *bête à bon Dieu*.

FIFTEEN

I must write quickly. It is the twenty-fourth day of June. The dragoons are in the shop beneath me, incensed and drunk. They've threatened Serge, and I can hear in his voice that he may be badly hurt.

Moments ago, I lifted the children, Marguerite, François, and Annette, through a small hole we made in the forge's roof. If they can get across to the Diderots' house and down to their donkey's stall from there, they'll be able to hide until they can steal home unnoticed.

I've chosen not to follow them. With Serge suffering for my safety, I cannot bring myself to walk away. He has a wife and children. They will not lose their father because of me today. Once I've written these words, I'll escape through the roof as the children did and climb down to the street, then surrender to the soldiers in the forge as if I haven't been hiding here. I pray they'll spare my rescuer because they've caught their prey.

I know this is the end. I sense it in my spirit, yet the peace I feel despite my fear can only be from God. His strength in me is greater than the vise grip of my terror, and it is sturdier than despair. My balm, in this moment, is the promise I perceived on the night our family parted. Though these may be my final breaths, I know in my heart that my Julie will be safe. She will live on to embody the kind of faith man's cruelest ploys will not be able to destroy.

Though I cannot fathom what lies beyond this realm, I believe in the celestial place where grief and pain no longer reign. I am resolved to reach its shores with unsurrendered hope, having endured with courage, resisted with wisdom, and persisted in faith until I could no more.

⸙

Grant turned over the last page of Adeline's notebook and I held my breath, hoping there would be more, but certain her story ended with those words.

"That's it," he said.

We sat there for a while in silence. "She died, right?" I finally asked.

"It sure looks that way. Death or—or something worse. She humiliated the dragoons by eluding them for so long, so . . ."

The silence stretched again. I didn't know what Grant was thinking, but my mind reeled with scenarios that all ended in horror. "The children . . ."

"She said they got out," Grant said, his expression grim. "Across the roofs."

"But Serge . . . ?"

He leaned back in his chair and rolled his shoulders to release some tension. We'd put off work to finish the translation that afternoon, and the uninterrupted hours of concentration had taken their toll. "In my mind, he went down fighting."

"They wouldn't have let him go."

"No."

"So . . . they both died?"

"That's what I'm thinking."

I'd felt a darkening in my spirit as we translated the last increment of Adeline's account. There was something about her unembellished storytelling that had compelled me from the start, and as her life turned into tragedy, her straightforward narration had forced my mind to fill in the details she'd left unspoken.

As I sat in the conservatory, wearied by the effort of translation and the story it had revealed, I felt vestiges of Paris stirring again. It was just a low hum at first. But as my mind reached for something else to focus on, it found only her agony.

The air around me felt saturated with Adeline's brutal end. Claustrophobia gnawed at the edges of my consciousness. I stood up, anxious to escape into the cool air of the courtyard.

"You okay?" Grant asked, as Patrick had so many times. I felt the fabric of my resilience begin to tear.

"I'm fine," I said, my voice unsteady. "I just need to—"

A tractor backfired in the lane outside the windows. It was a sound I'd heard nearly every day I'd lived in Balazuc, but this time it exploded against the backdrop of my memories, in a visceral remembrance of Adeline's end and Patrick's absence.

And it undid me.

I stumbled, sending my chair crashing to the ground behind me. I felt my control slip as terror surged into the loaded air.

"No, no, no . . . ," I heard myself mumble. I closed my eyes and willed the images away.

"Jess?" Grant's voice reached me from a distance.

Sights and sounds swirled as I was sucked into a vortex filled with the shattered remnants of my life before the Bataclan. I saw the concert hall, the crowds jerking to the strident music shrieking off the stage. The lights flashing and the bassist grimacing as he played.

Grant's hand on my arm forced a measure of reality into my reeling thoughts. I tried to speak, but couldn't. He hurried to the door and called for Mona. She was beside me quickly, her concerned face hovering in my fast-decreasing range of vision.

"Jessica, honey, what's going on?"

Patrick's face superimposed itself over hers,

just as sincere. Just as earnest. "Use your words, Jess," I heard him say from beyond the grave.

I sensed Grant moving, carrying an armchair from the alcove to where I stood. Mona tugged at my arm. "Why don't you sit down . . . okay, Jess? Sit right here and try to take a breath."

My legs buckled as I lowered myself into the chair. As my mind clung to the tangibility of these strangers enveloping me with their words and concern, the sights and sounds of the recent past launched themselves against the flimsy barriers that had kept memory at bay.

"Use your words, Jess," Patrick said again from somewhere above me, from somewhere inside me.

I shook my head. "I can't."

"Jessica, what can't you?" Mona's face swam into focus again.

"You can," Patrick whispered.

"I can't . . ." I felt a wail surfacing and tried to silence it. What escaped instead was a long, low moan.

"Should we call Docteur Fabian?" Grant asked.

"Give her another minute. I'll get a cool wash-cloth."

I was vaguely aware of her leaving the room and of Grant crouching in front of me. He looked unsure but determined. "Jessica," he said. I felt him grip my forearms and shake them, demanding my attention, my focus. "Jessica, look at me."

I dragged my eyes from the carnage in my mind

179

to the kindness in his gaze. "What are you seeing?" he asked, his voice firm.

"No . . ."

"Jess." He shook my arms again and leaned sideways to intercept my gaze. "Jess, what are you seeing?" When I shook my head, he said, "Whatever you're trying to control—Jess, whatever's in there, it's got to come out. It's eating you alive."

I opened my mouth to refuse again, to curl into the cowardice of numbness—of blankness. Every iota of my will begged for the solace of oblivion. I felt the past receding, the memories fading from red to gray, from shrill to muffled.

Then Grant said, "Jessica—use your words."

My eyes snapped to his face. "What did you say?"

Mona held a damp cloth to my cheeks, my neck. I brushed her hands away and leaned toward Grant, who was still crouching near my chair. "What did you say?" I heard the shock in my voice and saw confusion in his face.

"Use your words . . . ?" he said again.

In an instant, the chaos howling though my thoughts was sucked into abeyance. The lucidity that followed was blinding and excruciating. Its substance settled, cold and clear, and words that had until that moment felt deficient converged and subsided into meaning.

Mona dragged a chair from the table to my

side. "Jessica?" she said, perhaps sensing that this moment should not be let go.

"I was in the Bataclan," I whispered. "Vonda and I. And Patrick. We were in the Bataclan." I swallowed against the sobs lodged in my throat and took a breath. Then another.

I looked at Mona and saw kindness I could count on. I looked at Grant and saw courage I could borrow. And in fits and starts, with a rawness that shredded caution, I returned to a crowded concert hall, to rowdy spectators in a darkened room, and saw the night unfold again.

Sixteen

I was skirting the crowd of concertgoers, iPhone in hand, trying to get a clear view of the band. I'd left Vonda holding our spot at the front of the balcony to venture into the crowd packed around the stage, hoping for a good angle and a few snapshots I could text to Patrick.

I jumped a little when the first firecracker exploded, surprised that any sound could pierce the throb of electric guitars, drums, and strained vocals. I smiled at the yelps that followed the first blasts somewhere by the main doors and raised my phone for a shot of the stage.

The next sounds were closer. Well inside the concert hall.

And they were not firecrackers.

Three long bursts roared over the heavy metal. On my phone's screen, I saw members of the band fumble. Their faces blanched as they lowered their instruments and stared aghast toward the back of the room. There seemed to be a moment of absolute silence. Then a single female's voice shrieking into the deafening panic.

More shots exploded, and I saw two bodies projected forward. The crowd surged away from the fallen forms and jolted as another shot rang out.

"*Sortez*! *Sortez par la scène*!" a woman

shielding two teenagers screamed over her shoulder as she pushed them toward the stage and away from the gunfire.

Then, in an almost simultaneous, spontaneous reaction, the spectators dropped to the ground.

I'm going to die. The thought flashed across my mind right before it slowed to stunned disbelief. The rounds were coming faster than I could count—long bursts that seemed to travel from one side of the room to the other. I wanted to get up and run. I wanted to dig through the floor to safety. I wanted to breathe, but even that seemed impossible in the unfolding horror.

A man screamed, *"Non! J'vous en prie—pas ma femme!"* *Please. Not my wife.* Three shots in quick succession. Someone wailed.

I felt my body turn cold as my mind began to comprehend the full horror of what I was witnessing. There was someone lying across my legs. A stranger behind me breathed fast and loud, swearing under his breath as more shots rang out. I lay motionless, staring at the shoulder of the woman in front of me. She was facing the other way and visibly shaking.

"Cachez-vous!" one man yelled from the balcony, his scream cut short by shots fired in that direction.

Hide? I thought, looking around for an escape. I was near the front of the hall, where metal barriers kept the crowd from accessing the stage.

With a side wall at my back and the killers firing from the room's main entrance, where could I possibly . . . ?

Vonda. I moved just enough to steal a glance toward the balcony, but Vonda wasn't where I'd left her. There was movement by the door on the far side, and I could see crouching forms pushing through it. Vonda.

The shooters sounded closer now. I could hear them loading their weapons and speaking to each other in what sounded like perfect French.

"*Ça, c'est pour la Syrie.*" The voice sounded young and casual. *This is for Syria.*

Another shot. "*Mon Dieu,*" someone wailed. *My God.* Sobs mingled with screams as terrified spectators used short breaks between bursts of gunfire to try to escape the concert hall.

I couldn't breathe. I still held my phone, frozen in the act of documenting happy mayhem as the world fell off its axis and tumbled into terror. It took all the effort I could muster to bring it into view. I reached up with my other hand to swipe the phone on, then hit the dictation button in the messaging application. "Patrick," I whispered. "I'm at the concert—"

"*Non!*" The hissed order came from the man lying behind me. An arm reached around me and a hand gripped my wrist, pushing the phone out of sight. "They kill you if they see you," a gruff voice whispered in heavily accented English. I couldn't turn to look at him. I didn't need to. The urgency in his words was persuasion enough.

I couldn't see beyond the woman prone in front of me, but my peripheral vision registered two figures rising from the ground. I lifted my head as they took off running for the stage, wanting to scream at them to stay down. Stay out of sight. The shots that stopped them came from the middle of the room. The first victim fell sideways over the barriers between the floor and the stage. The other fell forward as the side of his head exploded.

I took a breath, desperate to scream and let some horror out, but the same hand that had gripped my arm earlier dug deeper.

My vision seemed to darken. The room tilted. A heavy pulse pounded in my ears. More bursts of gunfire rang out and seemed to last forever. I looked down at the people lying beyond my feet. A blond man with blood seeping through his shirt from his abdomen. A woman nearby, her horrified gaze on him, her mouth open in silent sobs—love and survival battling in her eyes.

My body began to shake as my breathing accelerated. I couldn't get enough oxygen. I was suf-focating—drowning. I pushed up off the floor. I had to move. I had to run. I had to get out before . . .

Another muzzle flash. Up there. Off to the right. Then another on the other side of the room. Aimed toward . . . aimed toward me.

The arm reached across me and pulled me back down to the floor. I struggled against its weight. "I can't . . . I—please," I begged, straining against the torture of immobility.

"No," the man barked English. "You stay! You stay!" He forced me back and held me down. Several spectators clambered onto the stage and took off running for the wings. A long burst of gunfire. A middle-aged man crumpled without sound, but the rest of them got away.

"I can't," I said, my voice barely above a whisper, tugging at the arm that held me down. "I need to—I don't want to die—" I glanced down at the blond man at my feet and felt bile rising in my throat. He lay immobile, dark blood now saturating his shirt.

"I will help you," the voice behind me said. "When it's the right time, I will help you run. Okay?"

I nodded. There was something about the urgency and weight of his voice. I believed him.

With eyes half-closed, I watched a shooter calmly making his way around the room, ignoring some who lunged away from him and shooting others point-blank. A woman crouching behind a large speaker whispered into her phone, tears streaming from terror-stricken eyes. He saw the light of her screen, raised his rifle, and ended her life.

Another burst of gunfire traveled across the

room, hitting wood, walls, and human flesh all around. The sound of agony was overwhelming, the silence just as strident as the screams.

"When I tell you," the man behind me said. "That's when we run."

Shrieks erupted from the space behind the bar. Voices begged. Glass shattered.

"*Regarde moi, fils de pute!*" one of the shooters yelled. *Look at me.* He was standing on the bar, aiming his gun behind it. I could see the shooter closest to me moving toward the back of the room.

"*Tu sais ce qui se passe en Syrie?*" My mind struggled to translate what I was hearing over the roar of terror in my ears. *You know what's happening in Syria?*

There was an unintelligible answer.

The second shooter joined him and said something. They laughed—they laughed like twelve-year-olds. A third terrorist came into view. I heard him say something, but couldn't make it out. Four shots. More laughs and a high five. The taller of the three motioned with his gun toward the stairs that led to the balcony. One of them took off in that direction while the other two inserted fresh clips into their rifles. I saw people rushing toward the door in the balcony above the room. Hushed, urgent voices. They knew the shooter was coming.

Vonda.

"They're getting away up there!" the men below yelled at his comrades.

"Now!" the man behind me hissed.

"Wha—?"

He was on his feet, dragging me up by the arm and shoving me toward the barriers between us and the stage. "Go now!" he spat. "Go!" Then we were running. I could see others running too—risking their lives in a flight toward the exits.

There was nothing in my mind but the desperate need to move, to get out, to escape. The man pushed me over the barriers hindering our access to the stage. There were bodies in the pit. Blood-drenched and shattered. I couldn't falter. I couldn't hesitate. I took two more steps, feeling bone and flesh under my feet, then reached the stage. The man heaved me up as if I weighed nothing. Bullets sprayed into the wood to our right, so we dodged left.

It took an eternity to reach the wings. The stage was small, but my terror made it feel immense. Behind me, the man yelled, "Go—go—go!" More bullets lodged in the wood beneath our feet as we careened into the wings.

Without thinking, I followed those who had made it there before me to a door toward the back, the elation of impending freedom mixing with the horror still quaking in my body.

I stopped so suddenly that the stranger ran into me, propelling me forward into two others.

The door was open, but there was nowhere to go. No exit into the Parisian streets. It was a closed space—a dressing room. And it was already so packed with terrified strangers that there was no space left for more.

I heard a low moan—like a wounded animal begging for mercy. Then I realized the sound was coming from me.

Another series of shots rang out—perhaps the longest yet.

The stranger didn't hesitate. He pushed me farther to the back of the stage and pulled me down next to him behind a pile of sound equipment cases. I cowered against the back wall, curled into a tight ball, and felt death crawling toward me like an inescapable tide. A violent shaking began at my core and spread outward.

That's when the tears started. When the shock began to wear off and the certainty of death set in.

SEVENTEEN

"Américaine?" the stranger asked.

My tears had ended. There was no room for them—the terror was too deep. Too numbing. My body ached with tension. We'd sat behind the pile of equipment for what felt like hours. It was probably only minutes.

"Yes," I answered, my voice unsteady. "American."

He ventured out from behind our protective barrier, crawling far enough to get a look at the other side of the stage. His jaw was set when he returned.

He seemed to search for the English words. "The exit," he finally said. "It's on the other side."

"On the other side of the stage?" Despair gnawed at my courage. "But . . . how can we get there?"

He shrugged. It was such a French gesture that it almost elicited a smile from me. Then the enormity of the risk set in. We could either wait in the dead end of the wings and hope that no one would come looking, or we could try to escape across the stage, exposed to the killers, and find the emergency exit on the other side.

From the sounds reaching us, I could only imagine the horror still playing out in the Bataclan's concert hall. Mingling with the screams and agonizing groans, the distinct voices of the terrorists spoke to each other between bursts of gunfire—one of them tense, while the others sounded calm and measured. There were fragments of sentences I understood. Something that sounded like, "Tell this to your president" and "Now you know what it feels like."

The pleas of victims. "I beg you. Please."

"*Allahu Akbar*." Softly spoken. Followed by two shots and a laugh from somewhere in the room.

A protracted, high-pitched scream broke through the stupor in my mind. A shiver crawled down my spine as my lungs spasmed over constricted breath. The stranger leaned out from behind our precarious shelter and froze. I leaned out too.

A young man moved into my line of sight, crawling from the stage toward the door of the dressing room where dozens of people waited for death or deliverance. He used only his arms to drag his limp body. There was blood spatter on his face, a look of disbelief and terror in his gaze. I heard steps following him. He looked forward, into the shadows of the wings, and saw me cowering behind the sound equipment.

"*Aidez-moi*," he mouthed as his eyes shifted to my rescuer. *Help me.* "*Aidez . . .*"

A shadow stepped into sight, outlined by the lights still streaming from the stage. The young man looked back—slowly, agonizingly. "*Non*," he begged. His eyes skimmed over me as he turned forward again and tried to crawl farther with his arms, the lower part of his body lifeless.

I heard a metallic click. He inched a bit farther. "*Aidez-moi*," he begged of no one in particular, his voice hoarse and breaking.

Another metallic sound. Metal against metal. An arm came out in front of me and pushed me farther into the darkness. Two quick shots and the sound of a slumping body.

I began to scream, but the stranger covered my mouth before any sound escaped. He backed me against the wall and brought his face within an inch of mine. "No," he hissed, his eyes fierce with fear, his hand still on my mouth. He brought a finger to his lips and motioned for me to be quiet, but my body was no longer responding to my mind's commands. Sounds of disbelief and horror rose from my chest like vomit, desperate to escape, frantic to be heard.

A spasm arched my back and seized my lungs. My rescuer's gaze softened as he moved his hand over my nose. I kicked and tore at his fingers, craving oxygen. "Stop," he whispered, tears in his eyes. "Stop. Please."

Darkness crept its way into my terror. It softened the sharpness of my desperation. Consciousness diminished. Rigid muscles grew limp. My legs stopped kicking. I looked into the stranger's eyes as my body struggled to breathe and my mind surrendered to the darkness.

● ● ●

When I came to, he was still beside me. I could hear my pulse beating in my ears and breath returning to my tortured lungs. There was no color in his face. "I'm sorry," he said when I stirred, shaking his head. "I hurt you . . ." He glanced toward the landing, where the boy's body still lay. "I had to. If the terrorist had heard us . . ."

He leaned against the wall beside me, a pallor to his face that hadn't been there before. Something in his expression scared me—something fragile. I sat up and turned toward him. His breathing seemed labored. Sweat stains ringed the collar and armpits of the gray T-shirt he wore.

"I need to know your name," I whispered.

"*Quoi?*"

"I need to know your name." His face swam out of focus as my eyes filled with tears. Tears of terror. Tears of shock. Tears of gratitude. "Before we . . ." I glanced at the stage. "Before we go out there," I said, hiccupping on a sob. "I need to know your name."

"Bernard," he said, his voice gruff.

"Jessica."

He nodded, perhaps understanding my need for a semblance of humanity in the evil permeating the concert hall. He winced and dropped his head back against the wall.

"Bernard, are you okay?" I kneeled in front of him. "Bernard . . ."

He took a deep breath and shook his head as if to clear it. "Yes," he said, wincing as he shifted his position. "Yes. I think maybe I got a bit hurt. When we . . ." He jutted his chin toward the stage. "When we were running."

That's when I saw the blood seeping around from the back of his shirt. I felt myself blanch. "Bernard . . ."

"*C'est juste une égratinure*," he said, smiling bravely. "Just a—how you say it?—a scratch."

I moved to his other side and helped him lean forward from the wall. I couldn't tell whether the bullet had penetrated his body or just skimmed it, but from the amount of fresh blood coming from the wound halfway down his rib cage, I suspected the injury was serious.

"It's more than a scratch . . ." A new wave of fear washed over me.

"We need to get out," he said. I saw courage and determination come over his face like a mask. He took a deep breath and rose to a kneeling position. Then he put out his hand for me to help him to his feet. I wanted to curl into a corner, cover my ears, and surrender to the shock that muddied the edges of my consciousness, but a visceral survival instinct drove me to do everything to escape.

We edged forward together. From our position, I could see across the expanse between where we sat and the wings on the other side. Discarded instruments still lay where they'd been dropped.

The monitors still hummed. The exit was close and unimaginably far. I tried not to picture myself being shot—dying—in the distance between cornered and free.

A burst of bullets slammed into the back wall as more spectators tried to escape onto the stage. I didn't stop to wonder how many had died this time. It was no use. The carnage, I knew, was already beyond measure.

"We wait until they're shooting again," Bernard said beside me. I looked into his grizzled face. Into the kindness and resignation of his gaze. "More than one. When more than one of them are shooting at . . . at someone else. That's when we run. Yes?"

I nodded, trying not to imagine those whose deaths would distract the killers while we attempted to escape.

We crept closer to the light coming off the stage. There was no gunman in my line of vision, so I inched farther yet. The smell of gunpowder was overwhelming. I could see bodies. Pools of blood.

Bernard leaned in behind me as we surveilled what we could from our vantage point. At the back of the room, behind the sound station, four people stood and ran in a crouch toward the main entrance. Two men and two women. Utterly silent. Bullets hit the edge of the balcony as they ran beneath it and rushed toward the lobby. A burst of gunfire hit the pillars from another angle.

"Two shooters," Bernard hissed. "Two shooters. Go—go—go!"

I ran. I ran and tried not to scream and kept moving past corpses sprawled across the stage, and when I stepped into blood and stumbled to my knees, my legs kept pumping, sending me slowed and crawling toward the safety ahead. I felt the bullets flying around me more than I heard them. I was still four feet from the wings when Bernard's hands gripped me by the shoulders and pulled me to my feet. I felt his chest behind me the moment before he propelled me forward with a guttural cry.

Then I fell hard on the floor inside the wings and looked over my shoulder to Bernard, my protector. The stranger who had rescued me. He lay on the stage, his face turned toward the exit, but his eyes stared blankly. Blood poured from a wound just below his collarbone and from his shattered shin. "Bernard!" I screamed. Then I screamed his name again. I waited a moment—an eternity—for him to move, desperate for a sign of life. There was none. I pushed myself up, crying out in pain, and I ran.

Through the metal exit door stained with bloody handprints. Over the wounded and dying in the alley beyond. I ran—screaming—until the pain in my abdomen halted my flight.

When I looked down, I saw blood dripping from my sweater's hem.

The pulse pounding in my ears drowned out the muted sound of gunfire still exploding from within the hellish concert hall.

Darkness swirled closer, suffocating and blessed. Extinguishing my will to fight. I felt my knees buckle.

Then nothing.

Eighteen

I didn't look up when I finished telling Grant and Mona about the events of November 13. I knew Grant sat in his chair by the table. I'd felt him move there as I related the details of Bernard's death and my survival. Mona sat in a chair right next to me, her hand on my arm. She'd barely moved since I started telling my story. If anything, she'd leaned in closer, shielding me from my own memories as she wiped tears from her face.

We sat in silence for a while. I fixed my eyes on the tattered fabric under my hand, gold and blue threads loosened by time and wear. Across the room, Grant sat with his elbows propped on his knees, hands tightly clasped as they had been throughout my retelling. I could hear him breathing.

After several minutes, he broke the silence with a single word. "Patrick?"

I braced myself for an onslaught of tears and was surprised when they didn't come. It was as if my ability to feel had been snuffed out by the exertion of recollection. I told them about Patrick's decision not to join us at the concert, and about his change of mind.

"I didn't know until . . ." I breathed deeply. "I didn't know until later that he'd come to the concert to find us. Vonda told me he was at the doors when they began to—when they began to shoot."

"Oh, Jessica . . ." Mona's voice broke as her grip tightened around my arm again. She looked at Grant, who still hadn't moved. "What can we do? How can we . . ." Her words trailed off.

I shook my head. "Nothing. There's nothing you can do that you haven't done already."

"Do your parents know about the . . . about what you've been through?"

"They do," I said. "They found out from the police that I'd been shot, and they called me in the hospital—"

"Wait," Grant said, his voice sharp. "Shot?"

I realized I'd left that part out. "In the waist," I said. "Right here." I pointed to the spot where the bullet had entered. I told them about surgery and recovery. "One inch higher or lower and the damage would have been so much worse."

"It's a wonder you're alive," Mona whispered, and I felt guilt wash over me.

"So many aren't."

I was grateful that she didn't answer.

"Bernard?" Grant finally asked.

"I don't know. I . . . I wasn't myself after the attack and I—I haven't really had the courage to look anything up since I got here and . . . remembered."

"Do you want to know?" Grant asked, somberness in his voice.

"I don't know. Maybe." Fear tingled on the edges of my consciousness. "Maybe later."

He nodded.

"When Patrick convinced me to go ahead with this trip after the attacks—" I caught myself. "When *I* decided to drive south, like we'd planned, and landed here, I didn't realize what I was carrying with me. And you couldn't have imagined when you took my reservation that I'd still be here all this time later . . ."

Mona sat back a little. "Listen, if you're working your way into an apology, I'm going to stop you right now. You're exactly where you need to be."

I didn't know what to say, so I stayed silent. Grant rose from his chair—slowly, it seemed to me—and walked to the door. It clicked closed behind him.

Mona watched him go. "He's pulling a Grant," she said. "Think now, speak later."

"It's a lot."

"It's a lot," she agreed.

The sound of Grant chopping wood in the courtyard reached us through the thin, ill-fitted windows of the conservatory. "That would be Act II of 'Pulling a Grant,'" Mona said, getting up and stretching her back. Her eyes fell on me. "I want you to know how honored I feel that you shared this with us. And I can see it's worn you out," she said with her usual kindness. "I have questions, but they can wait until later. In the meantime . . ." She put out a hand to help me up. "I could use a strong cup of tea, and I'm guessing you could too. What do you say? Earl Grey and snickerdoodles until I get Connor from school?" She smiled. "I'm pulling a Mona: eat now, talk more later."

I felt a subtle brightening. The memories still hummed in the darkness of my mind, but I knew they were no longer only mine to know. There was relief in that. "Connor won't be happy we started without him."

"I believe in an early introduction to disappointment," she said with a quiet laugh. "Life's full of it, right?"

I contemplated the statement. Disappointment, yes. And more crippling forces too.

"Thankfully, it's also full of snickerdoodles," Mona said, linking her arm through mine as we walked toward the kitchen.

-3◦8-

With no more translation needed, Grant and I crossed only at mealtimes after that day, or in my walks across the courtyard from the manor to the cottage. I saw the glances Mona cast in his direction when he joined us for lunch and dinner and her pinched lips when he answered questions with short replies, his voice hard, his features set. Even Connor seemed to sense the discomfort of our interactions.

"That's an upside-down smile," he said as we were finishing dinner one night, leaning out of his booster seat to poke at his uncle's chin. "*Un sourire à l'envers.*"

Grant wrapped his fingers around Connor's hand and pulled it away from his face. "What are you talking about?" His tone always softened when he spoke to his nephew.

"A smile is like this," Connor said, contorting his face into a broad, gap-toothed smile. "But a frown is an upside-down smile. See?" He twisted in his chair, bending over as far as he could in an attempt to demonstrate what he was describing. "This is what you look like," he said, his voice squeaky from the awkward posture.

"I have to say he's got a point," Mona said. She'd been rinsing our dinner dishes in the sink and placing them in the dishwasher.

I felt Grant look at me as I shoveled our leftovers into plastic containers. "Want to chime in, too, and make it a consensus?" he asked.

"Chime! In! Chime! In! Chime! In!" Connor chanted.

Grant wrapped an arm around him and covered his mouth with his hand, pulling him back into a mock-angry hold. "Aren't you supposed to be on my side?" he growled into the boy's ear.

Connor pulled Grant's hand off his face and craned his neck to look up at him. "But you're being a poopy face!"

Grant ruffled his hair and released him. "Great ally you are."

"All right, young man," Mona said, wiping her hands on her apron and helping Connor out of his chair. "Enough harassing your uncle. Bath, pj's, and bed—in that order."

"But it's not dark yet!"

"It's dark enough. Scoot!"

His bottom lip came out as he crossed his arms, hunched his shoulders, and marched out of the room.

"Of all the things I wanted him to learn from you," Mona said to her brother as she followed Connor, "your poopy face was not what I had in mind."

That made Grant smile.

I concentrated on finding the right lids for the containers I'd filled, avoiding eye contact as he sat there in silence. After a moment, he stood and came around the island to the counter I was cleaning. He leaned a hip against it and let out a breath.

"You don't know what to do with me," I said before he had the chance to speak.

"Pardon me?"

"You start working on a translation project with a woman who turned up at the B&B with an imaginary friend and a truckload of baggage, and you somehow manage to overlook some of her weird behavior—weird enough to make you call the village doctor. And then you find out

203

there's even more in there. The kind of 'more' that makes you wonder if she's going to go full-throttle crazy the next time. Not to mention the amount of time she's spent living in your space without paying any rent at a time of year when you could be making money if you just kicked her out." I shrugged so he'd know I wasn't upset. "I get that I'm—that my situation is off-putting."

"Are you done?"

"Except for the part where I say thank you. Because you've been really understanding and good to me. And I want you to know that I feel worse and better since the other day. Worse because I can picture it all now. And better because someone else knows. Two someone elses, to be exact. That doesn't make me sane, but it makes me . . . I don't know. Maybe less of a time bomb." I looked at him as earnestly as I could, so he'd see I was sincere and not hurt by his change of attitude. "It's still not fair to dump all this on you and Mona. I called my dad. He's working on a ticket out of Marseille, so . . . I won't be interfering with your Christmas too."

"*Now* are you done?" He expression had grown more somber as I talked, which was the opposite reaction of what I'd hoped for.

"I think so."

"I'm sorry about what happened to you."

"Grant—"

He held up a hand. "Please—let me say this."

"Okay."

"I can't imagine what it's like to live with the memories you have."

I didn't know what to say, so I let the silence stretch.

"After you told us about the Bataclan, all I could feel was this mind-numbing anger. This—this intense impulse to . . . to lash out at something or someone. I was livid. Still am. What they did to you—to your friend. What they did to the families who lost loved ones that night . . ."

"So you went out and chopped some wood."

He grinned despite the anger still flashing in his eyes. "Was it that obvious?"

"You have enough kindling to last a few years."

He hung his head and was silent for a moment. "I couldn't get the images out of my mind. What you must have seen. And that man—Bernard?—putting his life on the line to help a stranger . . . to help you get out alive."

Guilt tugged at my conscience. I closed my eyes hard to blot it out.

"But my next thought," Grant finally said, "nearly right on top of the anger—my next thought was that we have to go to England."

My eyes snapped open. His expression was unchanged—reluctant and uncomfortable. "I'm sorry," I said. "What did you—"

"I think we need to go to England."

"What does England have to do with—with what happened to me?"

"I don't know," he said, exasperation in his voice. He raked his fingers through his hair and took a moment before speaking. "I don't know why we have to go. It's just this . . . this feeling I have. And I'm a 'trucks and hammers,' not a 'feelings' kind of guy. But Patrick told you to follow the sewing box where it was leading you, that it found you for a reason. And yo trust him, right?" When I didn't answer, he shook his head and sighed. "And Adeline died believing that her sister would survive but never knew if she really did. And . . . this whole thing just feels really . . . unfinished to me. And I'm a finisher. I want to see things through." His smile was sheepish and a bit embarrassed as he shrugged.

"You know you can't catch crazy, right?"

He went back to the island and slid onto one of the stools. Then he looked at me so seriously that I knew this wasn't a whim. I saw in Grant a protective instinct frustrated by the lapse of time. The same that had sent him out of the room after I'd spoken of the Bataclan. It was that impotence that had fueled his anger.

He cast a rueful smile my way. "So that's my thinking," he said, rolling his eyes a little. "You survived the Bataclan. And Patrick said the box had something to tell you. And Adeline would want to know if what she sensed from God was true—if Julie would survive."

His logic eluded me. "Those aren't related things."

"I know. But it's—it's what I've been thinking. And not liking."

"Hence your poopy face?"

"Are we really calling it my poopy face?"

"We are."

"Okay. So yes, hence the poopy face." He smiled.

Mona came into the room and found Connor's sword propped against the island. "Sir Swords-a-lot can't take a bath without his weapon," she mumbled, glancing up at us. She stopped short when she saw our expressions. "Something I need to know?"

Grant said, "We're going to England."

Her eyes got wider. "I'm sorry, we're what now?"

"Going to England."

She turned on me. "You know what he's talking about?"

I hung the dishrag I'd been using over the faucet. "He says he has a feeling," I told her.

"A feeling," she repeated.

"A feeling," Grant confirmed.

She turned back to her brother. "And when, pray tell, are we going to find time in the renovation schedule to take a vacation?"

"I'm thinking soon," Grant said, his expression almost sheepish. "Maybe after Christmas?"

Mona propped both fists on her hips. "Is this what's been turning your smile upside down?" she demanded.

"Maybe."

There was a moment of silence while brother and sister faced off, then Mona slid onto a tall stool next to Grant's and smacked him in the arm. "Get me your laptop."

He looked startled. "Why?"

She glared at him. "Just get it."

Grant returned moments later and opened his MacBook in front of his sister.

"Is Adeline's journal on here?" she asked.

"In the dock."

"Good." She handed him Connor's sword. "Now go get your nephew ready for bed while I adjourn to the conservatory and do some reading. It's time I acquainted myself with the mystery woman wreaking havoc with this household."

A little over an hour later, after Grant had put Connor to bed and joined me in the living room to talk about our trip, Mona walked in, wide-eyed and shaken. "That's quite the story," she declared.

"It is," Grant said.

She bit her lip and frowned. "I don't think she survived."

"Agreed."

"She'd want to know what happened to Julie. Right? She'd need to know."

Grant leaned forward. "So . . ." He let the word drag out.

Mona threw up both hands and, looking more confused than convicted, declared, "So we're going to England!"

Part 2

Persist

NINETEEN

After her initial reticence, Mona took to Grant's plan with surprising willingness. "Don't get me wrong, I love Balazuc, but the thought of seeing new horizons—new horizons that aren't up to us to renovate—that sounds absolutely divine."

Grant and I spent hours during the next few days going back over what we'd read in Adeline's account, looking for clues in the details she'd related, then using Monsieur Vivier's books to do research into the French Protestants who left the country at the end of the seventeenth century.

We'd decided to begin our trip right after New Year's so we could make some progress on our various projects before heading out of town. We'd take a train under the Channel from Calais to Folkestone, get a nice B&B in the country outside of Rochester for a few days, and use the city's Huguenot Museum as a hub for our exploration of the Baillards' fate.

In the meantime, there was a five-year-old who was counting down to Christmas. The exuberance that defined him only increased as the big day drew nearer. His tantrums got louder, his laughter got brighter, and his fantasies got wilder. We told him about the bed-and-breakfast we'd booked, and he seemed only moderately interested until

Grant mentioned that it was on a working farm and that the stay included daily rides on the horses they kept for their visitors.

"Horses?" he yelped, eyes wide and disbelieving. "Like . . . *real* horses?"

All we'd heard from Connor since then were tales of horses and farmers and castles and wars.

"You sure you're up for travel with a five-year-old?" Mona inquired after a particularly dramatic reenactment of a cavalry battle that ended on a pirate ship.

"I think I can take it." There was something about the simplicity of Connor's worldview that was comforting to me.

The days before we left were hectic. Grant had decided to hire a local carpenter to do some work while we were away and had to bring him up to speed on the quirks and demands of turning a barn into a youth hostel. Mona's energy went mostly to Connor, whose surplus of free time had finally turned into a mantra of "I'm bored! I'm bored! I'm bored!"

And while Grant focused on construction and Mona on Connor, I found my energies torn between a growing sense of urgency and a muddy sense of strain. The urgency was about Adeline—the impatience of setting out on the search Patrick had inspired.

And the muddiness was about fear. I realized it now. Fear of getting woven, by time and circumstances, into the fabric of Mona's, Connor's, and Grant's lives. As my comfort level with them increased, the tension of both wanting and fearing connection did too. And every thought of Patrick—every reminder of his absence—only magnified the threat of allowing it again.

-꒦꒷-

On New Year's Day, Mona and I set to work putting away the Christmas decorations. She handed me a shoe box with Connor's name calligraphed on top. "His ornaments go in here."

"He's got his own ornaments?"

"One for each year of his life . . . plus a few extras from his grandparents and friends. It's a family tradition."

"And the rest of these are yours?" I asked, motioning toward the mismatched decorations crowded on the tree.

"A lot of them," she said. "This little skier girl is from the year we went to Aspen. I think I was eight or nine at the time. This scroll is for high school graduation, and this three-tiered plastic cake," she said, grimacing a bit as she pulled it from the tree, "is for the year I married Fred." She dropped it into a larger box without bothering to wrap it in tissue, then made a production of wiping her fingers on her jeans.

"I'm surprised you still have it."

She pursed her lips and reached for another

ornament. "The way I see it, we can't understand the present—much less make better decisions for the future—if we don't acknowledge the good, bad, and ugly of the past."

I stopped and watched her for a bit. "That's remarkably rational."

She smiled. "If anything proves that there is a God, it's Mona being rational . . ."

"And this one?" I held up a small figurine depicting a rock climber hanging by one hand from the edge of a cliff.

"That's from the first Christmas after Fred left." Mona laughed, taking the ornament from me to wrap it in tissue. "Believe me, the symbolism is an understatement."

"What kind of Christmas store carries this kind of thing? The least they could do is put a Santa hat on the guy's head."

"Oh, it's not intended to go on a tree. Grant found it in an REI store and drilled a hole through it for the hook so I could remember every Christmas just how far I've come."

I watched as Mona laid the figurine in the box, alongside the rest of her life's story told in tacky Christmas fare, and marveled at her sanity.

"So . . ." The tone of Mona's voice made me look up with suspicion. "You know the French expression for changing topics without warning in the middle of a conversation?"

"I don't think I do."

"It's called 'jumping from the rooster to the donkey.' "

"Okay."

"And you're about to meet the donkey."

I forced a smile and took another ornament from the tree. "Oh boy."

"It's about you and Grant . . ."

I froze.

"Preferred the rooster, did you?"

"I just have a feeling I know where this conversation is leading."

But there was no deterring her. She put down the ornaments she held and turned to look at me. "I want to say a couple things. Not because I'm worried. Just because . . . because I need to say them."

"Mona . . ."

"Grant is a good man."

I put up a hand to stop her, disturbed by the confusion her words were exacerbating in my mind. She ignored the gesture.

"He's a good man," she said again, "and . . ." She paused for a moment. "The fact is, all you know of Grant is what you've learned about him here. And he had a different life before he came to France. A complicated life."

"What are you trying to say?"

"What I'm trying to say is that he wasn't in a good place when he got to Balazuc, and you're— you're in a tough place too." Her voice and face expressed reluctance and pleading. She was clearly as uncomfortable with this conversation as I was, but determined to see it through. "I know it's easy to get attached to someone and feel like that person is part of the healing process, but the way I see it—"

"Mona . . . ," I tried to interrupt her.

"Lost finds lost. That's all I'm saying. And in my experience, lost finding lost only multiplies the lostness. I just don't want either of you to get hurt by thinking that the other is capable of 'fixing' you."

"Please. Stop." There was sharpness in my voice. "If you think you're seeing something between Grant and me, you're imagining it. We've been together a lot because of Adeline's journal and now planning for this trip, but I'm not looking for someone to . . . to fix me. Mona, that's the last thing on my mind."

She sighed and waved a hand as if to erase what she'd said. "I'm sorry. I shouldn't have—"

"How long have you been sitting on this little admonition?"

She held up her hands. "It's just that men like to be needed, and women . . ."

Something cold and bitter trickled down my spine. "You don't have to worry about me needing anyone," I said, my voice low.

"No," Mona said before I could go on. "No, that's not what I meant, Jessica. It's just the timing.

That's all I was talking about." She seemed to rack her mind for the right words. "Just be careful," she finally said. "That's all I'm trying to get across. With what you've both been through . . . Just be careful. I've said as much to Grant, and he was about as pleased as you are."

I wasn't sure if I was shaking because of the cold in the manor's living room or the intrusion of Mona's words. The muddiness I'd been fighting hardened into something solid, impenetrable, and irrevocable. "Grant and I, we've been working hard—for Adeline. That's all. And when this trip is over, I promise I'll be on the first plane out."

She threw up her hands. "I knew when I opened my mouth that I should just shut up, and yet . . . Please, Jessica, forget that I said anything. I've loved having you here—and I do not want you to hop on the first plane out. You've been good for me, for Connor, and for Grant. I just wanted you to be careful, and I've opened my big mouth about things that are none of my business. Can you forget what I said?"

I could tell by her expression that she was sincere, that her words had probably come out more strongly than she'd intended. But I also knew they'd anchored deep. I tried to focus on the concern that had motivated her comments rather than the response they had elicited in me. "You're imagining things," I said again.

"I know. I know I am."

We finished our task in awkward silence, then Mona apologized again and went upstairs to bed.

⁂

As we continued to prepare for the trip, I caught myself being more guarded when I was with Grant. We still spent time together and engaged in conversations that felt casual, but I retreated to the cottage more often during the day and feigned fatigue earlier at night. Part of me wanted to resent Mona for the warning she'd given, but the other part of me knew that her concerns were founded. Lost seeks lost. Broken finds broken. I'd seen it happen before, and I knew I'd be safer pulling back than leaning in.

TWENTY

After a ten-hour drive to Calais and a short night in a Formule 1 motel, we took our time visiting the city before driving our car onto the train that would take us to England.

We passed the Jungle on the way to the station, a huge refugee city that stretched out of sight just off the highway, its makeshift tents tattered and clustered close. Children clung to the chain-link fence as we drove by, their faces dirty, their hands extended, their eyes imploring.

"Are they in prison?" Connor asked.

"They're refugees," Grant said.

"What's a refugee?"

Mona patted his knee. "They had to leave their countries because they weren't safe there, and now they're waiting to go across to England."

"Like us?"

"Well . . . kind of."

The political standoff that had resulted in the Jungle was too complex to explain to the curious five-year-old. I knew the arguments on both sides of the issue—I'd seen them flash across my computer screen and heard them debated on the radio station Grant played in the barn. But as I looked into the faces on the other side of the fence—a boy in a green hoodie peering out with solemn eyes and an older one who watched the traffic with frustration in his gaze—my only thought was of the men I'd seen in the Bataclan. All I could feel was distrust. Fear too.

The sheer cynicism of my response made me look away. *They're only kids,* I told myself, loosening my white-knuckled grip on the magazine I'd been reading. *The men who killed Patrick were kids once, too,* another voice replied inside my head.

The reminder made me shiver. I focused on the signs counting down the kilometers to the Eurotunnel and tried to take deep breaths, stilling the panic that seemed to surge when I expected it the least.

The thirty-five minutes we spent crossing under the Channel were uneventful. We exited the train in Folkestone and followed the flow of traffic toward the motorway we would take toward London. After a few minutes, we made the mistake of veering off main roads to find a place for Connor to take a potty break and were instantly introduced to the perils of driving on the left through towns whose narrow streets were obstructed by cars parked on both sides.

Because we were driving a French car, Grant's vantage point around corners and obstacles was diminished by sitting on the left, leaving me in the unenviable position of estimating distances between us and the curb and warning him of oncoming cars and trucks. I took deep breaths and tried not to grip the dashboard, disoriented by exit ramps that went off to the wrong side and traffic circles we navigated clockwise.

I could hear Mona trying to distract herself by focusing on Connor in the back seat, but the occasional tense intake of air told me that her attention hadn't really strayed from the close calls of driving for the first time in England.

"Well, I'm glad that's over," I said when we finally made it onto the broader lanes of the A2, headed toward Canterbury and London. "How's the adrenaline over there?"

"Pumping nicely," Grant answered, his fingers relaxing a bit on the steering wheel. His jaw was set, but there was a flush in his cheeks that I hadn't seen before.

"Loving it or hating it?" I asked.

He pursed his lips for a moment. "Both," he answered as his smile spread.

"Men and cars," Mona said from behind us, shaking her head. "Nothing like a little seat-of-your-pants driving to perk up the testosterone."

-⊰∘⊱-

We stopped to buy a quick lunch from a Tesco supermarket outside Canterbury on our way to Rochester, eager to get to the Old Schoolhouse B&B Mona had booked for four nights in Burham, a small town in the southeast corner of England.

Connor hadn't stopped talking about riding horses since we'd mentioned it to him, and we wanted to get there with time to spare before it got dark.

"Find it here all right?" a young woman asked as we got out of the car around three that afternoon. Her accent was lilting, her pacing slow, her expression as friendly as Mona's had been when I'd arrived in Balazuc, but mellowed by British sobriety.

"We did," Mona said, lifting Connor from his car seat and setting him on the gravel drive.

"I'm Renée," our hostess said, shaking each of our hands, even Connor's, when she reached the car. "I'm delighted to welcome your little family to Burham."

Grant smiled. "We're a bit of an eclectic assortment."

"Brother and sister," Mona filled in, pointing at each of them. "My son, Connor, and . . . his Aunt Jessica."

Grant raised an eyebrow at me and I shrugged my consent.

"Lovely," Renée said. "You've certainly picked the perfect days for your trip—these are the warmest temperatures for January since 1974."

She led us into a beautiful old house restored to its nineteenth-century splendor. The front door opened into a small sitting room where the remnants of a fire glowed in a stone-framed fireplace. I could see Mona taking in every detail of the décor, the authentic floral prints, antique sconces, and Victorian furniture.

"Don't get too many fancy ideas," Grant said as Renée led us up the stairs to our rooms.

"Who, me?" Her response sounded too coy to be genuine.

My room was the epitome of vintage country charm, bright and busy, with a view of the North Downs extending out of sight. After helping us to bring in our things, Renée pointed out the landing's window to the stone-and-steel barn behind the house. "If you'd like a quick ride on horseback before dusk, I'll let Clive know you're on the way."

"Horseback!" Connor exclaimed, striking a superhero stance.

"That sounds like a resounding 'yes,' " Renée said, laughing.

Minutes later, we made our way around the Old Schoolhouse to the barn. Clive was an amiable and soft-spoken man. He suggested that Connor ride the pony on a lead around the enclosure while the rest of us followed a well-marked circuit in the fields along the edges of the B&B's property.

"Would you like that, Connor?" Mona asked.

He was too busy jumping up and down in excitement to form an answer.

"I'll stay with him, and you and Grant can take the trail," I suggested.

"Honey, this body is not heaving itself onto a horse."

"But you're the one who picked the place precisely *for* the horses!"

"I picked the place because Connor would love it," Mona corrected me. "Never once have I implied that I'd be riding too."

"So it's just you and me," Grant said to me. "You up for it?"

The long drive had left the area around my wound feeling a bit tighter and sorer than it usually was, but I wouldn't let the Paris attack deprive me of this chance for a horseback ride at sunset across the North Downs.

"I think so," I said, my greater concern more about the time alone with Grant than the discomfort of riding.

My eyes met Mona's. I saw both apology and encouragement on her face, as if she were trying to convince me that she no longer had any qualms. "You go—I'll stay with Connor," she said.

Uncomfortable and uncertain, I looked at the horses staring at us over their stall doors. "Have you done this before?" I asked Grant.

"Yep. You?"

"Does riding my grandfather's quarter horse when I was six years old count?"

"You bet."

"I'll saddle two horses," Clive said.

"Tame ones, please!" I called to his retreating back.

"Scaredy-cat."

I rolled my eyes in Grant's direction.

-§«§-

Just a few minutes later, we were riding Kimble and Mable through the gate Clive held open for us.

"Just follow the orange arrows," he instructed for the third time. "They'll get you back here in about an hour if you take it slow. There's a lookout just past the fourth marker if you want to rest a bit."

"Doing okay?" Grant asked over his shoulder as he took the lead to the broader path that circled the fields around the B&B.

"For a girl who'd rather not fall off a horse but is currently riding one? Yep, I'm doing fine."

"Did you ever fall off the quarter horse?"

"I only rode it a couple times."

"And?"

"Didn't fall."

"There you go."

I watched his easy sway as he rode. "You've clearly ridden before."

He reigned in his horse long enough for mine to come alongside his as the man-made path broadened. "Once or twice."

"As a kid?"

He nodded. "Worked at the local stables so I could compete in barrel racing growing up."

I laughed. "Of course you did."

"Not sure how to take that!" His chuckle was rich and mellow.

When we reached the fourth marker, Grant motioned to a bench just off the path. "That must be the lookout Clive mentioned. Sit a bit?"

Grant helped me off Kimble and we tied our horses to a tether pole, then walked around the bench to sit at the edge of an outcropping overlooking the Downs. The sun was low, nearly touching the outline of the soft hills that spanned the horizon. The only sounds we heard were of nature: branches creaking in the light breeze, birds, animals burrowing in the leaves nearby, and the contented munching of our horses, their heads hanging low over grass left green by the winter's mild temperatures.

"Gorgeous," I said—nearly whispered—as much to break the silence between us as to comment on the idyllic setting.

"Agreed."

We took in the lengthening shadows and darkening colors for a few moments.

"Feels good to be out of the car," Grant said.

I nodded and hugged my arms closer, the windbreaker I'd put on an hour ago not quite sufficient in the cooling air. I thought of Patrick, of the hues and nuances his artistic eye would see that were invisible to me. I started to imagine what he'd say if he were sitting there with us, then stopped the impulse. It would only make me miss him more.

I racked my mind for neutral topics to fill the lull, but found that after so much time together, we'd exhausted every casual subject I could think of. As the silence began to feel more uncomfortable, despite Mona's warning still ringing in my ears, I voiced the question that had been niggling at my mind since New Year's Day. "So . . . I'm wondering. What was your life like before France?" I heard the awkwardness in my own voice and wording, and could have kicked myself the moment the words were out.

I could feel Grant smiling beside me. "That's a pretty subtle discussion starter, Jessica."

Something stirred in me as he said my name. I didn't like the feeling. To distract myself from it, I prompted, "You flipped houses, right?"

"I did."

"And then you flew to France."

"I did."

"Listen, I'm happy to be the discussion opener on this little horseback ride, but at some point you're going to have to jump in too."

He shifted and turned a bit toward me on the bench. His arms were crossed, but his expression was open. "I flew to France to help my sister."

"Because . . . ?"

"Because her husband had just left her."

"Fred, right?"

"Fred. Visionary loser," Grant said.

"So you really liked him."

I smiled. Grant smiled too. Some of the awkwardness diminished, and I felt myself tense up as it did.

"He was only there a year before he bailed."

"Was it a surprise?"

Grant sighed and turned front again. "To me? No. To Mona—most definitely."

"She seems so—I don't know—casual about it now."

"You should have seen her right after it happened. Connor was only about two. They'd just opened the cottage to the public and listed it online, and Fred informed her that he never really wanted to move to France—or to marry her, for that matter—and that he was heading to Florida to learn massage therapy and work on a cruise ship."

I was speechless for a moment. When Grant finally looked at me, eyebrow raised in question, I stammered, "I'm sorry, I'm . . . I've got to admit that of all the scenarios I'd imagined, Fred leaving her and Connor to become a masseur on a cruise ship never crossed my mind!"

Grant laughed. "And the kicker is that it was Fred who talked her into buying the property in Balazuc and converting it into a B&B. Told her he'd do the hard labor, she'd do the hosting, and they'd make a mint in no time flat."

"But—what kind of handyman was he? I mean, I can see someone like you taking on the building remodel, but a guy whose new dream is a career in massage therapy doesn't strike me as the Bob the Builder type."

"Exactly."

I shook my head. "Poor Mona."

"Yes. And poor Connor. I didn't fly over intending to stay this long, but . . . when I saw what still needed to be done and how much Connor was struggling . . ."

"You decided to stay."

"I did. And now I'm trying to decide when to leave."

That took me aback. "You're leaving?"

"At some point," he said, a bit of frustration creeping into his voice. "The fact is, if I stay in Balazuc until the construction is finished—converting the barn, finishing the manor house—there's no telling how long I'll be there."

"Mona's been talking about developing a brocante during tourist season, too, so . . ."

"Please—don't even let her contemplate that option!" He chuckled and leaned forward, propping his elbows on his knees. Then he turned his head and looked at me, as if weighing what he'd say next. "Mona needed my help—that much is true. But I needed to get away more than she needed me. And now . . ." He looked forward again. "Now I have to figure out when it's time to go back and start living differently."

After the silence grew uncomfortable again, I asked, a bit reluctantly, "Differently?" When he pinched his lips and looked off thoughtfully, I added, "No need to answer. Really. We should probably be getting back to the farm anyway, now that the sun has gone behind the hills."

I was just pushing off the bench when he said, "I had a really good thing going back home. Great life, good friends, steady income. My college buddy started a flipping business on a whim a few years ago and recruited me as a partner. Turns out we were good at making money. Jack was the brains behind the oper-ation—CEO, CFO, and promoter-in-chief. And I was the project manager. A dozen people reported to me on any given day—carpenters, roof layers, painters, tilers . . . a well-oiled machine that eventually got us all kinds of attention. Headlines, sponsorship offers, inquiries from reality shows."

"Sounds . . . great?" I couldn't figure out why he'd leave it all for France.

"It was—for a while."

"And then?"

Grant hung his head for a moment. "At some point, Jack started asking me to cut corners. It was pretty harmless at first. Mostly cosmetic—overcharging for low-quality paint and cheaper windows. Billing for high-end floors and installing something inferior. Typical stuff in that line of work. Then he insisted that we skimp on more important things. HVAC. Structural. Electrical. If it increased our bottom line, Jack didn't over-analyze it. And me? I did what he asked, kept my mouth shut, and tried not to listen to my gut."

Grant stood and took a couple steps to the edge of the outcropping, stretching his back, then standing there, hands on hips, looking out. I saw the carriage of his shoulders harden as he stood in front of me admitting to a level of complacency that seemed completely out of step with what I knew of him.

"There were threats of lawsuits," he continued. "Just a handful of them from disgruntled buyers. But Jack had a crack legal team, and they shut them down pretty fast. The fact is, those people were right to want to sue. I knew they were, but . . . Jack was a friend. And the income was great. The exposure too. And . . ." He smiled self-deprecatingly. "And my girlfriend at the time—Audrey—she really liked the perks of dating 'that guy from TV.' "

He turned to look at me then, frustration in the tightness of his jaw. "I let it go on way too long. I guess I liked the perks of it too." He went silent for a moment.

"But you did eventually quit, right? To help Mona with the B&B."

"Yeah, I quit. But only after a substandard wiring installation in one of our houses caused a fire that landed a nine-year-old girl in the burn unit."

"Oh, Grant . . ."

Frustration turned to anger. He shoved his hands into his pockets and turned toward the distant hills. "We knew the electrical was bad—it dated back nearly fifty years to when the house was built—but we weren't making a whole lot of profit on that particular flip, and Jack figured if the buyers didn't know about the problem . . ."

Silence stretched for a few moments more. Then Grant looked at me and said, "After the girl's parents went public, Jack's shysters cried defamation. Said the homeowners had known about the issue and opted not to have us fix it. They were just speaking up now because they saw money to be made—you know the drill. When they denied it, it became our word versus theirs. Nasty stuff all played out in public . . . while their daughter lay in a hospital bed with burns over 20 percent of her body."

His smile was completely devoid of humor. "Great stuff, right? Respectable behavior from someone who's always claimed to look out for the little guy."

"It just—it doesn't seem like you."

He answered my statement with a look that said it all. Regret and self-disgust. He walked back to the bench and lowered himself slowly. "So . . .

I told the investigators what I knew to be true, then I went to Jack's office and quit. And about a week later, Audrey quit me. So when Mona called to tell me about Fred, I saw the B&B as the perfect way to escape my old life. I flew to France to redeem myself one eighteenth-century structure at a time."

He blew out a breath and stared at the reddened sky. "So I might be doing a good deed by helping my sister," he said, "but a knight in shining armor I'm not."

"And yet you're riding a horse over the Downs." I hoped my smile communicated that I wasn't judging him.

He got up and stepped toward our horses, releasing their reins and handing Kimble's to me. "The reason I want to go home, probably in a couple of months, is to prove to myself that I can do things right the next time around." He cupped his hands under my knee to help me into the saddle.

I hesitated. "Thanks for telling me about . . . about what happened. You didn't have to put up with my prying."

He looked up at me, his expression unguarded. "It was hardly prying. Besides, we're friends, right? Friends know."

I remembered Mona's admonition and felt a wall come up as my own qualms intensified. "More like treasure-hunting partners," I said, a bit too eager to reduce our connection to a project.

He frowned and hesitated. "Sure."

We rode mostly in silence on the way back to the Old Schoolhouse, Grant no doubt rehashing the mistakes of his past and me trying to understand why my final words had left me feeling so unsettled.

TWENTY-ONE

Connor was not impressed with the full English breakfast Renée served us the next morning.

"I want Cheerios!" he proclaimed loud enough for the neighbors to hear.

Mona tried to convince him that there were some things on the plate in front of him that he liked, but he wouldn't back down. So while the rest of us devoured the eggs, bacon, sausage, baked tomatoes, and fried toast Renée had made for us, Connor ate a bowl of cereal. By the end of breakfast, I wished I'd done the same.

We left for Rochester and its Huguenot Museum—the only one in England—shortly after we'd finished eating, armed with Mona's GPS and a quick lesson from Renée on the myriad rules for navigating English traffic circles. The driving got a bit more tricky as we exited large motorways and drove into the city. Twice, Grant instinctively pulled into the right lane as he turned onto a new road, and twice he was brought back on track by Mona mumbling a tense, "Left rudder, left rudder" from the back seat.

As we circled the center of the historic district looking for parking, we passed between Rochester's cathedral and its castle, eliciting an avalanche of questions and exclamations from the five-year-old in the back seat. Mona decided to take Connor on a tour of the castle while Grant and I did our thing in the Huguenot Museum. Though I agreed that our research would be more efficient unimpeded by a little boy's attention span, I still felt a bit uncomfortable walking off alone with Grant.

We'd made a request to use the archive room and its resources a few days before, but it still took us a while to find someone who would guide us downstairs to it.

"We've brought in some books you may find helpful, given the subject and era of your search," a young man named Peter told us as he ushered us into a blue-walled room where two desks sat under a frosted-glass window. "We don't allow our historic manuscripts to be touched, but they've all been scanned. Here's a list of the ones our curator suggested." He handed Grant a sheet of paper with handwritten notes on it and pointed at the laptop on each desk. "You can access them from our archives. And once you're into the collection, of course, you might find something else that catches your eye. All the documents are searchable by key word or topic."

When Peter had left and we sat at the side-by-side desks with our laptops open to a welcome page, neither of us moved.

"I'm not sure how to start," I finally whispered, daunted by the stacks of books and the online resources we had to peruse.

"Maybe one of us should take the books and the other the scanned archives," Grant said just as quietly.

"I'll take online."

"Then I'll take the books."

"You think we need to be whispering?" I asked, giggling a bit at the notion of two adults in a closed space speaking as if someone were eavesdropping.

"Probably not," Grant whispered again. Then he cleared his throat and said in a full voice, "Probably not."

I cringed. "Let's keep whispering."

"Agreed."

He reached for the top book on the desk, and I logged into the catalogue of documents that dated back to 1695 and the five years following.

We spent nearly two hours skimming huge amounts of information, sometimes pausing long enough to fill the other in on what we were learning. We were allowed only a pencil in the archive room—no photographs or duplications permitted—so the research had to be done in real time, not taken home.

"Listen to this," Grant said, holding up a book that covered the exodus of nearly a hundred thousand Huguenots to England in the sixteenth and seventeenth centuries. "They fled from every major city along the Channel coast— Calais, Dunkerque, Cherbourg—some dressed as soldiers or clergy to ensure safe passage. And

King Louis XIV posted guards everywhere he thought he could catch the Huguenots trying to escape. Bridges, passages through the mountains, ports."

"Ports?"

His expression was somber as he returned my look. He glanced down at the book again, summarizing what he saw. "He ordered his men to . . ." I saw a muscle twitch in his jaw. "They fumigated the holds of ships where they suspected people were hiding. Burned or sank others. Tortured captains who were sympathetic to the Protestants until they were sure they weren't ferrying anyone to safety."

I shook my head, trying not to imagine what the hidden Huguenots might have endured. "Even if Charles, Isabelle, and Julie made it to the coast—even if they made it onto a boat bound for England . . ."

"There's no guarantee they actually made it here," Grant concluded. He blew out a breath and looked up at me. "Find anything on your end?"

"Nothing worthwhile. A couple of Baillards in the last wills and testaments, but they came from another region of France. Maybe distant relatives, but not the family we're looking for." I felt frustration growing. "How do we even know if they listed their real names? They might have traveled and settled under assumed identities just to be safe."

"Did you search for Gatigny?" Grant asked.

I threw up my hands. "*Gatigny!* Why wasn't that the first word I looked for?"

"Because you're hunting for people, not places," Grant said.

I turned back to the laptop and entered *Gatigny* into its search field. When the next page came up, it showed hits in four documents.

"Grant," I whispered, a flutter of excitement rippling through my chest.

"We're back to whispering?"

I looked at him and felt myself smile again. "Four hits!" I said more loudly. "For *Gatigny*. I have four hits."

His eyes got wider, and he rolled his chair closer to mine so he could see the screen. "Well, click on one of them!" he said, his voice tight with anticipation.

I clicked on the first link and found the highlighted *Gatigny* in the translation of a document describing the region around Privas at the time of its siege.

"Nothing there."

Clicking out of the first link, I selected the second one and opened it. This time it was a genealogy that referenced Gatigny in the thirteenth century, well before Adeline's time.

"Come on," I muttered as I moved the cursor back to the list and clicked on the next link. The first words I saw were: *"son of Pierre and Constance of Gatigny France."* Both of us froze.

241

Then Grant leaned back in his chair and let out a "Yes!" that might have been heard in the museum upstairs. "Open it! Open it!" he said, sounding for all the world like his five-year-old nephew.

I used the mouse to open the document wider and scrolled to its first line.

In the name of God, Amen, the Fourteenth day of April in the year of our Lord 1735 I Charles Ballard of Canterbury in the County of Kent son of Pierre and Constance of Gatigny France.

My breath caught. "No way . . ."

"It's *Ballard* instead of *Baillard,* but . . . son of Pierre and Constance." He shook his head, incredulous. "We found him," Grant said.

I pointed at the year the will was written. "If he was thirteen at the Revocation, and he was, what, twenty-three when they fled . . ."

Grant did the mental calculation more quickly than I could have. "He would have been fifty-five when he wrote his will. Probably a ripe old age in those days."

"We found him," I said, repeating Grant's words from moments before. I leaned over so I could see the screen more clearly, now that Grant had swiveled it a bit away from me. "Keep reading," I said, surprised by the excitement in my voice.

Grant heard it too. He turned his head and smiled, the glint of victory in his eyes. Leaning in as I was, our faces were close, but the proximity didn't matter in that moment. I smiled back and nudged him with my shoulder. "Keep reading," I said again.

His smile deepened as he turned back to the screen and started to read out loud, stumbling a bit over spellings and sentence structures dating back nearly three hundred years.

I Charles Ballard of Canterbury in the County of Kent, son of Pierre and Constance of Gatigny France, Carpenter, being sicke and weake in Body, but of Sound minde and perfect memory (praised bee God for the same) doo Make, Nominate, Constitute, and Ordaine, this my last Will and Testament in manner and forme following.

First and Principally, I comend my Soule into the hands of God my maker, hoping through the Merits of Christ my Redeemer, to receive full Pardon of all my Sins and to Inherrit Everlasting Life after death.

I give and bequeath unto my wife Isabelle Ballard the sum of Thirty Pounds

I give to my Daughter Jane Burnell wife of James Burnell of Rye in the County of Sussex the sum of Fourty shillings

All the Rest of my personall Estate whatsoever I give and Bequeath to my Loving Sonne Christopher Ballard of Hawkhurst in the County of Kent whom

I doo make full and Sole Executor of this my last Will and Testament, and Doo hereby Revoke Disanull, and utterly make void all former Wills, and Testaments, by mee made, and this and noo other to Stand, for my last Will and Testament.

"A daughter in Sussex and a son in Kent," Grant said when we'd sat in silence for a few moments.

"But no mention of Julie."

He looked back over the text and shook his head. "No mention of Julie."

We searched a bit more for her name, now spelling it *Ballard,* and found nothing in the museum's archives. There was no evidence that Julie had ever lived in England.

Charles's line was easier to trace. There were censuses indicating that his son's ancestors had stayed in Kent—though their numbers seemed to dwindle steadily until the mid-1900s. His daughter and her husband had sailed across the Atlantic to settle in the New World and put down their roots in New Rochelle, in the modern state of New York.

As intriguing as those branches of Charles's lineage were, it was uncovering Julie's fate that felt most urgent to me. I suspected, from Grant's stubborn searches, that he felt the same way.

"She may have died in the crossing," I said. "Or before they even got to Calais."

"Or she could have made it here and just died before her brother did."

"But she was ten years younger."

"And living in a time when the flu or even childbirth were life-threatening things."

"There'd still be a trace of her, wouldn't there?"

I watched as Grant moved the mouse over yet another document. When he opened it, we found it had nothing to do with our Baillard family.

"Strange that he changed the spelling of *Baillard* to *Ballard*," Grant said.

"It might have been easier to pronounce in English."

"Charles Ballard, the Canterbury carpenter." His mind seemed to be skipping from one detail to another as quickly as mine was.

"I like the sound of that." I pictured Charles raising his children far from the horrors he'd witnessed in his youth, contributing his skills to the adoptive land that had granted them safety. Happiness—the kind that had felt elusive for weeks—began to bloom in my spirit. Part of me wanted to tamp it down. But we'd found Adeline's family, connecting her in spirit to a brother who'd lived on, had children of his own, and founded his future in a country she'd rejected out of love for her students.

"Charles lived," I said. I laughed and shook my head in amazement at our discovery.

"Freedom-giving," Grant said.

"Pardon me?"

"It's how Adeline described the laughter of her students. Freedom-giving."

She was right. It was. And guilt-inducing too.

Grant must have seen my countenance change. "Hey, that's supposed to be a good thing."

My smile felt forced now. "I know."

He cocked his head, but remained silent.

"It feels disloyal sometimes."

"Laughing?"

"Just being lighthearted."

"Because . . . ?"

"I don't know." It was an honest answer. I knew Patrick would want me to laugh. I knew it was the equivalent of thumbing my nose at the perpetrators' attempts to eradicate joy. But that I would be the one laughing—that I would be the one who ran out of the Bataclan's side door and lived while so many others died inside . . . It felt an insult to their memory to laugh and be carefree.

"Canterbury tomorrow?" Grant asked, shifting my attention back to the present.

My eyes met his. "Just . . . because?"

"Seems like the logical next step, given that Charles and Isabelle settled there." He frowned. "Adeline believed that Julie would survive . . . I just don't think we can stop looking for her yet."

His doggedness was comforting. "So you still think we can find her?"

"I do. I don't really know how, but . . . I feel like we need to keep trying."

I knew the anticipation on my face reflected Grant's. And in my mind I heard Patrick say, "Grab a shovel and believe in gold!"

TWENTY-TWO

We dropped Mona and Connor off at Howletts Wild Animal Park the next morning and left the car in the parking lot so Grant and I could take the bus into Canterbury without worrying about traffic in the city. They'd spend a few hours with the exotic animals of Howletts, then join us in town a bit later.

Grant and I boarded Coach 5 headed for Canterbury and found seats at the very front upstairs. We were silent as the bus turned onto the motorway, content to watch the rural scenery rushing by. We entered the city from the north, and I found myself straining to take it all in— the contrast of modern structures and historic landmarks, of traditional sobriety and multi-cultural community. When our bus turned the last corner before the stop nearest the cathedral, the close-up view of its spires and buttresses took my breath away.

"Wow," Grant said beside me.

"Wow," I concurred.

We hurried down narrow stairs to exit the bus and walked the short distance between the stop and the cathedral's entrance, which was under an archway in its surrounding wall.

Grant asked for two tickets and handed over

the payment. "Is there any chance we could see the Huguenot chantry?" he said through the small opening in the glass.

We'd done some reading about it the night before. There was a small chapel tucked away in the cathedral's crypt, where Canterbury's Huguenots had worshipped after their escape from France.

The ticket seller behind the glass, an efficient young man who'd barely made eye contact, gave us a long-suffering look. "The chapel's not part of the cathedral tour," he said.

I stepped forward. "It's just that we're doing research on a specific family that came over from France during the persecution, and we're hoping there might be a connection."

"I'm sorry," the man behind the window said. "It's off-limits to tourists." He stared at us with resolve, and I felt my hopes deflate.

"Are you sure you can't make an exception?" Grant asked.

A wiry woman well past retirement age who had been standing nearby restocking supplies of pamphlets and maps leaned in to address us through the hole in the glass partition.

Her warm voice and friendly expression were a welcome departure from the young man's contention. "There is information about the chapel in the visitor's center just to the right when you pass through this arch," she said, smiling kindness at us. I glanced at her name tag. It said Nelly D.

"That's the best we can do," the young man said.

The woman patted his shoulder. "Arthur, luv, would you be a dear and tell Sue that Alan won't be in today? She'll need to sort out the breaks to make sure we're fully staffed."

He seemed displeased with the suggestion but got up anyway, leaving his chair empty for Nelly to occupy. Once he'd left the office, she leaned in, her expression conspiratorial. "Research, you say?"

"I—" I glanced at Grant, who gave me a nod. "Yes. Yes, research."

"For a book perhaps?"

This time Grant shrugged when I looked his way. "Sure. I mean, yes. It's for a book."

She softened visibly when Grant smiled at her. "And you'll both want to see the chapel?"

He leaned in. "If that's possible."

She tore two tickets from the pad in front of her, assuming an enigmatic expression. "Well, we usually don't allow visitors into the chantry other than two hours on Sunday afternoons but . . ." She looked directly from Grant to me, emphasizing her next words. "But *since you're doing official research for a book you're writing,* I think we can make an exception just this once."

"Are you sure?" I asked, pleased and surprised by her willingness to bend the rules for us.

"I'll call for a verger to meet you at the chapel entrance in thirty minutes. Can you make it there by then?"

"I—yes! Of course."

Grant leaned in again. "You've been a godsend, Nelly. Thank you so much."

She blushed when he used her name and waved away his thanks. "Nothing at all, luv. We make exceptions for authors wanting to shine a light on the history of the cathedral." Handing us our tickets, she added, "The verger will be waiting for you. To the right when you enter the crypt. Look for a sign above the door that says *Église Protestante Française*."

Grant seemed surprised. "That sounds like an authentic French accent," he said.

Nelly tapped her name tag and smiled. "The *D* stands for *Durand,* luv." She pointed at the line growing behind us. "If there's nothing else I can do for you . . ."

"You've been more than helpful," I said. "Thank you—thank you so much."

"Lovely. Now hurry up and get to the visitor's center for the information they can provide you, and give yourselves some time in the cathedral too. Might as well see it all as you've come from so far!" She turned her attention to the people in line behind us as Arthur reentered the office.

We hurried off, feeling elated and just a bit guilty.

"You realize we're going to have to write a book now, right?" Grant said.

"Small price to pay."

⤞⟡⤝

I had to pause as we entered the cathedral. The grandeur of its vaulted nave was arresting—the sheer height and heft of its elements a gravity-defying feat. The silence of the tourists who had come to visit that day reminded me of the sanctity of the space.

We wandered slowly down a side aisle, past rows of chairs framed by graceful arches, stopping to read the plaques under the sculptures of centuries-old tombs and paintings depicting the history of the church.

After a while, Grant realized how much time had passed and whispered that we needed to get to the crypt. We went down several steps into the dark grayness of a space devoid of the art and artifice we'd seen above and found Nelly standing by an arched door under the wooden sign that read *Église Protestante Française*.

"I was beginning to despair," she said in lieu of greeting, a broad smile on her face.

"Nelly! What happened to the verger you were sending?"

She leaned in. "I decided to send myself, don't you know." She unlocked the door and ushered us in. "Welcome to the Black Prince's Chantry."

252

The first item that caught my attention was a small, colorfully painted pipe organ by the door, but as I turned to survey the space, I found myriad details begging for exploration—inscriptions on the walls in the same Old French we'd spent hours translating, the Huguenot cross on the bright-blue pulpit cloth, the open Bible on a wooden table in an alcove beneath a window.

Nelly must have seen my eyes darting around the room. "It's rather a lot to take in, isn't it? Such a small space holding so much of our history."

Grant had found some printed pages on a sideboard and was leafing through them. "There are still services?"

"Every Sunday afternoon. Nothing like they used to be, of course, but still mostly descendants of the Strangers, as our ancestors called them."

"I expected it to be bigger," I said, taking in the smallness of the space and remembering the number of Protestants who'd chosen to flee to England. "There had to be more Huguenots than these pews could fit."

"Oh, there were! Probably two thousand of them worshipped in the cathedral by the end of the 1500s—most of them Walloons who fled the Netherlands during the Inquisition. The French Huguenots came later and added to their numbers. They met in the crypt back then, but even that was likely too small! With the Edict of Nantes making things a bit better for Protestants of France, and with assimilation, of course, their numbers began to fall in the decades that followed, but when the Edict was revoked, a new wave of refugees made their way here, and service attendance surged again."

"So . . ." I was confused. "This chapel . . . ?"

"It's only held the Huguenot church since the end of the 1800s. They met in the crypt for quite some time, then were forced to relocate to the south aisle when their attendance dwindled, and finally to this chantry."

"So if the Huguenots we're researching had been in Canterbury at the end of the seventeenth century?" Grant prompted.

Nelly pointed over her shoulder. "They would have met out there. But there are items here that would have been in the crypt when your Huguenots came to services."

"If they did," I interjected.

"You're not sure?"

"We know Charles and his family lived in town, but have no evidence that they came to services here."

"If they were Protestants and lived here, they likely did. They would have seen those boards," she said, pointing to the walls on either side of an alcove. "That's the Lord's Prayer and the Creed, and across from that, the Ten Commandments. The only French version I know of in this country."

Grant and I wandered closer to the boards where

gold lettering stood out against a dark, painted background.

"These date back to the seventeenth century?" I asked Nelly.

"Right around there, I think." Waving a hand, she added, "I'll let you take a look around."

From the boards, we walked over to a list of former pastors carved into a stone plate on the wall. I scanned it quickly, hoping for something to connect this church to Charles. When I found nothing there, I turned my attention to a sculpted Huguenot cross hanging in an alcove.

Grant caught me twisting it on its hook to check the back side of the piece. "Looking for CSF?" he asked, right behind me.

I nodded. The carpenter's mark on the bottom of Adeline's sewing box continued to mystify me, and my mind seemed to be constantly scanning for the three letters—in lists of genealogies, historical documents, and handcrafted crosses hanging on chantry walls. The letters couldn't be Charles's initials or they'd have ended with a *B,* so who was it that he'd honored with the last gift he gave his sister? I shook my head and sighed. "Maybe we're not meant to figure it all out."

Nelly sat in a pew by the door as we walked the perimeter of the room, taking in the details of a space rich with history. There was a large portrait of Gaspard de Coligny on one wall, a general whose life span preceded Adeline's. Near the door was a verse from Ecclesiastes. Nelly saw me looking at it. "Probably here well before your family arrived," she said. "It's original to the chapel."

We lingered a few minutes longer. I marveled at the juxtaposition of old and new—service schedules printed on dog-eared paper hanging next to verses hand-painted in flowing calligraphy centuries before. It was all fascinating, but my spirits sank as nothing seemed to point toward the family that had sent us on our impromptu trip to England.

Perhaps sensing my discouragement, Nelly patted the spot next to her on the pew. "Come—tell me what exactly has you so interested in the Huguenots of Canterbury."

I moved to sit beside her, and Grant settled on the pew in front of us. He turned toward us and I felt his eyes on me, his silence indicating that this story was mine to tell.

"We're trying to trace the family of a woman called Adeline Baillard—Ballard," I corrected myself. "We think she died in 1695." I told her the rest of the story in broad strokes, starting with the sewing box that had sent us on our search. "I think part of me hoped we'd enter the chapel and find a bust of Charles Ballard sitting on a stack of documents pointing us to the sister we've lost track of, but . . ."

"Aren't you the epitome of optimism," Nelly said.

"I'm actually not." I felt frustration swell inside me. Frustration at myself. At having found nothing. At having hoped we would.

"We uncovered some details in Rochester yesterday," Grant said into the silence. "They led us to believe that Charles and his family settled here after crossing the Channel, but there was nothing about a sister in his will. We're still hoping to track her down."

Nelly sat with her lips pursed for a moment. "It's a puzzler, for sure," she murmured.

"We don't even know precise dates," he said. "They left home in June 1695, but we have no idea when they made it to the coast. All we know is that the three of them traveled together and that Charles's wife was expecting their first child. We assume they headed for Calais, then Dover, but we have no proof of that."

"Or Sandwich. It was a common arrival port back then." Nelly sat thoughtfully for a while. "That's not a lot to go on, is it? But—if you don't mind, I'd like to pass the information you've given me on to a few friends and see what they can uncover. We Huguenot enthusiasts tend to be a well-connected group. It's a bit of a shot in the dark, of course, but what have you to lose by enlisting strangers' help?"

"Nelly . . ." I was so taken aback by her offer to assist us that I didn't know what to say. "Are you sure?"

"I'm absolutely sure. Life around here tends to get dull as ditch water at this time of year, and I could use a bit of a mystery to perk things up."

"We'd love for you to help," Grant said.

"Give me your contact information and I'll follow up here while you continue with your research. Of course, with the secrecy and violence surrounding that period of history, you'll likely find holes in the story big enough to drive a lorry through, but there's always a way, don't you reckon? There's always a way."

"I hope there is," Grant said.

Nelly pulled a notepad and pen out of her purse and started scribbling. "Let me just write down a few things while they're on the tip of my mind. Baillard, right? Then Ballard?"

We filled her in on the pertinent details again. When we were finished, I reached into my purse so I could write down her contact information and felt the plastic sheath surrounding our Bible pages. "I forgot I brought these with us," I said, pulling the documents from my purse. They were pressed between two layers of cardboard for protection.

Nelly's eyes grew wide as I uncovered them and handed them to her. "These were in the sewing box too."

"Just these three?"

"We learned that some churches split up their Bible among families when they disbanded," Grant said.

"And then distributed the pages among their members," Nelly filled in, turning Adeline's over in her hands, a mystified expression on her face. "I've heard of the tradition," she said.

I felt a flutter in my stomach. "You have?"

"I wonder if searching for other orphaned pages might give you some direction."

"We did that before we left France," Grant said. "Hoping to find the ones the Baillard parents took with them to the caves. We didn't find anything."

"But we searched for them in French," I said to him. "Using French key words. It never occurred to us to do a search for the same kind of pages in England—in English."

"If all the children were given their share, those belonging to Charles and his sister Julie might still be out there just waiting to be discovered," Nelly said, a gleam of intrigue in her eyes.

Grant and I looked at each other. "If we can find some more of these pages . . . ," he began.

"They might point us to Julie," I concluded.

"There you go then! Something for the lot of you to investigate while I do a little digging of my own." Nelly handed Adeline's pages back to me.

"We'll look into it," I said, excitement—maybe hope—stirring again.

Grant gave Nelly his phone number and email address, then warmly shook her hand, thanking her for her help.

"And whether you find your missing girl or not,"

she added, "you simply mustn't leave the country without trying fish and chips. And a cream tea too!"

"We'll try to fit those in," I said, laughing.

"Both should come with a doctor's warning, but you're young enough to indulge without risk." She said *indulge* with so much drama that I laughed again.

When I gave her a hug, she whispered, "Lovely to see such a beautiful young couple off on an adventure together."

"Oh . . ." I pulled away and glanced at Grant. "We're not a couple—"

"Nonsense!"

Grant feigned deep interest in an announcement pinned to a corkboard, but I could tell from his frown that he'd heard Nelly too.

TWENTY-THREE

We took our time leaving the cathedral, stopping to read the plaques and admire the art. I couldn't help but wonder, as we passed the impressive woodwork in the quire, if Charles or his descendants had had a hand in carving any of it, if his family had walked on the tiles under my feet or occupied the pews where Grant and I sat when we'd finished our tour.

"I was so sure we'd find something here," I said.

He nodded. "Me too."

"I guess we found Nelly instead."

"And maybe she'll dig something up . . ."

Though he'd meant to sound positive, there was defeat in his tone. "That's the problem with gut feelings," I said.

"What's that?"

"No guaranteed outcome. Just a whole lot of hope."

We sat silently for a while longer, then Grant said, "Maybe all we were supposed to find on this trip to England was evidence that Charles survived."

"I guess I should be satisfied with that." But I wasn't. And I knew Adeline wouldn't be either.

A woman's voice came over the loudspeaker system, intrusive despite her softly modulated tone. She invited those present to pause wherever they were and join her in reciting the Lord's Prayer in the language of their choice. What little bustling noise there had been in the nave stilled to absolute silence as visitors stopped walking and recited the words in unison.

I saw Grant glance at me and realized my lips were moving, mouthing the prayer I'd grown up saying with my classmates at the beginning of every school day. I bit my lip to stop myself from reciting the rest of it.

The disembodied voice continued to speak once the recitation was over, pleading for God's mercy on a broken world and entreating us to live faith-filled lives despite the uncertainty and violence surrounding us. There were amens murmured all around us at the end of her prayer, then the tour guides and tourists went back to their business. An elderly couple not far from us remained kneeling for several minutes, and neither Grant nor I spoke until they left their pew.

"You know the Lord's Prayer," he said.

"Eight years under Headmistress Heaton's thumb."

"Catholic school?"

I nodded. "Best education in town. We said the Lord's Prayer before class every day."

I tried to remember the exact wording of the line that had stood out to me as we'd listened to the reading over the cathedral's loudspeakers.

" 'Open our hearts that we may see you at work in the world.' "

"Right. I caught that too."

I really didn't want to get into the topic—it felt too broad and intimidating to tackle—but the grand serenity of our surroundings prompted me to speak my thoughts. "I guess I've seen a lot of humans at work in the world, but not a whole lot of divine intervention." When Grant said nothing, I added, "Look at the Huguenots. Just believing the way they chose and getting exterminated for it."

"By a king whose faith wasn't all that different from theirs."

"I would have abjured," I said, sure of my conclusion. "I'd have been the first person to raise my hand and say, 'Okay—I give. Call me Catholic, call me Buddhist . . . whatever it takes to spare me and my family.' "

"But the Baillards didn't."

"Why didn't they?" I asked after a brief hesitation. "Surely it was something more than stubbornness. Even the hundreds—thousands— who fled to England. To Canterbury. They could have kept everything if they'd just . . ."

I shook my head and let my gaze travel along the pillars and arches of the cathedral's nave. "Losing everything—their possessions, their children, their country, their *lives*—for a God who didn't seem to step up to protect them."

"What was it Adeline said? In the last few pages we translated." Grant frowned, searching his mind for the words we'd read again just a few days ago. " *'For all its scars and strife, this world still speaks the beauty of its Maker.'* "

The sound I made was cynical. "That's awfully optimistic from a woman facing a violent death." I remembered my friend. "But Patrick probably would have agreed with Adeline."

"He was an optimist?"

I nodded. "Through and through. He used to drive us crazy singing 'What a Wonderful World' in the worst possible Louis Armstrong impression." Grief tugged at my resolve again. I shook it off. "Anytime he saw something beautiful—mountains, a sunset, puppies, for Pete's sake—he'd launch into a full-out performance."

"Good song."

"Great song," I agreed. "And he really believed it. Wonderful world. People are good if you discount the rotten apples. Yada yada." I heard the edge creeping into my voice as I contemplated his fate and tried to tamp it down. I felt myself frown. "How could the Baillards, from Pierre down, believe God was working in the world and be witnesses to . . . to the kind of violence that can only be pure evil? It's so—I just don't get it."

Grant cleared his throat. "I don't get it either," he said. "But as much as it confuses me, it also . . . I don't know. I look at Connor and hope they're right."

"And I think of the Bataclan and can't believe they are."

"I guess—" Grant seemed to catch himself. I turned so I could see his face. He was watching the elderly couple who had been sitting near us during the time of prayer. After speaking with a priest at the front of the cathedral, they were making their way to the exit now.

"You guess . . . ?"

He nodded toward the couple. "They get something from believing." He paused, then quoted Adeline again. *" 'The peace I feel despite my fear can only be from God.' "*

I knew what he was getting at, but I dismissed the implication. It was all well and good to assign beneficial side effects to a belief in a higher power, but I was still living with the pain of his failure to intervene.

❈

I found it hard to concentrate for the rest of the day. We met Mona and Connor at the bus stop a while later and spent some time walking around the city, then we had dinner in a quaint, historic pub on The King's Mile.

Connor slept for a while during our bus ride back to Howletts, then Grant carried him to the car for our drive back to the Burham B&B.

"No message from Nelly yet," Grant said, phone in hand, as he folded himself into the driver's seat of the Peugeot.

We drove the fifty minutes home mostly in silence. With Mona dozing in the back, it fell to me to point to the left side of the road when Grant automatically turned into the right lane.

"You'd think it would feel more normal by now," he muttered.

"It takes more than two days to undo decades of habit."

He shook his head. "Has it really only been two days?"

I laughed. "Could make a person miss the slower pace of renovating a barn."

"You doing okay?"

I looked at him, confused by the question. "Sure."

"It's been a long day—a long couple of days—and with your injury so recent . . ." He paused, then said, "Let's stay home tomorrow." Glancing at Mona and Connor in the rearview mirror, he added, "No use staying in a rural B&B if we're never there to enjoy it."

Much as I liked the thought of staying put for a day, I felt disappointment stirring.

"What do we do if Nelly doesn't call us?" I asked, voicing the concern I'd felt since leaving Canterbury.

Grant was silent for a while. Then he said, "She'll

get back to us. And until then, maybe we can try to find more Bible pages like the Ballards'. Want to give it a shot in the morning?" He glanced in my direction. "Only if you're up to it."

As much as I distrusted hope, I felt a vestige of it still motivating our search. "You can go ahead and assume that I am."

TWENTY-FOUR

I read a magazine in the sitting room downstairs after breakfast the next morning while Grant went out back with Mona and Connor to get his nephew set up for another ride. Then he joined me with his laptop and sat on the couch next to the Victorian chair I occupied.

"So," he said, lifting the lid and opening a Google page. "What do we search for?"

Over the next hour, we tried every conceivable combination of words like *Huguenot, France, England, Bible, pages, tradition, and divided.* I got Mona's laptop from her room and entered my own combinations, clicking on the first several search results each time and finding nothing related to what we were hoping for.

"I fell off the pony!" Connor yelled, bursting in through the front door and striking his usual superhero pose. There was mud in his red hair and up the left side of his body.

Grant looked up. "You did what?"

"He fell off Gretel," Mona explained, coming in behind him. "Our resident pirate got a little carried away with a Blackbeard battle reenactment and slid right off her back."

"He realizes Blackbeard traveled on a ship, not horseback, right?" Grant said.

"We're going to the river to float paper boats." Connor paid no attention as Mona tried to get him out of his muddy pants. "Wanna come too?"

I looked at Grant. The invitation sounded like a welcome reprieve from a fruitless search.

"Up you go!" Mona said, swatting his behind.

Connor leaned back as his mom took his hand and pulled him toward the stairs. "Wanna come too?" he said to us again, straining against her.

I closed Mona's laptop with a resolute *click.*

⁂

I suspected Grant had deliberately left his phone behind as we trekked off to the stream that flowed between the B&B and the neighbor's land. It felt good to be forced to live in the simple present, unable to check for messages from Nelly or run searches for documents related to Adeline's past. We made paper boats, some more seaworthy than others, and raced them downstream. Then Connor decided he needed to build a dam, and he and Grant took to the challenge with gusto as Mona and I sat on a bench nearby, shivering in the cold.

We talked about Connor and his extraordinary enthusiasm—which Mona called "happiness on crack"—then the conversation turned to more serious things.

"So . . . ," she began, "how have you been sleeping the last few nights?"

I glanced at her, surprised by the concern in her tone. "Why do you ask?"

There was gentleness in her smile. "The walls are thin, and your bedroom's next to mine."

I knew exactly what she was referring to and hung my head. "I'm sorry," I said.

"No need to be."

"I hoped no one heard."

"Nightmare?"

I nodded. "I had them a lot those first few days after the . . . after Paris. The screaming, thrashing-around kind. But lately it's been more the terrified, cold-sweat variety. I don't know why last night's was so . . . I'm sorry I woke you up."

"Don't worry about that. I'm a mom. I'm used to getting woken in the middle of the night. I was just worried about you, but when I didn't hear anything else for a while, I figured you were okay."

I remembered the dream vividly. The face of the young man I'd seen standing behind the fence of the Jungle refugee camp in Calais. The one with the pleading eyes and vulnerable stance. I'd seen him transform from pitiful to menacing in my nightmare. His eyes turned red and fiery. His body expanded and broadened as he tore through the chain-link fence and charged me, wrapped an iron grip around my neck, and threw me to the ground. He hovered over me, heavy and suffocating, and hissed, "This is for Syria" in French as the knife he held above my heart slipped deeper into my chest.

I woke up screaming—a hoarse, pained, panicked scream that ripped my mind out of the blackness of terror and into the predawn quiet of my bedroom in the B&B. I never went back to sleep.

"Were you reliving the Bataclan?" Mona asked gently.

I shook my head. "Not really. It was just—a face. And fear."

"I'm sorry, Jessica."

"It was the man from Calais," I admitted, wondering if identifying him would steal some power from the dream. "The one we saw behind the fence as we were driving by the Jungle."

"The little boy in the green shirt?"

"He wasn't a little boy in my dream."

I realized in that moment how thoroughly the attack had warped my perception. It didn't matter that the boy had been trapped behind chain link, probably hungry and cold, waiting for a chance to experience freedom. All I'd seen was the color of his skin, the texture of his hair, the shape of his face—and that had been enough to morph him into the terrorist who had haunted my nightmare.

"You must see them everywhere." Mona's empathy was an almost palpable force. "The men who attacked the Bataclan."

"I can't control it."

"I'm guessing it's absolutely normal." She reached across to grab my hand and gave it a firm squeeze. "I know you'll figure it out in time Get it all straight in your mind again. But for now . . . ," she said, earnest and sure, "with all you've been through, I think you're doing great."

That made me laugh, though I heard little levity in the sound. "Every so often I start to think that too. Then I get broadsided by a memory or dream or a sound that feels like Paris and . . . I may be doing a bit better, but I'm still a long way from doing great," I conceded. Even that mitigated statement felt like an affront to those who'd died.

"If it happens again and you need some company, come find me, okay?" Mona said, releasing my hand and turning to watch Grant and Connor hard at work on their dam. "I'm a world-class nightmare wrangler."

"Connor?"

"When all the lights come on in my bedroom in the middle of the night, I can assume that a little body is about to crawl into bed with me and tell me to sing Barney to him."

"The dinosaur?"

" 'I love you, you love me . . . ,' " she quoted. "Seems to calm him down. So I sing the song and I pray for him. By then, he's usually fast asleep again." She smiled. "I'll do the same for you if you need it."

"Well, I'd be up for Barney, but I'll pass on the prayer."

"Keep the purple costume, scrap the deity?"

"At least I'm sure Barney's a man-made thing."

She was silent for a moment. "And God?"

"I don't know—maybe real, but more likely some form of Great Delusion."

That seemed to take her aback. "You don't really believe that," she said after another moment of silence. Her voice held no condemnation.

"The Bataclan," I answered. "ISIS. September 11. I'd be a fool *not* to believe it."

"Connor. The bed-and-breakfast. You."

I shook my head. "I don't follow."

Mona turned toward me on the bench. "Here's what I figured out a few months after Fred left us," she said. "God layers good over the bad."

"Is that a verse or something?" A hard edge had crept into my voice.

"I wanted to blame God for what Fred did. And trust me, I gave it my best shot. But two years later, with a bit of a step back, I understand better that *Fred* did that. Fred and his juvenile ideals. Fred and his impulsive and selfish pursuits."

"But God didn't stop him. If he's really God, he could have. Isn't that guilt by omission?"

"I don't know. I don't think so." She sighed deeply, then added, "Sometimes I think there are things we're just not meant to understand from a human perspective. But . . . I guess I'm beginning to see the stuff I couldn't when I was neck-deep in the bad. The good stuff. Don't get me wrong, I'm not ignoring the bad. The abandonment, Connor's trauma, the fear of losing everything . . . Leaving us was Fred's choice, and it was devastating. But there is still good in my life. There's a lot more good than I realized."

"And that makes it okay that Fred walked out on you?"

"No, but it makes it survivable—laying blame where it belongs and measuring the good. Especially measuring the good. If I hadn't married Fred, I wouldn't have Connor. And if Fred hadn't moved us here, I wouldn't have known France. I wouldn't have met you." She nodded as if reaching the same conclusion all over again. "God layers good over the bad. It's what he does. And the more of the bad life dishes out, the more good God dishes out too. We just get so blinded—legitimately—by what hurts that we can't see the good brightening the darkness."

"What about those who don't get to see it?" I mumbled before I was able to stop myself, echoes of the attack thundering in my mind. "What about those whose lives get stolen by the bad?" I took a deep breath. "If God would just stop it before it happened, he'd spare himself a step in the process."

Mona looked at me, sadness and understanding on her face. "I just think it's easy to blame God for the stupidity of humans. The cruelty too." She saw my involuntary grimace and laughed. "And I'm *also* guessing you'd rather talk about anything but this," she said.

"I would."

"Great, because there's something else I need to say to you."

"Oh boy."

"Listen, I don't get you to myself very often, so I might as well make the most of it, right?" She watched Connor and Grant dragging a fairly large hunk of rotted tree toward the creek. "I need to apologize."

"Mona . . ."

"What I said about you and Grant, back in Balazuc . . . It wasn't about you."

I looked at her, shaking my head. "No, you were right. I didn't want to admit it, but—you were absolutely right."

"I wasn't."

I frowned, confused and a bit uncomfortable.

Mona went on. "Lost finds lost. That much I can stand by. But . . ." She stopped speaking as Grant slung Connor over his shoulder in a fireman's hold and leapt across the creek with him, eliciting a shriek from his nephew. He put him down next to a pile of sticks, and they carried them to their makeshift dam.

"I think I was talking about myself," Mona said. "When I warned you about Grant. Fred and I—we were as lost as it gets. I was insecure and scared of taking risks, and he was immature and needing to feel loved. Our combination of lost was doomed to self-destruct. But that doesn't mean yours is too."

I wasn't sure how to respond. "You were right, though," I told her, needing to believe it. There'd been relief in heeding Mona's warning, in deciding that the wisest course was to maintain a safe distance from Grant. "I'm not just lost. There's a part of me that's broken, and . . . broken doesn't make for good relationships."

"You are not broken."

"Wounded, then."

"Wounds heal."

I shook my head. I couldn't imagine being able to live beyond the horror someday while every moment, to some degree, was still steeped in its agony. "Sometimes they don't. Sometimes they *can't.*"

She grasped my upper arms and made eye contact with me. There was nothing belittling on her face. Only concern and determination and something that looked like love.

"You are strong," she said, intensity in her voice. "Stronger than you think."

I felt tears burning my eyes. "I'm not."

"You may not feel like it, but . . . Jessica, you carry within you the strength of those who have loved you best. I'm guessing Patrick was chief among them. You are not broken," she said with so much conviction that I almost believed her. "You've been shaken."

I laughed at her choice of words and heard the cynicism in the sound. "You make it sound so benign."

"But this isn't over yet. You'll find your way back to yourself, Jess, I'm sure of it. And if you and Grant can help each other toward that kind of healing . . ." She smiled. "Sometimes lost *needs* lost—because lost *understands* lost. Will you please ignore what I said before? I was projecting my mistakes onto you. And you and Grant—you're the furthest thing from Fred and me."

It took awhile longer for her to release my arms. I couldn't look at her, so I let my eyes linger on the birds lined up on the phone wire above us, the clouds rolling in from the west, and the knee-high dam made of sticks and rocks now spanning the creek.

"I promise not to speak of this again," Mona said. "But I wanted to set the record straight, just in case. What I said before—it was self-centered and misguided."

Connor leapt across the creek with a little help from Grant, jabbering about forts and floods and victories. "I'm not in a relationship with your brother," I said quietly.

"Just in case," Mona said again.

I caught Grant's eye. He looked suspiciously

from me to his sister. She waved and yelled that she was ready to head in.

"We'll dismantle the dam and be right there!" he called back.

Mona and I walked across the field to the B&B together.

TWENTY-FIVE

"I'm giving this one more shot, then declaring that we've done our best," I said to Grant later that evening. We were in the lounge at the bottom of the stairs with our laptops again. Clive had lit a fire in the fireplace and I sat on the floor, leaning back against its hearth, enjoying the warmth.

Grant hadn't said much since our return from the creek. I'd caught a couple curious looks as we sat around a table at the local pub for dinner, but Connor and Mona had steered the conversation to trivial things. She was upstairs putting him to bed now, which tended to be a rather long process, and Grant and I had met by unspoken accord to dig a little more into Adeline's Bible pages.

"Everything okay with you and Mona?" he asked.

I paused in my typing for a moment and opted for a simple, mostly true answer. "Yep."

He got the message. Pulling his laptop closer, he smirked and said, "All right. Nice chat."

I continued to search for various combinations of key words, grouping them together in quotation marks in an attempt to reduce the number of hits. On a whim, I added *"Kent UK"* to the series of key words I entered into the search bar, remembering that Charles's family had settled in that county.

I scrolled down, expecting again to find nothing pertinent in the results, and saw an entry whose title read: "Sandhurst Baptist Church Reveals Historic Donation."

I clicked on the link, and the first few lines I read were:

> Pastor Ken Slater of Sandhurst Baptist Church revealed this week that a donation made to the parish in 1972 will be offered for public viewing in the sanctuary on Rye Road, Sandhurst, Kent. The single page, torn from an historic edition of a French Bible, arrived in Sandhurst in what might best be described as an intriguing manner.

Grant must have sensed the excitement. His eyes were on me when I looked up. "Found something?"

I couldn't speak, so I nodded instead. Grant was sitting on the floor beside me in an instant.

"Whoa," he said after reading the first lines of the article. He moved closer and continued to read aloud.

> Pastor Slater invites curious minds in Sandhurst and beyond to join the congregation at a social on May 7, 2002, during which the entirety of the Huguenot Bible page's known history will be revealed. It's a tale that extends back in

time to England's great wave of religious refugees. Light snacks and refreshments to follow in the annex. All are welcome.

We sat motionless and silent for a while, rereading the short blurb on my screen. I could hear Grant taking the kind of loud breaths that had signaled deep concentration since the beginning of our search. They came more quickly this evening, the adrenaline of discovery likely heightening his senses as it had mine.

Grant finally retrieved the laptop he'd left on the couch and sat back down next to me, typing furiously. He brought up Google Maps and entered *"Sandhurst Kent UK"* into the search bar. We watched the map appear, its red marker on a spot directly south of us. He clicked Directions and entered our B&B's town of Burham into the second space, then waited for a route to appear.

"Less than an hour," he said. "Wait."

The suppressed excitement in his voice got my attention. I leaned closer as he zoomed in on the map and pointed at a town not far from Sandhurst. "Isn't that where Charles's son lived, according to his testament?"

"Hawkhurst . . ." I racked my mind, visualizing the notes I'd taken. "Yes. Grant, yes, I'm pretty sure that's what it was."

I hurried upstairs to my bedroom and found the notepad I'd used at the Rochester museum.

I dropped it on the floor next to Grant when I returned to the sitting room, standing over him with my arms spread wide. "Hawkhurst."

He laughed and I sat back down, trying not to let our discovery get my hopes up too high. I retrieved my laptop and clicked on the link to Sandhurst Baptist Church in the announcement I'd found. The church's home page opened, and I scrolled down.

"There's a 'Contact Us' link."

There was something so carefree and joyful in Grant's eyes when I looked up at him that I felt my hope buoyed by sheer proximity.

"It may not be from Charles's or Julie's pages." I had to say it.

"But it could be."

"It could be."

"Well, write them a note!" Grant said when I'd just stared at him for a while. "If that Pastor Slater is still there, he may be willing to give us an encore performance of the story." He smiled again, so broadly that dimples I'd never noticed before appeared high in his cheeks.

"What if he isn't there? Or if they've sent the page to a museum or something? This article was written in 2002 . . ."

"We won't know until we ask."

I clicked on the link and composed a short note explaining who we were, that we were in Burham for a couple more days, and that we had some interest in the page from a French Bible that had been mentioned in the local paper on May 7, 2002.

"Should I say more than that?" I asked Grant. "Something about the pages we have or Adeline's story?"

He shook his head. "Let's wait and see what he answers."

I clicked Send, and we sat without moving for a bit longer. That we may have found another connection to Adeline—and maybe Julie—was dumbfounding.

⚜

I kept the laptop in my bedroom so I could check my emails first thing when I woke up. I hadn't anticipated the sleeplessness that had me checking for new messages at regular intervals throughout the night. The answer from the pastor of Sandhurst Baptist Church landed in my inbox around six the next morning.

> Dear Jessica,
> We still have the Bible page displayed in the church. You're welcome to visit, but it is a long way from Burham. If you'd rather I email you the information I've gathered, I'd be happy to do so.
> Kind regards,
> Ken Slater

Grant must have spent the night as I had. I found him in the sitting room when I came down an hour or so before our scheduled breakfast time, nursing a large mug of coffee, his eyes a little bleary.

"He answered," I said, sitting next to him on the couch and showing him the response from Pastor Slater.

"Want him to just send the information by email?" he asked.

I didn't give it a moment of thought. "No—I want to go see for myself."

"I was hoping you'd say that."

"Leave after breakfast?"

I loved the look of adventure on his face. "If this page in Sandhurst is connected to the ones we have . . ."

"Adeline would be pleased," I agreed.

"Imagine two sets finding their way back to each other . . ."

I wrestled with myself, wanting to tell him what had been occupying my mind for much of the night, but unwilling to give space to the emotions. "Patrick would love this," I finally whispered.

Grant looked at me but said nothing.

"He'd have left last night—probably would have started yelling at us to get ready and shoving all our belongings into the car the moment we found that article about Sandhurst." I laughed. Then the enormity of missing him cloaked my levity with loss. "He'd have loved this," I said again, as if the words could make him more present.

"What was he like?" Grant asked, sincerity in his voice. "If you're okay talking about it."

It struck me at that moment that I wanted Grant to know him. They'd have probably become friends if they'd met, Patrick drawn to Grant's no-nonsense practicality and Grant entertained—and likely annoyed—by Patrick's indefatigable gumption.

"He was . . ." I searched for the right word. "He was luminous," I finally said. "Witty, adventurous, intuitive." I glanced at Grant, gratified that he seemed to be listening. "He'd get these inklings—these ridiculous notions would cross his mind—and he'd somehow will them into becoming a reality. His store. His art studies in Paris. He loved beauty," I said, and realized the sentence encapsulated his spirit. "Creating it, finding it, sharing it . . ." I let my voice trail off as Patrick's face drifted to the foreground of my mind, his energy and optimism a nearly palpable force. "He was obstinate too. And sometimes so blunt that he made people angry, but . . . he was luminous."

I could see Grant measuring his next words. "And you two were . . . ?" He gave me an awkward smile and hunched a shoulder, almost apologetic in his attempt to be considerate.

"Oh," I said, surprised by what he was hinting at. "We were friends. Just friends."

285

"I figured, but . . . just wanted to be clear."

After a few moments of silence, I said, "People were always making assumptions about us, and I get why they did. There was something between us that just . . . clicked. He dragged me out of the restrictions of being responsible and measured at all times and . . ." I laughed. "And I think I dragged him kicking and screaming toward a reluctant sort of restraint."

"So this trip," Grant said, kindness in his tone. "This hunt for Adeline's survivors. It's actually more like Patrick than like you?"

"I guess his impulsive streak was contagious."

Grant's smile turned compassionate. "I guess it was."

I glanced at him and shook my head, trying to clear it of the seeds of anger. "Death is so . . ." I searched for the right word. "Final. It's just so *final*. I keep having these reflexes. Wanting to tell him about the cathedral yesterday and the food and . . . all of this," I said, pointing to the laptop where Pastor Slater's email was still displayed, then to the exquisitely decorated room that would have sent Patrick into creative overdrive. "But . . . death is just so final."

"It is."

The tears I'd been stifling pushed past my reserves. I covered my mouth with my hand and tried to steady myself, but my shoulders shook with restrained sobs.

Grant seemed to hesitate for a moment, then moved closer. He took my free hand in an awkward gesture and held it in both of his. "I'm sorry," he said. They were simple words, but they soothed the jagged edges of Patrick's absence.

When I could breathe again, I let my head fall back against the tall backrest of the Victorian couch and whispered, "I miss him."

Grant nodded but didn't speak. I leaned forward to swipe at new tears, pulling my hand from Grant's grasp. Then I looked at him, hoping he'd understand, and whispered despite the caution tugging at my conscience, "I'm just so scared that we're not going to find anything. I hear Patrick in my head telling me to keep hunting—to keep following the journal, the Bible pages, the . . ." I swallowed hard against a sob. "But I'm terrified that I'm going to miss what I'm supposed to find."

I bit my lip and strove for composure as Grant pulled me into his chest, rested his chin on the top of my head, and held me there.

For the first time in a long while, I felt anchored. I sat immobile, letting the tears run down my neck, unwilling to break Grant's hold by shifting enough to wipe them away. My body softened into his as tension seeped out of my shoulders.

"We're not finished yet," he said after several minutes of silence.

I pulled away—reluctantly—and reached for

a box of tissues sitting on the end table beside the armchair. "But we don't know if we'll find anything. If that page in Sandhurst doesn't belong to the same Bible . . ."

"We'll keep hunting," he said.

"Why?" I finally voiced the question that had been lingering just out of reach in my mind. "Why are you doing this?"

"Going off on a wild-goose chase with a woman I didn't know two months ago, dragging a sister and a five-year-old nephew along?" He grinned.

I bit my lip. "Yeah—that."

He leaned back into the corner of the couch and crossed his arms, his eyes on me but his thoughts clearly elsewhere. "I guess I get the sense that there's something more to this, that maybe the box was supposed to find me too."

I caught myself smiling. "That sounds a little mystical for a trucks-and-hammers kind of guy."

"And then there's you," he said, serious.

Panic fluttered in my stomach. I tried to disarm it with humor. "The woman you nearly committed to an asylum three days after she arrived in Balazuc."

It took him a while to answer. I fiddled with the fringe of a pillow I'd pulled onto my lap and hoped he'd let the topic slide.

"Mona gave me the same warning she gave you," he finally stated.

Silence stretched taut again. Then Grant said, "I think she suspects there may be more to this collaboration than a shared curiosity about the Baillard family."

"She's a sister," I said, hoping my tone was light and airy. "Seeing romantic pitfalls around every corner is part of the job description, right?" I suddenly regretted the vulnerability that had enabled this conversation. "I assured Mona that her concerns were absolutely unfounded," I said when Grant didn't respond, my flippant tone jarring on the heels of our more serious conversation.

He sat for a moment without saying anything, then nodded imperceptibly and pushed off the couch. "I'll go tell her we're driving to Sandhurst."

He went upstairs to our rooms.

TWENTY-SIX

We were on the road by ten, our GPS set for Sandhurst, our minds preoccupied with what we'd find when we got there. Sandhurst Baptist Church was a couple miles out of town, its red brick and hedgerows blending into the fields and woods surrounding it. We pulled into its gravel parking lot with a few minutes to spare before our scheduled rendezvous with Pastor Slater.

As Connor had finally fallen asleep after whining most of the way there, Grant cracked the back windows so we could leave him where he was.

We passed through a wrought iron gate and went around the end of a hedgerow to access the graveyard that nearly circled the church. Then we wandered slowly among the tombstones, some so old and worn that only a trace of their engraving remained.

The crunch of car tires on gravel alerted us to the pastor's arrival.

"I'll come to you!" he called over the shrubbery separating us from the parking lot. He looked to be about sixty years old, his gray beard and hair cropped short. He'd worn a slate-colored suit to meet us, and his bright-yellow tie spoke of a cheerfulness that hadn't translated in our email exchange.

"Have you been waiting long?" he asked as he reached us, extending a hand to Mona and to me, then to Grant.

"Lovely to meet you, Pastor Slater," Mona said. "We got here a bit early—I hope you don't mind that we wandered into the graveyard."

"Not at all!" he answered, his voice deep and resonant, his accent soft and somehow welcoming. "And I'm Ken, by the way. No need for formalities. You must be Jessica, then?"

"That's me," I said, putting up my hand like a schoolgirl, my poise a bit rattled by the excitement of seeing the page donated to the church. "This is Grant and his sister, Mona." I pointed to our car. "Connor is still sleeping in the back seat."

"Lucky boy. I miss the luxury of a good midday nap! Have you been around back?" he asked, pointing toward the other side of the church.

"Not yet," Grant said.

Our host motioned for us to follow him. "I don't know why you're wasting your time here when there's something just around the corner much more pertinent to your research. Come," he said, setting off in the direction he'd pointed. "I think you'll appreciate this."

He led us past the front entrance of the church and around to the graveyard that extended in the back. "This one here is what you'll want to see." He led us to a wide tomb—probably six feet across—covered by an arched layer of red bricks. "That curved shape is typical of Huguenot graves," Pastor Slater said. "Easy to pick out if you know what you're looking for." He motioned toward the weatherworn marker above the grave. "See the angel in the pictogram there? And the smaller figures clinging to each of his arms? Those are refugees being guided out of France. A powerful image, even in its eroded state."

"Any tombs here with the Ballard name on them?" Grant asked, using his phone to take pictures of the grave.

"Not to my knowledge, but so many have been worn down by the elements that it's a bit hard to tell." He turned to me. "Right, then. Remind me how you found our little country church?"

"We've been doing some research," I said, reaching into my purse. "I found these pages of a Huguenot Bible in an antique sewing box in southern France, along with the journal of its last owner, and we're trying to trace her descendants."

Grant pocketed his phone and took over. "We were able to find her brother's last will and testament in the Huguenot Museum in Rochester. Then yesterday we decided to search for something similar to these," he said, pointing at the pages the pastor now held. "We somehow came across an announcement from 2002 about the event you organized here."

"Ah, yes. Our storytelling evening! One of our many attempts to invite new blood into our congregation," Pastor Slater said, chuckling. "I think we had a grand total of three visitors come from outside the church, and two of them left before we got around to the history lesson." He turned our pages over and studied them intently. "Remarkable, really," he said.

"Are they anything like yours?" Mona asked, voicing the question I'd been trying to suppress.

He looked at each of us in turn, then handed the pages back to me and fished around in his pocket for a set of keys. "I think you'll be intrigued," he said a bit mysteriously, leading the way to the side door of the church.

I barely heard Mona say, "I'll stay out here and keep an eye on Connor."

We followed Pastor Slater into the modest sanctuary of Sandhurst Baptist Church. He stopped when we reached a small wooden frame hanging under an arched window toward the front. "This is what you're after," he said, and Grant and I pressed forward to see what was behind the glass.

"Good Lord," Grant said.

The pastor chuckled. "Well, you're certainly in the right place for that sentiment."

The first word I saw was *Ezekiel* in bold letters at the top of the page. When I looked beneath it, I recognized the same type of script and anomalies as I'd seen in ours.

I reached for Grant's arm instinctively. "Grant . . ." I heard the awe in my own voice.

"Looks familiar, does it?" Pastor Slater asked. Grant took our pages from my hand and held them up to the one hanging on the wall. They were a nearly perfect match—the typesetting, the margins. Our pages lacked the stains and discoloration of Pastor Slater's, but they seemed ripped from the same Bible.

Ken lifted the frame off its wall hook and brought it to the small table at the front of the sanctuary. He flipped it over and laid it down so we could see the other side through the double-glassed mounting. We leaned in again, taking in the details. There was a page number in the upper-right corner.

"Four sixty-seven," Grant said.

I flipped over our pages. "Four seventy-three to seventy-eight."

"Close enough."

"Tell me it's a match," Mona said, walking in with a groggy Connor at her side.

"It's a match," Grant confirmed.

"It's a—" A hand fluttered to her chest as her eyes got wide. "It's a match?" she asked, incredulous. When Grant nodded, she hunched down in front of Connor so they were eye to eye. "Connor, it's a match. We found a treasure!"

He frowned at her. "Can I have a juice box?"

She laughed and straightened. "So much for family bonding!"

Grant looked from the framed page on the table to Pastor Slater. "Just finding Charles's name in Rochester felt like beating the odds, but this . . ." He shook his head, a smile softening his features. "This is astounding."

"And in this country," our new friend said, "this kind of 'astounding'—and anything else, really—is celebrated with a steaming cup of tea. So . . . how would you like to adjourn to the church kitchen so we can connect our pieces of this puzzle? You can tell me all you know, and I can tell you all I know and—Connor, is it? He can have a go at the toys we just bought for the Sunday school room. How do you feel about that, young man?" He bent down to look into Connor's surly face.

"Can I have a juice box?"

"I think we can rustle something up."

Minutes later, we sat around a Formica-topped table in the church's kitchen, the framed page lying between us. We told Pastor Slater the rest of Adeline's story while Connor played with Legos on the floor. Mona prompted us for details we overlooked in the retelling, and I tried not to laugh watching Grant drinking his tea with a barely perceptible grimace.

"You never told us how your page got to the

church," Grant asked when we'd finished our story and answered the questions Pastor Slater asked.

"A bit of a mystery there—and short on details, I'm afraid," the pastor said.

"Whatever you can tell us will be more than we know now." I smiled my encouragement.

"Right. Well, as the story goes, in November 1972, someone knocked on the manse door and my predecessor opened it. He found a stranger standing there, an elderly man who seemed in poor health. He said he was the final descendant of a family that had fled from France to England, and that he wanted to leave a sort of memento with our church, something that had been passed down for generations. He didn't come inside and didn't offer any information beyond that—not even his name. He essentially bequeathed his document to us for safekeeping and walked away."

"How did you know it was something special?" Grant asked.

"I'm afraid none of us did for quite a while. When I arrived in the late eighties, we performed a bit of a purge. My predecessor had been reluctant to throw anything away, you see, so I declared the rubbish bin a sacred space and filled it as often as possible in my early days here. When I came across the page tucked into a file with a brief account of its mysterious arrival, I was tempted to discard it too. It's the historic French

296

that kept me from it, at first. And the more I researched it, the more I realized that it was worth keeping. It's from a rare edition, you may know, and such a fascinating vestige of a Huguenot tradition.

"So we framed it and hung it on the wall, and in 2002 we tried to use it to draw new people into the congregation." He smiled. "And all these years later, here you are."

"Here we are," Mona repeated.

Grant spoke up. "We've been hoping to find something that proves that the younger sister survived their escape from France. But I'm guessing this page comes from Charles's side of the family, not Julie's, since his son lived just a few miles away in Hawkhurst."

"And in the last will and testament," Pastor Slater said. "Nothing about her in there either?"

I shook my head and tamped down a feeling of defeat. "We've found no trace of Julie," I admitted. "Nothing since the day they left Gatigny."

"There would have been so many hazards to a voyage like theirs." Our new friend shook his head, likely imagining the challenges the Baillard children encountered.

"But this is good," I said, nodding toward the frame in the center of the table. "We found one of the pages Charles carried to England, and that will have to be enough." I corrected myself. "It *is* enough."

We talked a bit more about our quest, the village of Sandhurst, and the weather. And when Connor got antsy again, we said our good-byes.

"You're brave people going on a grown-up adventure with a squirrelly little boy."

"Oh, he hasn't exactly suffered," Mona said. "With all the bribery we've resorted to, this may turn out to be the trip of his lifetime!"

"And what does he get for the stop in Sandhurst today?"

"Two hours at a playhouse near Maidstone on the way home," Grant said.

"Yay! Yay! Yay!" Connor yelled.

"Blessings, my friends." Pastor Slater stood by the car as we prepared to drive away. "Remember that the right side is the wrong side on our roads!" He leaned down to wink at me. "You'll keep him sorted out."

⸺�⸻

With Mona and Connor deep in conversation about the realness of Bigfoot, Grant and I rode in silence for a while. I wondered if this was the beginning of an ending. For our vacation. For our search. For our partnership. I watched Grant's hands on the wheel, his driving strong and self-assured, and I found it hard to imagine the person he'd been before coming to France. He'd brought the same protective impulses to Adeline as he did to Connor every day. As he did to me in different ways. I could scarcely envision the failures he'd described.

"I'm sorry about this morning," I murmured, surprising myself almost as much as I seemed to surprise him.

He glanced at me, then looked back at the road. "No need for that."

Now that the topic was broached, I wasn't sure how to proceed. "I was . . . blunt."

He shrugged. "You were honest."

I wouldn't have called it honest. Wise, maybe— that's what I'd told myself when guilt had stirred during our day in Sandhurst. By saying what I had that morning, I'd protected myself from the hazards of attachment—from the quicksand of need. But in a part of my mind I still couldn't quite control, I felt the looming threat of trying too hard to stay safe.

"And we're okay?" I asked the man whose sturdiness of spirit was a quieting force.

He took his eyes off the road again long enough to cast me a thoughtful smile. "We're fine," he assured me.

I hoped we really were.

Grant's phone rang just as Mona and Connor's debate about Bigfoot was reaching a conclusion. He took the phone from the console where it was charging and glanced at the screen. "Unknown caller."

I put out a hand. "Want me to answer it?" He handed me the phone and I swiped it on. "Hello?"

"Jessica, dear. Is that you?"

I recognized her voice immediately. "Nelly?"

"Indeed! Calling with disappointing news, I'm afraid. After speaking with you, I called every Huguenot-savvy acquaintance I could think of, but the only suggestions they offered for your little search were things you've already done."

"Nelly—"

"So, much as I dislike having to concede defeat, I'm afraid I must throw in the proverbial towel—"

"Nelly," I tried again.

"Yes, dear?"

"We found another page from the same Bible."

"You did!" Her voice went up a notch with excitement. "Like the ones you brought with you?"

I spent a few minutes explaining how we'd found Sandhurst and filling her in on the new information we'd gleaned. "I don't think we can hope for much more," I said in conclusion. "We know Charles survived, and we found another page of the Baillard Bible. We'll have to be content with that."

"So it's just Julie you're missing."

"Yes, but we're not even sure she made it across the Channel."

"The Channel . . . ," Nelly said thoughtfully.

Something in her voice caught my attention. "What are you thinking, Nelly?"

"I've got to hang up," she said so loudly that I pulled the phone away from my ear. "I'll call you back the moment I've confirmed a little hunch I have. Cheers!"

And the line went dead.

-ஃ~ஃ-

She called back when we were at the playhouse. Mona and I sat in the coffee shop while Grant helped Connor negotiate a climbing wall.

"It's all as it should be," Mona said. "The women sipping coffee and the men watching the children."

I looked at the phone's screen when it vibrated and felt my pulse accelerate. "Hello?"

"Jessica, luv, it's me! How do you feel about a quick trip out to Somerset?"

I mouthed to Mona to get Grant and said, "Tell me what you've found," into the phone. I had that feeling—that Patrick-esque feeling—that our quest wasn't quite over yet.

"Your comment about the Channel got me to thinking, and I just might know someone who can advise you on your search," she said, her voice bright and animated. "Last we spoke was probably thirty years ago, so it took me a while to find his most recent known address . . . and longer than that to remind him of who I was once I tracked down his current phone number. I must warn you that he's an original. About as warm and fuzzy as a prickly pear, and obsessed with the strangest things, one of which might be of interest to you. Corbin Owens is the name—are you writing it down, dear? But he goes by Corb or 'Captain Corb.' Not a real captain, mind you, never has been, but he likes the prestige of the title. That's my guess."

I was frantically taking notes with the phone on speaker. Grant had joined Mona and me while Connor burned energy in the bouncy castle with a new friend. "Nelly, who's Captain Corb?"

"Well, that's a long story that barely bears repeating. We were sweet on each other once. Met at university . . . and you know what they say about opposites attracting. We were just crazy for each other until our opposites did what they tend to do second: repulse. But that has no relevance to the investigation you're conducting.

"Captain Corb is absolutely barmy for old ships' logs. He's collected them since uni and become a sort of reference on all things related. Made quite a name for himself in dusty historian circles. So if you've got the stomach for a probably less than civil encounter, I'd suggest you find a little town called Dunster on your map or your phone or whatever you techie-types use, and get your American fannies to the lovely county of Somerset."

"Does he think he can help us?" Grant asked.

"Oh, hello there, young man! I didn't know this was a party call. I'm confident he can at least give you some direction on the matter. I've shared with him all the information you gave me, and he'll use the time until you get there to peruse the mounds of ancient, musty tomes he calls a library."

She gave us his number and his address and signed off with a cheerful, "Now you go find that pot of gold!"

TWENTY-SEVEN

It took us six hours to get from Burham to Dunster the next day. On the edge of Exmoor National Park, just a stone's throw from the Bristol Channel, it was a quaint and scenic town. In tourist season, it would have been overrun with vacationers, but it felt nearly deserted on a damp January day.

We found our hotel and moved our bags into our rooms, then Grant and I set off toward Captain Corb's place while Mona, Connor, and his scooter headed toward a bakery the check-in clerk had told us not to miss. I marveled at the beauty of Dunster. Everything we saw seemed saturated with the past. The church, the narrow and cobble-stoned streets, the castle perched high on a hill above the town. It was the stuff of fairy tales and make-believe.

"Brace yourself," Grant said as we arrived at the door of a row house whose white façade seemed to have been recently painted.

"Maybe Nelly was exaggerating . . ."

The door opened before Grant had the chance to knock.

"You Nelly's friends, then?" Corb's accent was thick and coarse. So was his voice. He looked at us through bloodshot eyes, his coveralls straining against a huge beer belly. Wisps of gray hair escaped a stained, beige, knitted hat.

"We are," Grant said.

The old man looked at me. "You reckon I can help you?"

I quelled the urge to step back. "Nelly thinks you might."

"Old bat still off her trolley?"

"I—I'm sorry, I don't know what that means."

He turned and walked away. "Bloody Americans."

I looked at Grant, and he met my gaze, perplexed and amused. "You think we're supposed to follow him?" he asked.

"You'll protect me, right? If things get weird."

"I'll use my martial arts," he said, entering the house before me and following our host down a narrow, book-lined hallway.

"Barrel racing is not martial arts," I retorted.

I heard him chuckle and fell in behind him.

"Sit," Corb instructed as we took two steps down into a square room whose floor and walls were lined with stacks of books and maritime mementos. There was an anchor in one corner so large that I wondered how he'd gotten it into the house. An antique diving suit stood eerily in another corner, and I could see a captain's wheel, a cannon, and what looked like a treasure chest from where I stood.

"You sit there," Captain Corb said to me,

motioning to an armchair with tattered gray fabric and a sunken seat cushion. "You." He pointed at Grant, then motioned toward a wooden stool not far from the chair I now occupied. Grant checked its solidity before perching on it.

"So you're hunting for refugees."

I wasn't sure whether it was a question or a statement. Grant seemed to think the former was true.

"Yes—the Ballards or Baillards. They were Huguenots, and most likely left from Calais at the end of the 1600s."

"And what makes you think they used Calais?" Corb asked with overt derision.

I looked at Grant and saw a glint in his eyes. "It's the shortest distance between land masses," he explained. "So it seemed to make sense that—"

"Make sense? Of course it makes sense."Corb reached for a pipe and took his time lighting it. "King knew it too. Calais was crawling with his goons, all liquored up to hunt the fugitives."

I cleared my throat. "So . . . where do you think they would have sailed from?"

"Cherbourg, most likely. Less risk." He sat back and inhaled from his pipe, letting the smoke out slowly, his eyes on me, then on Grant, then back on me again. After what felt like an interminable pause, he said, "Nelly told me about the family. Brother and sister from the Vivarais region."

"And a wife," I interjected. "She would have been pregnant."

"You going to do the talking or am I?" He waved his pipe at me, eyebrows raised.

"I'm sorry—"

"Don't be sorry, be quiet!"

"Nelly warned us about you," Grant said, his voice low and measured. I looked at him and saw a muscle twitching in his jaw. "All we came for is answers. If you can help us find some, great. But if you don't have anything for us, we'll let you get back to whatever we interrupted."

"Look at you," Corb sneered. "Fancy peacock preening for his mate."

Grant stood and held a hand out to me. "Come on," he said. "Let's go."

I was about to get up, somewhat relieved to be leaving so soon, when Corb let out a laugh so loud that both Grant and I jumped. "Sit down!" he bellowed, slapping his leg and reaching for a half-dozen books stacked by his chair. "You Americans and your namby-pamby feelings. Wouldn't have opened the door if I didn't have something for you. Now sit down and cork it so I can tell you what I've found."

He tossed a leather-bound book at Grant and another one at me. We went back to our designated chairs with them and waited for Corb to continue. "Found your Charles bloke's name on a ship manifest from December 14, 1695."

"How did you get ship manifests from that far back?" I said, then kicked myself for speaking out of turn.

Corb leaned forward. "Ever heard of the Internet?"

I sat back and said nothing. From the corner of my eye, I could see Grant grinning.

"That book there is the actual captain's log," he said, pointing at the one Grant held.

I was dumbfounded. "The captain who brought them over to—?"

His glare stopped me short. "Lucky thing for you he was the talkative type. Got a transcript here, too, if you don't like his chicken scratch." He flipped through the printed pages he held. "December 14—says a family of three approached him through the usual connections." He looked up. "They had runners back then. Whole network of allies." Looking back down at the notes, he continued. "Says it was a couple and a brother wanting to get across to Portsmouth."

Grant leaned forward. "It would have been a sister."

"Unless the sister was dressed as a boy," Corb said slowly, as if talking to a child.

Grant frowned. "What are you saying?"

The older man leaned back and took a long drag from his pipe, then he tilted his head and blew the smoke straight up. "I'm saying a boy getting caught by the goons was one thing, but a girl . . ."

He didn't need to elaborate more. I'd read enough about the atrocities perpetrated against the Huguenots to understand why Julie might have wanted to wear men's clothes.

"So they're in here?" Grant asked, holding up the log.

Corb ignored his question. "Where you staying?"

"The Castle Hotel."

"Take that," he said, pointing at Grant's book. "Start on the date I told you." Then he turned on me. "And you take that one. You'll find they supplement each other." He handed me the transcripts. "Here. You'll likely do better with the sissified English."

I wasn't sure whether he was being kind or insulting. "I . . . thank you."

"Get them back here by the same time tomorrow, or I'll come to the hotel and get them myself, you hear? Just push 'em through the slot in the door so we don't have to do all this again."

"And if we have questions?"

He just stared at me.

"We'll try not to have questions," I amended.

"Get outta here, the lot o' you! And don't you make me come after those logs!" I could have sworn I heard a smile in his voice.

Grant and I hurried up the steps, down the hall, through the door, and made it back to our hotel in record time.

TWENTY-EIGHT

We didn't start on the project until after dinner, and what we found kept us up most of the night. We read every word—even the accounts that had nothing to do with Charles and Julie—drawn in by the storytelling of a captain who'd risked everything to help the Huguenot refugees he ferried out of harm's way.

The transcripts Corb had given us were incomplete, so we had to go back to the originals again and again to piece together the missing elements of the story we uncovered. It left us burdened with more questions.

Connor took one look at us the next morning and said, "Do you need to take a nap?"

"That obvious?" Grant asked.

Mona walked into the breakfast room behind her son. She saw the page markers sticking out of Corb's old logs and squinted at us, probably trying to gauge whether we'd found something or not. "Any luck?"

Grant and I looked at each other. Then he pushed the book Corb had given him across the table.

"So this is what a captain's log looks like," Mona said, picking it up.

Grant nodded. "More like a blow-by-blow

account of everything he witnessed as the go-to Huguenot smuggler of Cherbourg."

We spent breakfast filling her in on what we'd uncovered. Charles Baillard and his family had found their way to Captain Jonathan Fletcher several months after they'd left the South of France.

"No way of knowing what took them so long," Grant said. "Illness. Weather conditions. Maybe they just took long breaks as they trekked across the country."

Fletcher had described them as gaunt—Isabelle sickly but brave. He referred to the third member of Charles's entourage as Jules, which supported Corb's suspicion that Julie had been traveling as a boy.

The captain's logs alluded to heightened scrutiny at the time the family reached Cherbourg, and we knew from what we'd read in the Rochester museum's resources that the king had ordered extraordinary measures to keep the Huguenots from fleeing. His dragoons had gone from searching random vessels to slashing into bundles of fabric and boxes of vegetables with their swords and fumigating entire holds where they thought escapees were hiding. If they found fugitives alive, they dragged them through town and made examples of them by torturing them in public squares or sending them off to the gallows. The dead were left hanging in the sun to decompose—a warning not to help the heretics in any way.

Still, Fletcher told Huguenot sympathizers on land that he'd get the Baillard family to Portsmouth if they could find a way to sneak them on board.

"With Cherbourg's port under heavy surveillance, they couldn't risk the family walking to the boat—even under cover of darkness," Grant said. "So they loaded them into empty wine casks in a town not far from the port and had them brought to the ship on a horse-drawn cart."

"The way Captain Fletcher tells it," I continued, "Isabelle got violently ill after deckhands rolled the casks onto the ship and into its hold. The only way for them to breathe was through a straw they could push through a small hole in the barrel, and the sicker she became, the more untenable it got. Fletcher could hear them screaming to each other as several dragoons approached the ship, then he heard Charles trying to kick his way out of his cask, presumably to help Isabelle out of hers."

"Did they get in trouble?" Connor asked, bread crumbs and Nutella stretching from his mouth across both cheeks.

"Should we . . . continue later?" Grant looked at Mona.

She pulled a phone from her pocket, brought up an app, and handed the phone to her son. "Why don't you go sit over there and make like an angry bird?" she said.

Surprised by the rare permission to use her phone, Connor scrambled off his chair and crawled into a window seat on the far side of the dining room. He hunched over the phone and started a game. "No sound insulation needed," Mona said. "Please—continue."

I motioned for Grant to take over. "Fletcher rushed down to the hold as the dragoons were preparing to board the ship. Found Isabelle slumped on the floor and Charles trying to pry the top off Julie's cask, but it was stuck and there just wasn't time to get her out before the soldiers got to them. Fletcher distracted the dragoons by putting up a bit of resistance when they found him in the hold, while Charles and Isabelle took advantage of the diversion to make it up to the deck unnoticed. His best guess is that they somehow slipped overboard while the dragoons were roughing him up, then either found their way to shore or died trying—in either case, there wasn't anything he could do. So he headed for Plymouth, never knowing what became of them."

"Wait—Plymouth?" Mona asked. "Weren't they supposed to sail to Portsmouth?"

"That's where it gets confusing," I said. "Portsmouth is where Fletcher had promised to take them, but he described letting Julie out of her cask in the Plymouth port."

"Why would he change the itinerary?"

Grant sighed and leaned forward to gather our logs and transcripts into a stack. "He mentioned a storm—it could have been that. Or maybe he knew something we don't and decided to take Julie to a safer location. Or maybe it was just a change of plans. We didn't find anything that hinted at a reason."

Mona shook her head. "So this—what was she? Twelve years old?"

"Probably thirteen by then," I said.

"This thirteen-year-old gets loaded into a ship's hold, hears her brother kicking his way out of a wine cask and freeing his wife, crosses the Channel in a sealed container with just a straw for air, and lands on the other side in the wrong place with no idea whether Charles and Isabelle are alive or dead and joining her or not?"

"Pretty grim, right?" Grant said.

I tried not to picture the teenager crawling out of that cask on foreign soil, staring into the faces of strangers and coming to grips with being stranded alone.

"Is that it?" Mona asked, appalled. "That's all we know? She got off the ship in the middle of the night and . . . what?"

Grant glanced at me. "There's just a bit more."

"Fletcher found a refugee family that was headed from Plymouth toward London and asked them to take her along."

"A refugee family." Mona seemed as troubled

by the saga as Grant and I had been. "He just . . . found somebody to take her and went on with his life?"

I rubbed my hands over my face and tried to make sense of the myriad details I'd absorbed during the night. "The captain sounds like a good man," I finally said. Tentatively. Hopefully. "I don't think he would have just . . . abandoned her. And he calls the family who took her 'refugees,' so maybe they were Huguenots too. French people who knew what she'd been through, who spoke her language . . ." I tried to conjure up what we couldn't know of Julie's fate. "Maybe the family took her to Portsmouth to meet up with Charles and Isabelle."

Mona shook her head. "But we don't know when they finally made it across. It could have been months later."

Grant reached for the second book we'd spent the night scrutinizing. "Actually, we might," he said. "A Captain Paul Robinson. Short on words and details, but we think we've figured out why Corb gave us this log too."

"Charles and Isabelle?"

"He doesn't use names," I said. "But he talks about a couple from the Vivarais with a newborn baby that he took across to Portsmouth about five weeks after Julie made the trip."

"Except that she went to Plymouth," Mona stated. There were tears in her eyes, the uncertainty of Julie's fate wounding her mother's heart.

"Right," Grant said. He leaned back in his chair and scratched his head, frustration in the gesture. "All we can know for sure is that Charles and Isabelle made it to Canterbury. We have ample evidence of that. But Julie . . ." He let his voice trail off, looking from Mona to me. "And since there was no mention of her in Charles's will—"

"That doesn't mean she didn't survive!" Mona interrupted Grant, perhaps more forcefully than she'd intended.

Connor's head snapped up. "Hey! Hey! Hey!" All three adults turned toward him and he wagged a finger at us. "No fighting!"

There was a moment of silence as we realized we were being chastised by a child. "We're not fighting, kiddo," Grant finally said. "Just talking about serious things."

"Like lightsabers?" Connor asked.

I looked at Mona. She looked at me. "Sure," she said with a laugh. "Serious things like lightsabers."

That seemed to placate him, and he went back to his game.

"I don't mean to be a pessimist," Grant said, speaking softly enough that we wouldn't disturb Connor again.

I sighed. "I know."

"Even if Charles and Isabelle had tracked Fletcher down after they made the crossing, he'd have had no way of knowing where the refugee family that took Julie finally put down roots. Charles himself had intended to settle in London but ended up raising his family in Canterbury. It's just . . . unlikely—no matter how you look at it—that they would have found her again."

"She made it to England," Mona said. "Maybe we just need to be satisfied with that. She got away from France, away from the dragoons. She could have had a good life here, right? Even without her brother?"

"I just keep picturing her on that dock." There had been no description of Julie in Adeline's memoir, yet I could see her face as clearly as if she were sitting in that room with us. I stopped my train of thought before it led me into sordid scenarios. I strove for certainty and said, "Someone took care of her. That family stepped up and made sure she was all right."

"Like the angel on the tomb in Pastor Ken's cemetery," Mona said. "Right there with them, leading the refugees to freedom."

I looked at Grant and saw the disappointment on his face. This moment felt hollow and emptied of redemption. All we'd gained for our efforts were more unanswerable questions and a tattered kind of hope.

⁂

"You didn't have to come," Grant said as we walked down High Street to Corb's home.

"I'm just here for the brawn in case our friend gets out of hand."

Grant laughed. "We're shoving these books through the slot in his door and running away like we lit a bag of poop on fire."

I stopped, hands on hips, and tried for a disapproving look. "You've done that, haven't you?"

Grant stopped too. "What's the statute of limitations on having been a teenager?"

I swatted his arm and he grinned. "We may need those martial arts in a minute," he mumbled.

When we got to Corb's home, Grant pushed the first book through the hole in the door. I wasn't sure which of us jumped higher when it opened unexpectedly and Captain Corb bellowed, "Thought you'd get away, did you?"

I nearly laughed out loud at the look on Grant's face. "We're just doing what you told us to," he said, sounding for all the world like a teenager caught red-handed.

"Figured I'd spare myself bending down to pick 'em up," Corb said, motioning for us to hand over our books. I found him less intimidating standing in the light of day. "You find what you were looking for?"

"We found enough," Grant said.

"And?"

"They got separated—the brother and his wife from the sister—but at least they made it here."

"I'm hoping someone took her in," I said, wanting to convince myself that she hadn't been left to fend for herself.

Corb pursed his lips. "Wasn't just the captains who were good to the Frenchies in those days. Common folk were too. Took in the refugees and gave 'em places to live and food to eat. Work too. No doubt about it, your girl got helped." For a moment, he looked kind despite his gruff, off-putting way.

"So you think she was okay?" I asked as if he could know the answer.

Corb raised an arm and, in a voice so sonorous that it reverberated down the street, declared, "Valor is strength, not of legs and arms, but of heart and soul." He took a step back and closed the door.

We walked most of the way back to the hotel in silence. "You think that was a quote?" I said when we were nearly there.

"The bit about valor?"

I nodded.

"I don't know, but . . ." He stopped, his hands deep in his pockets, and hung his head. I'd come to recognize it as a thinking posture for Grant, so I stood by and gave him time. When he looked up, I saw conviction in his face. "Julie had valor," he said. "Courage. Or as Corb put it, 'strength of heart and soul.' Look at the family she came from—what they went through." He hunched a shoulder. "She was a Baillard," he said. "Valor is what they lived by. I think she found her way to a good life."

I felt hope try to breathe.

TWENTY-NINE

With one day remaining in our English vacation, we left early the next morning for Bristol, which Mona had discovered was Blackbeard's birthplace. We all agreed that a quick venture east would be our final gift to Connor on a trip that had, to his detriment, been mostly adult-driven.

We joined a tour of Blackbeard's favorite haunts, led by one Pirate Pete fully decked out in corsair gear, and while Grant and Connor stuck close to the guide, Mona and I darted in and out of shops, buying souvenirs we'd take home to France.

When the tour ended, Connor found us eating caramelized peanuts next to a statue of John Cabot. "I'm a pirate! I'm a pirate! I'm a pirate!" he yelled, letting out another heartfelt growl and pointing to the patch covering one eye.

Mona moved it to his forehead. "Keep it up there while we're moving, will you? You just ran over two innocent bystanders."

We headed back to our hotel in Dunster after lunch.

"Why don't you two do some exploring in town while I wrangle my little pirate?" Mona said as she helped Connor out of the back seat.

"You and Grant should go," I countered. "I'll keep an eye on Connor."

She dismissed the offer with a wave of her hand. "Absolutely not. It's your last day in this country, and all you've seen of it so far is archives and books and the occasional cathedral. So why don't you make like tourists and see what you can while the day's still young."

"Are you sure?" Grant asked.

"Go forth and conquer!"

⚜

Minutes later, Grant and I strolled down High Street looking in the windows of mom-and-pop stores, tearooms, and tourist traps. Learning of Julie's survival and finally admitting that there were things we would never know about the Baillards' fate had seemed to remove a burden from us both. It felt as though we were finally living in the present after so many weeks spent steeping in the past.

A handwritten sign across the street caught my eye. "We never *indulged*," I said, imitating Nelly's dramatic voice and pointing at the offer of cream teas for five pounds each.

"I don't do tea," Grant said.

"Come on—just this once. As an homage to Nelly."

He gave me a look.

"Tea for two?" the hostess asked as we entered the tearoom. She seated us at a small, lace-covered table in the alcove, took our order, and retreated

322

to the kitchen. I looked at Grant and had to giggle. He seemed so out of place in a space saturated with floral prints and delicate decor.

We talked about the trip and our morning's excursion to Bristol until our waitress brought our order: several scones, an assortment of jams, and a dish of clotted cream. "Scone, then clotted cream, then jam," she instructed us.

"Is it that obvious we're new to this?" I asked her.

She smiled. "I'll be right over there if you need further coaching."

"I asked for coffee, right?" Grant said to me, eyeing the pot of Earl Grey sitting between us on the table.

"I think laughing at you when you did was her very English way of saying 'fat chance.'" I stared at the white substance in front of me. It looked more like butter than cream. "Patrick would say to just rub it on my thighs in a circular motion. It's all going to end up there anyway."

Grant laughed and reached for a scone. I watched him spread a thick coat of clotted cream on it and top it with strawberry jam. He gave me a dubious look as he took his first bite, and I watched his expression morph into pure delight as he starting chewing.

"That good, huh?"

He rolled his eyes and motioned for me to try it too. I followed the same steps and, after sampling my own scone, reached for the pot of cream to set it down right next to me. "You can have the rest of that," I said, wiggling my finger at the scones and tea. "This little pot of decadence is entirely mine!"

Our hostess, who told us her name was Lydia, was attentive and entertaining. She brought Grant a cup of coffee when we were getting near the bottom of the pot of tea. "This one's on the house if you promise to leave some flyers lying around your hotel's vestibule."

Grant smiled. "For this cup of coffee, I'd have done a lot more."

She pointed at the empty dish in front of me. "Liked it, did you?"

"You could say that." I giggled.

"Well, it's a lucky thing you came to me for your first cream tea. Some other places in town serve whipped from a can, but this here's from our own cows on our own farm just up the road a bit."

Grant pointed out our alcove's window at an unusual stone-and-timber structure that stood in the middle of High Street. Its central pillar, dormer windows, and bell tower had piqued our curiosity. "We've been trying to guess what that is," he said to Lydia. "Know anything about it?"

"Do I?" She laughed and rested the cups she'd been removing on the edge of our table. "What you're looking at there is all that's left of Dunster's Yarn Market. It's from the 1600s, I believe, and rare because of its octagonal shape. This entire region was a hub of wool and fabric trade all the way back to the thirteenth century, and that little market is a vestige of the era."

"Sounds like you know your local history," Grant said, glancing at me. I knew what he was thinking.

"I know a little, mostly because I've been hearing my husband prattle on about it for all of my adult life. He's the true historian in these parts." She looked at us askance. "I'm assuming from the looks on your faces that you're history buffs too."

"Not exactly," I said. "We're just—we're intrigued by a span of several years at the end of the seventeenth century. Do you know if any Huguenots might have settled in Somerset?"

She held up her hand. "Stop right there. I can assure you that I'll have no answers to your questions." She leaned in and spoke in a conspiratorial voice. "But if you leave me a good review on Open Table, I may be able to point you toward someone who knows a lot more."

"Five stars," Grant said, leaning in as well. "The clotted cream alone put you over the top."

We hurried back to the hotel and told Mona where we were headed, then drove off toward Nether Stowey, our eyes peeled for a small farm on the outskirts of the village.

"Can I help ya?" a man called from the open door of his barn after we'd pulled into the driveway and exited the car.

Grant raised a hand in greeting. "Lydia sent us! I think she called to let you know we were coming."

The scrawny middle-aged farmer took a rag from the waist of his pants and wiped his hands on it, sauntering toward us. "Just rang a few minutes ago. Name's Roger." He shook our hands. His grip felt like leather. "You're the Americans, then?"

"Lydia told us you're the local historian," I said, curiosity and time constraints making me cut to the chase.

"Unofficially, but yes. What brings you to the farm?"

"Probably a wild-goose chase," Grant said, shaking his head. "We've been here for a few days trying to learn more about the Huguenots who escaped to England."

"Seventeenth century," Roger said. "Some in the sixteenth too."

"So you know of them?" Grant asked.

"Of course! A bunch of them settled in London—but you probably know that. Spitalfields, I think, is where the largest number landed."

He waved at us to follow him as he walked off toward a garage just behind the farmhouse. "Lydia tell you how history stole her parking space?" he asked.

Grant laughed. "She didn't—but I'm guessing there's a story there."

Roger unlocked the garage door and pushed it

up on its tracks, revealing rows of shelving lining every wall, each holding neatly organized and labeled items. "She regularly threatens to throw all this rubbish out so she can park her car in here again. And I tell her that I'd be happy to move it all into the sitting room if it will ease her mind. That generally ends the conversation!" He walked to the back corner of the garage and reached for something sitting high on a shelf. "This here's the only item I can trace back to the Huguenots."

He handed me what appeared to be a piece of rolled-up fabric. I spread it out carefully, revealing small slots hand-sewn into the faded, striped cloth. "Is it a pencil case of some sort?" I asked.

"Something like that. Could have been for art supplies too. Brushes and such," Roger said. "Don't know if you can tell, but that's silk. A little more coarse than what we see today, but definitely silk."

I finished unrolling it and held it up in front of me for closer inspection. Grant's intake of breath made me look over the pencil scroll at him.

"Turn it over," he said, his voice electric.

What I saw when I did made my heartbeat accelerate. I glanced at Grant again, then back to the cloth. There were three small letters embroidered in red thread in one corner of the fabric. The same three we'd found on the bottom of Adeline's box.

"Where did you get this?" Grant asked Roger.

327

"Found it at a flea market. Bridgewater, I think. Didn't have much use for something so pretty, but—"

"How did you know it was connected to the Huguenots?" Grant interrupted him, voicing my own question.

"Because of the note, that's why. It's the whole reason I bought it," Roger said with a broad smile. "There was a letter of sorts wrapped up in it, you see. Got it right over here." He reached for something that looked like an old photo album and turned a few pages, then handed it to me. "Stuck it in here with postcards and the like to keep it from getting damaged any more than it already was."

The yellowed pages, two of them, lay under a thin layer of plastic. The words on them were in tiny script, written in faded pencil.

"This roll . . . it came from somewhere near here?" Grant asked while I tried to read the note.

"I'm thinking maybe Holford." Roger pointed over his shoulder. " 'Bout two miles away. Seems a logical assumption, when you consider the mill."

"What mill?" I heard the tension in Grant's voice and felt the same expectation tightening my own lungs.

"Lydia didn't tell you? There's a silk mill in Holford. Story goes the Huguenots ran it back in the day—the handful who settled here. Not much left of it now, mind you. Just a few walls." He hunched his shoulders. "You can still get to it if you don't mind trespassing a little."

Something I couldn't define was making my skin tingle. Roger nodded toward the book I still held. "You able to make out what it says?"

I shook my head. "Not all of it. The writing is so small and most of it is faded . . ."

"Lucky for you I've had some time to look it over." Roger pulled a pair of glasses from the pocket of his plaid shirt and propped them on his nose, then took the photo album from me and began to read, his voice taking on a formal intonation.

My grandmother believed in the power of words, in the capacity of story to transcend both time and place. This scroll is evidence of the temerity of her escape, a tribute to the ancestors who lost their world to save their faith.

All I know of our story I learned from my grandmother, an overcoming woman who spoke often and profoundly of her flight from oppression, her stranding among strangers, and the joy she uncovered in the ruins of her grief. The history of my people is a tale that must not perish. I've told it to my children and they'll pass it down to theirs, not to boast of our resilience, but to bear witness to the courage we displayed because of God. These pages I leave here, inside the scroll her sister gave her, are the evidence of her enduring, woven as it is into the fabric of this place, this site of our restoring and rebuilding.

From the dungeons of our shock, wrapped in the chains of all our losses, we, the hounded Huguenots, may have doubted for a time, but we knew God in our core to be unshakable and real. My grandmother's survival is a tribute to that faith, a sturdy kind of certainty forged in the flames of man's worst deeds. She died believing still.

It is to honor her and those who went before us that my family and progeny will strive to live the truth we learned from her:

Roger glanced up long enough to say, "This next bit's in French, but I looked up the translation."

Enduring with courage, resisting with wisdom, and pressing on in faith.

"Persisting in faith," Grant whispered next to me, correcting Roger's translation, his eyes meeting mine. And with those words, we knew beyond a doubt that we had found Julie Baillard.

Roger closed the album and removed his glasses.

"I've read it a thousand times and it still gives me chills."

By unspoken accord, we let the silence deepen, honoring the history recorded by Julie's granddaughter.

Then Grant said, "Where can we find this mill?"

Roger went to a table near the garage's entrance and found a pad of paper in its drawer. "I'll draw you a map."

THIRTY

Grant helped me over the gate made slick by recent rain. We'd driven the short distance from Roger's farm to Holford, a village nestled in the hollow of two hills. Its main street was no more than a narrow lane bordered on each side by thatch-roofed homes. We could see little beyond the gate, but Roger's drawing told us the old silk mill was somewhere in the trees along the overgrown path that extended from where we stood down a slight hill.

Grant climbed over the gate clearly marked with No Trespassing signs and caught my eye as he jumped down. We hadn't said much, our minds still reeling from the sheer magic of our find.

We took a few steps, and Grant held out a hand. "Watch out, it's slippery," he said. I took it gratefully, mostly because my legs had felt weak since we'd left Roger's museum-garage.

"There it is."

I followed Grant's gaze to the small structure on our left. All that remained were stone walls, the roof, and windows long gone, but that they were still standing felt miraculous to me. About ten feet wide and thirty feet long, the mill stood in mute tribute to the history it had witnessed.

We circled it slowly, taking in the crossbars

still spanning window openings and the roofline overgrown with vines.

"Look at the arch," Grant whispered.

It took me a moment to understand what he was referring to, then I saw it—an arch of red bricks framed the top of the front door and extended several feet on either side. "Just like the grave in the Sandhurst cemetery," I said, remembering the arch spanning the ground where the Huguenots lay.

We walked over mounds of sticks and leaves to enter the small house. Grant pointed out the holes where crossbeams used to hold up the roof's timbers. The silk mill's walls seemed strong, unbowed by time and elements. I marveled that so much of it, despite the centuries, had remained standing.

As we stepped back out the front door, Grant pointed to two other structures just a few feet away—the remnants of a wall and, right next to the stream, the corner of a smaller building.

Then he nodded back at the larger edifice. "Probably the main house," he said. "And the ruins over here could have been the fulling mill. With the creek right there, they likely used water to power some of their machines."

"Like Pierre's inventions back in Gatigny."

"Julie would have told her new community about the machines he'd created."

We looked around in silence for a few minutes.

It wasn't until later that I realized my hand had been in his for most of the time we'd spent in Holford's glen. We moved slowly to a fallen tree propped a few feet above the ground next to the creek. I sat on its broad trunk as Grant leaned back against it, facing the house that stood like a ghost in the silent, darkening space.

"So this is where it ends." Grant's voice was low. I looked at him. His gaze was soft and bright. "She may not have known where Charles and Isabelle ended up, but she found something here. Had children. Continued with the trade she'd learned from Constance in Gatigny. Adeline would love this—to know her instincts had been right. That Julie had survived."

"I think she knows." Grant looked at me, and I met his gaze.

We let the silence stretch again. There was something about the glen that felt healing. I leaned sideways until my shoulder rested against Grant's, surprising myself and him. He hesitated only briefly, then shifted to draw me close. His arm anchored me to his side as his cheek settled on the top of my head. I turned my face into his neck.

There was a smile in his voice when he said, "Listen, I'm not complaining, but . . . is there something I should know?"

I laughed, but kept my head right where it was. "I think—" I hesitated, trying to find meaning in the muddle of my mind. There was relief. There was sadness. There was trepidation. Gratification. Need. Confusion. I didn't know how the emotions were connected to each other or which were the most important for me to speak to Grant.

A small movement on the periphery of my vision caught my eye. It drifted through the air, then settled on my denim-clad leg.

"A bit late for ladybugs," Grant said when I raised my head to look at it.

"The *bête à bon Dieu*," I whispered. I straightened and looked around, careful not to disturb the bug, half expecting to see Patrick standing by the house or sitting by the stream. But there was no one there.

"The French have a saying about ladybugs," Grant murmured near my ear, watching it fan its wings and move across my leg.

"God cries when they get hurt," I said, my throat constricted. Tears clouded my vision. "That's what Connor told me. God cries when the helpless get hurt."

I sat up straight, willing to speak, but words seemed insufficient for the thoughts that held me captive. In my spirit I heard my friend's voice saying, "Use your words, Jess. Use your words," as the ladybug flew off.

"I was so scared about what we'd find," I finally admitted. "I wanted to know, but I was so scared." I looked up. Grant's eyes were on me, concern in their depths. "What if we'd gotten to England and discovered that they'd all died before they made it here? What if the horror—" My breath caught, but I wanted to speak while my courage held out. "What if the horror Adeline lived with and died by had just . . . been it. Nothing more. Just death and destruction and evil."

Grant's eyebrows were drawn. He listened intently, his eyes on my face, and I knew he'd sense the meaning in the space between my words.

"Finding Charles's will and the page at the Sandhurst church—that was good. That was *great* . . ." I laughed, but there was somberness in the sound. "But I think this whole time it was Julie I needed to find."

Grant shook his head, perplexed. "Because . . . ?"

I bit my lip. "Because Adeline died. And I could have died too—like Adeline—but . . . but I survived."

I could see Grant understood. "And so did Julie."

"So did Julie." Tears filled my eyes and I didn't try to hide them. "You think she was happy? When it was all over. Do you think it's possible for someone who's lost everything to find happiness again?"

"I don't know," Grant said.

I realized how desperately I wanted him to tell me that she had. She'd witnessed the unthinkable and survived the unbearable, and . . . I let my memory flash back to the words Roger had found in the pencil scroll. "I think she did," I finally said, surprised by the certainty in my own voice. "I think she made a good life for herself here, like her granddaughter wrote, but I just—I don't know how she did it. How she managed to live beyond the fear and the abandonment and . . ."

I looked over at the silk mill's ruins and expelled a long breath. Then I looked at Grant, hoping he would understand. "I've felt incapable for so long. Just . . . fractured. Like everything was too demolished to piece back together again. My mind. My memories. My dreams. My . . . my everything. But if Julie somehow found a way . . ."

"You're not demolished, Jess," Grant said, reaching out to take my hand in a firm, comforting grip. He leaned so close that I could feel his breath against my skin. "Wounded, yes. Scared? Of course. But demolished?" He shook his head. "What happened . . . What they did—" He turned away from me, toward the stream, and I missed the warmth of his hand when he released mine.

He squinted up at the sky with something that looked like anger on his face. When he spoke again, it was in a rough voice. "Your story isn't over either," he said, his eyes locking on mine. "You can still steal it back from the forces that tried to end it."

I shook my head. "But—"

"Fight for it, Jess. Fight for yourself like Adeline fought for those children."

"But I'm not strong like Adeline," I whispered.

"You are."

The shame I'd spent weeks trying to tamp down came surging to the surface again. It scraped across my tattered self-control. "I ran, Grant!" I nearly yelled the words. "I ran and left Bernard lying on that stage." Images of his face crescendoed my distress. "Then I made up Patrick's presence so I could run again to the South of France. Grant, I ran! That isn't courage."

"You were in shock—"

"It's cowardice!" I stumbled to my feet, nearly gagging on the word, bent over at the waist, and braced my hands against my knees. I stood like that until the spasms in my lungs stilled and I could breathe again.

When I looked up, Grant hadn't moved. He still sat where I'd left him, his intense, unfocused gaze on the trees next to the stream. I took a step and a twig snapped under my foot, drawing his eyes to me. A muscle twitched in his jaw. The hands that clasped his leg were white-knuckled with strain. I saw him take a breath.

"When I think of what they did to you," he began. Then he paused and swallowed hard. "When I think of what they did to all those people and *might* have done to you." His face twitched with suppressed rage. "I've got to be honest, Jess, there are times when I wish I could have killed them myself." His eyes were fierce. "But not because they *demolished* you," he said, infusing the word with an ardent disbelief. "Because they hollowed out the part of you that Patrick filled."

I felt his words like a physical wave—a wounding, destabilizing, and liberating wave.

Grant must have seen my posture sag. He was at my side before I realized the moment had sapped the last remnants of my strength. He helped me back to the log, and I rested my weight against it, seared and soothed by the wisdom of his words.

"You ran because you saw the kind of horrors I can't even imagine," Grant said softly. "You ran because you're human—no one can fault you for that." I felt his hand on the back of my neck, strong and calming. "But maybe . . ." He hesitated. "Maybe you can try to stop running now. Because you're getting strong enough again and because Julie . . . She survived."

I shook my head. "I don't know how to—"

"Breathe," Grant whispered. "That's how it starts. Breathe. Discover, risk, create, sing, find beauty . . . Fill that empty space with the things Patrick loved—with the things you loved in him. Show the monsters who wanted to destroy you what it looks like to choose life in spite of fear and loss."

"Like Julie," I said as tears coursed down my cheeks and Grant rubbed calming circles on my back.

"Like Julie," he said.

I knew she'd been there—in Holford's peaceful glen. I sensed her survival in the stillness of the air and the goldening of the clouds now cloaking the village. I saw her sitting in her home, teaching her daughter to spin raw silk into thread. She'd honored the dead by living. She'd countered the atrocities she'd seen by simply breathing.

"Do you think this is why we came?" I asked Grant, Julie's survival lending me the courage to lean into him again. His arms came around me. They felt familiar and safe. "Is this what Patrick wanted me to figure out?"

"He loved you," Grant whispered against my hair. "He'd have wanted you to keep on living."

We sat there for a while, savoring the silence in the place of Julie's healing. When I finally pushed away to look at Grant, his face was so close that I could see the steadfast kindness in his eyes. "What about you? You've said from the start that you had to follow the pages, too, to find where they led."

Grant considered the question for a moment. "I guess I needed to know if Adeline had been right about Julie. If what God told her about her sister's survival was wishful thinking or some kind of sign. I'm a fixer, right? The guy who needs answers. I wanted to be sure."

Grant paused and smiled at me, and I felt the flutter of something warm unfolding. He shrugged a shoulder. "And I think I needed to help you find your answers, too, because . . ." He shook his head as if to clear it, then fastened his gaze on mine again. "Because I care. About Adeline and her family. But mostly about you."

I laughed, a bit of panic in my voice, and tucked a strand of hair behind my ear, focusing on anything other than Grant's face. Anxiety tugged at my nerves. I'd made my peace with grief, but connection—the kind of connection he seemed to be hinting at—it still felt like a threatening force.

Unaware of the discomfort his words had caused in me, Grant went on. "And I hate to admit it, but I think this was about proving Mona right too."

I shook my head. "You've lost me."

"He layers good over the bad," Grant said, quoting his sister. "She's been trying to hammer that into my mind since—since everything that happened before I got to France. And I think I had to see it happen in the Baillards' life to be able to imagine it in mine."

"It just sounds like a lot of happy-talk to me." I knew I didn't want to be convinced. "Optimistic mysticism or . . ."

"Except that it seems true." He shifted a bit and turned his gaze toward the remnants of the Huguenots' silk mill. "When I look back at all the bad—the kind that left Mona stranded in France and made me need to escape California and the horrible bad that made you run to Balazuc. If you hadn't found that box or discovered the hidden papers. If we hadn't uncovered that change in the

Baillards' name or run into Nelly on a fruitless visit to Canterbury. If she hadn't sent us off to Dunster to see a long-lost love . . . When I look back at all the pain and start to trace the good that happened in spite of it—and when I look at where we're sitting now . . ." His conclusion was evident in the sureness of his gaze.

I couldn't accept it. "So God or the universe or *whatever* wanted the Huguenots to be massacred so we could be sitting here today? He wanted the Bataclan to be attacked so I could see some good layered over the death of all those people?"

Grant heard the bitterness in my voice and held up a hand. "No—no, that's not what I'm saying." He blew out a breath and let his head fall back. "Truth is, I have no idea what I'm talking about. But if there is a God—the kind that weeps when the weak and powerless get hurt . . ." He looked at me. "I want to believe that there's a force for good in this world and that that force won't let the bad have the final word. It doesn't explain or undo the darkness, but . . . I think somehow it covers it with light."

I could feel myself frowning, unwilling to accept that Grant saw meaning in the meaningless. Unwilling to admit that the journey since my horror, the orchestrated coincidences I could see now, in retrospect, had been a guided thing. But the more I contemplated the sheer number of the "ifs" Grant had so easily laid out, the more sobered I became.

I wanted them to be an arbitrary confluence of random luck and fate. But they seemed far too measured to be just the work of chance.

A mist hovered over Holford's quiet glen. I watched it blanket stones and trees and felt my spirit's slow surrender to the things I couldn't prove but knew I needed to believe. "If Charles hadn't made the box for Adeline to keep her pages safe," I admitted, adding to Grant's list, "and if she hadn't made the pencil roll for Julie—"

Grant stood up so quickly that I nearly lost my balance. That expression was back on his face again—the one that spoke of discovery and excitement. "He gave her the box to keep the pages safe," he repeated.

I was confused. "Uh—yes."

A broad smile broke across his face. "He gave his sister the box to keep the pages safe!"

I just stared, completely baffled by what he was saying.

"Come on!" He grabbed my hand and practically dragged me up the hill to the fence.

"Grant, what on earth—?"

"I may be completely wrong about this, but I've got a gut feeling . . ."

I'd been around him long enough to know protesting was no use.

THIRTY-ONE

"Isn't this a lovely surprise," Lydia said when she saw us standing outside her front door. Though her expression was pleasant, I could see some confusion too. "Did you want to speak with Roger again or . . . ?"

"We do," Grant said.

"Right—well, he's out back. Probably tinkering in the garage he calls a museum."

"Mind if we . . . ?"

"Be my guest," Lydia said.

We found Roger cleaning the mechanism of an old mantel clock. "Fancy seeing you again!" he exclaimed. "Did you forget something?"

"We need to take another look at the pencil wrap," Grant said.

I stepped in. "What Grant means to say is, 'Hi, how are you, and would you mind if we saw the wrap again?'" I tried for a lighthearted laugh. "There's a chance he's lost his mind."

The silk wrap was still on the desk where Roger had left it earlier. He handed it to Grant. "Something troubling you?"

Grant rolled the fabric out and turned it over in his hands. He ran a finger over the *CSF* embroidered in red silk. "Would you mind if I split this seam?" he asked Roger, who was standing back, perplexed.

"You want to—what now?"

"If I could just pull out the stitching right along this seam," Grant explained, showing our host the hemmed edge of the roll.

Roger seemed unsure. "It will probably damage the fabric . . ."

"I'll buy it," Grant said, reaching into his back pocket for his wallet. "What do you want for it? Name a price and you've got it."

"I wasn't exactly planning on selling—"

"A hundred euro. Two hundred. How's that? That's, what, maybe a hundred and seventy pounds?"

"Are you . . . ?" Now Roger was shocked. His Adam's apple bobbed as he swallowed hard, then cleared his throat. "If you're absolutely sure . . ."

"Here," Grant said, smiling broadly as he handed a sheaf of bills to the bemused Englishman. "You got a knife?"

Roger reached into the drawer for a box cutter. "Will this do?"

Grant cut through one stitch and used the edge of the blade to pull out several more. When he could fit a finger into the gap he'd made, he used it to loosen the rest of the row. Then he pulled the two layers of fabric apart and held them under the lamp on Roger's desk. His fingers were shaking as he reached into the space and gently pulled a fragile sheet of paper free.

It had been folded over and over again,

dissimulated inside the silken pencil case, but it was unmistakably a match to Charles's and Adeline's pages.

"How did you know?" I breathed.

"The *CSF,*" he answered in a hushed tone. "It was on the bottom of Adeline's box and on this pencil roll . . . If Charles gave his sister that box to hide her pages, it makes sense that Julie would be given something to protect hers too."

"I take it this is something special," Roger said.

"It is," I answered, smiling unapologetically.

He winked. "Should've asked double!"

Grant laughed, loud and deep.

I shook my head and ran a finger over the red embroidery on the pencil roll. "If it wasn't for the monogram . . . ," I murmured.

"That's not a monogram," Roger said. "It's an acronym."

Grant and I froze. "An acronym?" I asked, adrenaline surging again. "For what?"

"It's right there in the letter," Roger said, reaching for the photo album that held Julie's note. "That French bit I read to you earlier, remember? The bit about courage, wisdom, and faith." He found the spot and pointed at it. "See how she used capital letters on those three words? Took me a while to piece it all together, but you can see it right there in the red embroidery. The *CSF* on that pencil wrap stands for *Courage, Sagesse,* and *Foi.*"

I looked up at Grant and knew my elation

matched his. "Endure with courage, resist with wisdom—"

"Persist in faith," he finished.

And somewhere in my spirit, in that bruised and healing space still filled with Patrick's love, I was certain I heard his irrepressible cheer.

EPILOGUE

Grant loaded my suitcase into the back of the deudeuche and placed the sewing box securely in the passenger seat. Adeline's and Julie's pages were nestled in its drawer with the sheaf of diary pages and a pressed leaf from Holford's glen. "You sure you don't want me to make the drive with you?"

I shook my head. "It's only seven hours. And it'll be good for me to spend some time with Patrick's mom and dad alone."

It was Vonda who'd tracked down his wealthy, estranged parents in the aftermath of the attack to tell them of his death. She'd told them about me too—about my closeness to Patrick, my injury, and then my disappearance. They'd been paying the rent on his studio in Paris for nearly three months, unwilling to face it until I could be there too— as if exploring Patrick's world with someone he loved would restore their bonds with a son they'd lost long before his death.

They'd finally found me through my parents after I returned from England and started communicating again, and I looked forward to introducing them to the man Patrick had become, to the places and possessions that so perfectly defined him.

"Call if you need anything," Grant said. He leaned in for a kiss.

"There's a chance I'm going to miss this," I whispered against his lips and felt him smile.

"See you in Denver?" he asked, pulling back.

It had taken us a while to figure out our next step. We'd finally settled on a plan that would give Grant the chance to make a new start and our relationship the time it needed to be explored and defined. So I'd be returning to Denver when I was done in Paris. I had mixed feelings about moving back into the townhouse I'd shared with Patrick, the home he'd left for me in his oh-so-Patrick will—*"My digs go to Jessica. My moped goes to Vonda. My clothes go to charity. All the rest is up for grabs."* His parents had stepped in to spare the townhouse from foreclosure, covering the mortgage in the hope I'd reappear. I'd tried to persuade them to rent it out or sell it, but they'd been firm in their desire to honor Patrick's wishes.

"I'll see you in Denver," I said to Grant, stepping in close to wrap my arms around his waist. He held me tightly and kissed my hair. He'd join me there when the barn renovation was far enough along to hand off to local artisans. He'd be starting again from scratch—getting his own place to live, then finding houses to flip and subcontractors to hire. He talked about it with anticipation and purpose, and I knew he'd make it work. Until he did, we'd share the revenue from Patrick's Trésor store, which I'd wrestled back from the landlord with Grant's encouragement and help. I'd rename it Ooh-Là-Là Chérie the minute I got home.

The future felt unwritten. It felt inviting too. And though there were still moments when the horrors of the past shoved their way past my defenses, I was learning more each day that I'd only been hollowed out—not demolished or broken. And I purposed to fill the empty space with the good I'd seen lived out by Adeline and her family, with a courage, a wisdom, and a faith I was just learning.

Mona gave me a hug and held on for a while. "You'll be missed," she said when she released me.

"But I'll be out of the cottage so you can rent it again!" I looked into her kind and compassionate face. "I know how much income you sacrificed to let me stay this long."

She shook her head and repeated, "You'll be missed," more seriously this time. "And this," she added, pointing a finger at her brother and me. "No pressure, but Connor has been calling you Aunt Jess in his bedtime prayers, so . . ."

I laughed. It felt good to be wanted.

"Wait! Wait! Wait!" Connor burst out of the house with a sword in each hand and ran down the steps toward me. "I've got a booty for you!"

I looked at Mona.

"Have you been letting him watch the Kardashians again?" Grant asked.

She smacked his arm. "We've been reading books about Blackbeard and they use 'booty' for treasure, so . . ."

"You may need to address that before he gets any older."

Connor leapt into the air and landed beside me in a defensive pose, feet planted wide and weapons crossed. "What's this booty you speak of?" I asked him.

"It's a present," he said, holding the pose.

"Hurry it up, young man," Mona said. "*Aunt Jess* needs to get on the road."

"You can't leave!" he growled in his best pirate imitation, showing a smile missing one more tooth since yesterday.

"Buddy," Grant said. "Your present."

"It's a secret," he whispered.

"Well, it won't be anymore once you give it to her."

"No," Connor said, rolling his eyes. "The present is a secret I'm supposed to tell her."

Mona looked at her son, head tilted to one side. Then she turned to me. "We've got a drawing for you, too, but let's get this out of the way first— whatever it is."

Connor dropped his swords and crooked a finger at me so I'd bend down to his level. I crouched in front of him and he leaned close, placing his hands on either side of my face.

"You ready?" he asked, eyes wide.

I nodded.

"Shiny ninja says believe in gold," he whispered.

He let go of my face when I pulled back. His eyes were sparkling, peaceful, and intense.

"Shiny Ninja said that?"

He nodded.

I felt something fluttering closed. "Is he gone?" I murmured.

The freckle-faced boy made a *whoosh*ing sound and raised his arms toward the sky.

I fought back tears and stood, my eyes lingering on the world I'd found by running from myself. I saw the beauty of the place that had cradled my remembering and the kindness of the strangers who had buffered my renewing. I visualized all the "ifs" laid out like paving stones behind me, leading from the scene of one of France's worst mass killings to the threshold of this moment and its luminous beginning. The orchestration of it all, in retrospect, felt overwhelming.

I looked into the faces of the family I'd found and saw it clearly now—the layering of light over the darkness of my past. The flecks of gold that shimmered in the debris of my loss.

DISCUSSION QUESTIONS

*Warning: Discussion questions contain spoilers!

1. After the Paris attacks, Patrick tells Jessica that fleeing back to the States would just be yielding to the terrorists. In your opinion, where is the line between caution and resistance? What would you have done?
2. When Jessica finds the sewing box, it feels like a coincidence. Only later does she realize how important that item will be to her healing. Can you think of "coincidences" in your own life that turned out to be divine appointments?
3. Why did Jessica's subconscious need Patrick to be alive?
4. What different responses to grief are demonstrated by the characters in *The Space Between Words*? Are some healthier than the others? If so, why?
5. What compels Grant to pursue the Baillard's fate? What compels Jessica to do so too?
6. When they drive past La Jungle, the large refugee camp on the coast of France, Jessica feels herself struggling, but can't really identify the source of her emotions. Given her recent history, what do you think it is that

gets to her as she sees those stranded children looking at her through the chain-link fence?

7. Mona states that "broken finds broken," implying that those who have been wounded or traumatized by life tend to associate with those who have experienced similar pain. In your opinion, is this true and is it always a detrimental thing? What does the novel indicate on that topic? Do Jesus' incarnation and life contribute to our understanding of broken identifying with broken?

8. Adeline stays behind to teach her students rather than fleeing into the hills with her parents. Is this misplaced loyalty?

9. Most of the Huguenots showed tremendous courage and faith in the face of unthinkable persecution. Adeline mentions that some did recant their Protestantism in order to save themselves and their children. How do you view them? How do you think God does?

10. Connor's Shiny Ninja sightings bring comfort to Jessica. Have you known people who've had similar glimpses of loved ones after they passed away? How do you explain them?

11. Mona states that "God layers good over the bad" and Grant expands on that by saying, "I want to believe that there's a force for good in this world and that that force won't let the bad have the final word. It doesn't explain or undo the darkness, but it somehow covers it

with light." How does the Bible support this view? Looking back over the worst episodes in the world's history, how do you see God layering light over the man wrought darkness civilization has known?

ACKNOWLEDGMENTS

Kathleen M. Rodgers: When a first attempt at Book #4 became mired in writer's block, I wrote to an author I'd never met before, prompted by the wisdom of her posts on social media. With kindness and grace, she led me back to the magic of passive inspiration and gave me the courage to pause with expectation.

Renée Grubb: This kindred spirit sat with me at her dining room table, just after I'd abandoned a previous draft, and countered discouragement with hope. The only nuggets of story I had in mind at that time were "Bataclan" and "Huguenot," but somehow she knew that if we just did some Googling, *The Space Between Words* would emerge. As it has so many times, her excitement galvanized my efforts.

Sally Phoenix: My travel companion and trespassing accomplice took the next step with me, happily ditching our established itinerary to track down a piece of Huguenot history hidden away in a small church in Kent. Two days later, we climbed over a fence (placarded with warnings) to explore the remnants of an old silk mill. This is my mom—fearless adventurer, my fiercest champion and dearest friend.

Pastor Ken Slater: This humble keeper of a

Huguenot treasure welcomed us warmly, then introduced us to the historic item hanging on his church's wall. A few minutes into our encounter, we were astounded to discover that we'd already met twenty-six years before . . . Shaking our heads at the serendipity of it all, we left his small town having found the clue that would become a driving force in *The Space Between Words.*

Alan Wharton: It was Alan's clerical collar and persuasive skills that granted us access to Canterbury's Black Prince Chantry, a sacred place for the Strangers who fled from France to England under threat of extermination. Nelly Durand and Captain Corb exist in this novel because of that rare privilege.

Greg Tharp: This trusted advisor and lifelong friend was the first to set eyes on the finished manuscript. I held my breath for days . . . When it came, his response assuaged my hesitation and elevated my confidence. His steadfast support, instinctive understanding, and wise counsel have been integral to every book I've written.

Becky Monds: I can't imagine writing without this masterful editor's guidance. Her enthusiasm is an empowering force and her humble command of mechanics and story are peerless. My favorite editor's email of all time came from her and simply read, "NOOO!!!!!" (I knew exactly where she was in the book from that exclamation.)

Chip McGregor: Without the support and savvy

of my agent extraordinaire, this novel would have found neither publisher nor bookshelf. I am blessed beyond words that he saw something in my writing that was worth endorsing and promoting.

ABOUT THE AUTHOR

Born in France to a Canadian father and an American mother, Michèle Phoenix is a consultant, writer, and speaker with a heart for Third Culture Kids. She taught for twenty years at Black Forest Academy (Germany) before launching her own advocacy venture under Global Outreach Mission. Michèle travels globally to consult and teach on topics related to this unique people group. She loves good conversations, mischievous students, Marvel movies, and paths to healing.

Books are produced in the United States using U.S.-based materials

Books are printed using a revolutionary new process called THINKtech™ that lowers energy usage by 70% and increases overall quality

Books are durable and flexible because of smythe-sewing

Paper is sourced using environmentally responsible foresting methods and the paper is acid-free

Center Point Large Print
600 Brooks Road / PO Box 1
Thorndike, ME 04986-0001 USA

(207) 568-3717

US & Canada:
1 800 929-9108
www.centerpointlargeprint.com